An impossible dream

Theo stared up at the posters she had pinned to the walls of her room. Was this as close as she would ever get to seeing the world famous horses that lived in the barns only two miles away? One poster showed Dan Patch hitched to a sulky, a driver perched behind him. The lean brown horse stood relaxed and attentive, his fine large head turned toward the camera, his ears pricked forward, his eyes deep and knowing.

Theo slipped from her chair and studied the way the driver's hands held the reins, and curled her own hands to mimic them. She sat on the chair again and propped her feet up against the bed. She closed her eyes and held her hands out in front of her. But it was no use pretending.

"Girls can't drive horses," she muttered. "Stupid."

To Race a Dream

Deborah Savage

HarperTrophy®
A Division of HarperCollinsPublishers

To Race a Dream
Copyright © 1994 by Deborah Savage
All rights reserved. No part of this book may be used or reproduced in
any manner whatsoever without written permission except in the case
of brief quotations embodied in critical articles and reviews.
Printed in the United States of America. For information address
HarperCollins Children's Books, a division of HarperCollins Publishers,
10 East 53rd Street, New York, NY 10022.
Published by arrangement with Houghton Mifflin Company, New York.
LC Number 93-37654
Trophy ISBN 0-06-440611-3
First Harper Trophy edition, 1996.

*This book is dedicated with love
to my father, Richard Savage,
and my mother, Judith Savage,
who always believed in my dreams.*

My deepest thanks and appreciation go to Jean Johnson, who was so generous with the many items about Dan Patch collected by her late father, Joe Egan. I also wish to thank Delvin Miller and Del Stelling for their help and suggestions during the research for this book. And a special thanks to Bill Streeter for his wisdom and "magic."

To Race a Dream

ᔐ Chapter One ᔑ

HER OWN VOICE startled her, breaking the heavy golden
stillness of the afternoon. "It isn't fair. It isn't fair." Theo's
words hung in the air like the heat, shimmering over the
meadow where the first hay was already swelling up past
her knees. She lifted her arm to drag it impatiently across
her eyes, then kept it there to shade out the sun. She stood
on a low rise, looking out over the fields rolling before her
down toward the Minnesota River. She squinted, trying to
focus through the warm spring haze and the black shadows
of the cottonwoods that grew along the stream. Beyond the
cottonwoods and the stream, beyond the far meadow rising
green and soft in the distance, Theo could just make out
the glimmering white buildings of the International Stock
Feed Farm.

It was like a page from an exotic fairy tale. The light hit
the buildings of the most famous harness-racing stables in
the world until the white paint glowed like flames. Magic
pulsed like a shield from the heart of the place, gleaming
off the graceful onion-dome roofs and making the bold, dark
designs on the outside of the barns dance. For almost a year,
Theo had come to this rise to stare off across the meadow.
It seemed to her that every question she had in the world
would be answered by that distant place. It seemed utterly
inaccessible to her, untouchable as the sun. She stared across
the fields today and felt it farther from her than ever, and
the choking feeling that had been threatening her since she'd

1

come home from school earlier that afternoon rose up and filled her eyes and throat.

"It isn't fair!" she whispered again, almost allowing herself to cry. "I'll never get there now. Never!" She kicked at the thick grass stalks. The spring juice ran down her boots and made dark tracks on the dusty leather. Theo leaned down to pull a tangle of grass from her bootlaces. The hem of her muslin dress was already streaked a bit with green stain from her angry run through the fields. She jerked her pinafore straight and screwed up her face in disgust.

It was the last thing Theo had heard her mother say, after the "wonderful news": "Don't you mess up those clothes, Theodora! We're leaving in two days and those things are the best you have. . . ." But Theo had slammed the door on Maud Harris, raced along the dusty street to the railroad tracks, scrambled down the bank, and beat her way through the hay meadow to her hill. She was sweating when she got there. It was unusually hot for May, even for this low riverland in southern Minnesota. The road leading out of the little town of Savage was hard-packed and as she ran, the fine silt-like dust had risen up and filled her lungs.

" 'Don't mess your clothes, Theodora!' " she mocked now under her breath. Maud had fine high ideas when it suited her. "As long as women must live in confining clothes, following confining rules, their thoughts and desires will remain confined as well," Maud always said, and when she was in the house she often wore her husband's clothes. Mrs. O'Leary, who cooked and cleaned for them, could hardly look at Maud when she was dressed "like a heathen." Sometimes what her mother said, and what she did, were very different. She would bend any rule if it would benefit Claudia. . . .

Theo pushed her way slowly through the hay to the fence

2

and leaned against it, resting her chin on her folded arms. Claudia. Claudia, her sister, nineteen years old, four years older than she . . . Claudia, the reason for everything. The reason for everything that had happened this afternoon, the reason for them all living here in this little river town of Savage instead of the busy, friendly city of Indianapolis, Indiana, where they had been until last October. October 1905 . . . it was hard to believe it had only been eight months since they moved to Savage, eighteen miles south of Minneapolis, so the family could be closer to Claudia.

The sun flared once along the tops of the cottonwoods far across the fields. Crickets stirred in the grass. Hidden down along the stream in the thickets, birds began to wake from the heat into the cool shade. Theo sighed, shut her eyes, and let the long day rush through her memory.

It had been difficult to sit still through the languid heat after Mr. Bernard's announcement. The principal of the little school had seemed so pleased with himself. "It took a bit of organizing," said Mr. Bernard. "But now it's settled. The ninth grade graduating class will have a tour of the International Stock Feed Farm, and Mr. Savage himself invited us to have a picnic on the grounds. I expect all of you to be on your best behavior. . ." Two days until the last day of school — and then, the indescribable wonders of that distant farm with its famous horses would be open to Theo at last.

And at lunchtime, Miss Schroeder had bent to whisper to Theo. "We usually don't tell," she'd said. "We like it to be a surprise. But this way, maybe your big sister could make it for the graduation ceremony, Theo. You're to receive the English Prize!"

It almost made up for all the long, awful winter in a strange town where she hardly knew anyone. By January,

3

when the year slipped from 1905 to 1906 in the dim shivering days of a Minnesota winter, Theo had never felt so alone. Week after week crawled through gloom and snow and deadly cold. The river froze, and the road that ran north through Savage toward St. Paul and Minneapolis drifted shut. Theo dragged herself to school every day to sit hunched over her desk in the tiny classroom, trying to soak up the heat from the old potbelly stove in the corner by Miss Schroeder's desk.

She hated the eight other students in the ninth grade class. Theo swung out thoughtfully from the fence and narrowed her eyes. The English Prize was the top award in the school . . . and she was a new student. That will show them, she thought.

"I bet stuck-up Carl thinks *he* won it," she said. Carl had had a good chance at it, she admitted to herself. He was better at exams. He was so quiet . . . conceited, she thought. And that idiot, Gyp Grimer, with his stupid giggles and mean remarks . . . and Amelia McCarthy, whose father was the bank manager . . . she hated them all. She hated being here. It was all because of Claudia . . . Claudia, who should be coming home to watch Theo receive the English Prize in front of the whole school.

But Claudia was not coming home. Instead, Theo was going *there*, to Minneapolis, with Maud and her father, Stevenson, to hear Claudia's debut with the City Symphony of Minneapolis. They were leaving in two days, missing Theo's graduation, the tour of the horse farm, the picnic, the awarding of the English Prize . . . everything.

Suddenly, as if in answer to her thoughts, the high trumpeting call of a stallion broke through the hazy stillness. Theo climbed the fence to sit on the top rail. She chewed her lip and peered through the distance toward the farm.

4

The stallion called again, the sound as wild and powerful as a clap of thunder over the prairie.

Theo leaned as far forward as she could without losing her balance. "I hear you, Dan Patch!" She braced her feet on a lower rail and slowly stood, lifting her head and sniffing the warm air, feeling the first breeze of evening sifting through her heavy dark hair. She shook her head and her hair came loose from the braid and fell like a mane down her back. The stallion called again. The girl lifted her head to answer him.

From the top of the Taj Mahal–like domes of the International Stock Feed Farm buildings fluttered the bright flags Theo could just make out over the distant cottonwoods. She did not have to see the words written on them to know what they said. DAN PATCH 1:55¼ was printed in bold block letters on the highest flag. On the lower flags were printed the names of the other champions: Arion. Cresceus. George Gano. She knew them all, their names and histories, their fastest times. She knew from photographs and drawings clipped from newspapers what the buildings on the farm looked like. She knew how the five wings of the giant central building housed the champions, how the onion-domes held the heating system for the whole complex, how the half-mile covered track — the only one in the world — lay just behind the main barn, and how beyond in the meadows lay the open mile track where the fastest horses in the world worked out.

And where her knowing ended, the magic began. Dan Patch was at the very heart of the magic; he created it. Last October, when Theo moved with her family to the big wooden house on Cargyll Street at the edge of town, Dan Patch shattered the world's harness-racing record in Lexington, Kentucky. Theo had the newspaper clipping care-

5

fully folded in her drawer at home. OUR OWN DAN PATCH BREAKS WORLD RECORD AGAIN! The headline in the little Savage newspaper was two inches high. "October 12, 1905," read the article, "a date that will go down in history. Dan Patch, owned by Mr. M. W. Savage of the International Stock Feed Farm in Savage, Minnesota, paced a mile in one minute, fifty-five and one-quarter seconds, breaking his own previous world record of . . ."

Theo knew every word of the article. She gazed across the fields. She knew the photographs and drawings by heart. But the distant farm shimmered like a mirage. She balanced tensely on the fence. How many times in the past eight months had she done this very thing, on this same fence? How could she have gotten through the whole awful year without this?

Even now, she could imagine them. In her mind's eye, the magnificent doors of the central barn opened and the stallions stepped forth. Oh, they commanded the very earth with their wind-fast hooves! They were as powerful as the summer storms that raced over the prairies. And in the front stepped Dan Patch, the fastest pacing horse in the world.

Theo lifted her arms in front of her. Her hands curled around invisible reins. She threw back her head and the soft afternoon breeze became the slashing wind of speed tearing through her hair. Her hands tightened on the reins. Yes. Yes! She heard the pounding hooves racing before her. Her eyes closed. The pounding enveloped her until she felt the great pumping heart as if it were her own, until her own muscles burned with the strain. She leaned into the wind and felt the immense power flying down through the reins into her hands. The pounding of hooves grew until the whole earth seemed to tremble.

She opened her eyes suddenly. Her spell came alive around her. The rumble of hooves filled her until her thoughts dissolved beneath the swirling dust of their approach.

"Come on!" she cried. From the deep black shadows along the stream bank the yearlings came, leaping and tossing their young necks. The last rays of sun spun to gold on their coats; Theo had to squint to watch them. They charged up the long slope toward her like a storm coming in from the west, their long legs churning the sweet grass. In a moment they were all around her, leaping until she laughed for joy.

She'd watched them grow all year, this crop of last summer's foals. They were filling out into first strength. Their necks had begun to thicken and arch, their chests were broadening with the powerful lungs that would carry them faster than dreams around the racetracks of the country. As she watched she called the names she had given them, names formed from the presence of each animal by a toss of a head, a leap, the drum of a natural pace or trot over the earth.

They swirled around her, knowing her well. Some of them — she did not know which — could claim Dan Patch as their sire. She laughed again. In the winter the snow had been almost too deep for her to struggle across the fields. The herd of yearlings had beaten a broad path from the stream to the fence where she would stand, out of breath, her face stung bright red from the cold. Their steaming bodies would warm her until she felt that only these horses stood between her and the numbing isolation and loneliness of her strange new home. They came from the distant farm and linked her to the dreams Dan Patch created. Someday, she did not know how, she would drive these horses.

The powerful call of the stallion came rippling across the

fields like a whip. The yearlings wheeled in excitement until Theo could not resist a moment longer. She jumped into the grass and ran with the horses.

They knew the game well, and did not leave her behind. They careened around the girl, who ran with them until she felt her heart would burst within her. The yearlings raced with her through the trampled grass. The sweet smell of their bodies and the crushed grass filled her with pure energy. They swept down the slope toward the shaded stream and stopped. In a few seconds they were grazing peacefully, and Theo leaned against a tree to catch her breath.

She looked down at her clothing. The boots were scuffed and dusty. The hem of her dress had torn loose and was dragging in the dirt. Her stocking was torn and she had lost the ribbon from her hair. She ran her hands down the dress helplessly. Now, on top of everything else, Maud would be angry, and probably her father as well, mild-mannered as he was. And when she saw Claudia, she'd look like something dragged under a train instead of the sister of the second woman violinist ever to play in the City Symphony.

The yearlings rustled softly in the grass as they grazed around Theo. Once or twice, one of them would raise a head and stare at her from great violet-dark eyes, fluttering curiously through nostrils soft as velvet.

"You always understand me," she said quietly, and they flickered their ears as she spoke. She ran her hand over the neck of the nearest horse. They had been handled by experts since they were born, and no human being had ever given them a reason to be afraid. But they felt especially comfortable around the tall girl who had become so familiar out here in the far paddocks. They listened for her voice.

Theo struggled to pull off her pinafore. "It'll be different next year," she muttered, half to herself and half to the yearlings. "I won't have to go to that stupid little school anymore, because I'll be in high school." High school was in Shakopee, twenty minutes' ride by train from Savage. "And there's bound to be people there who aren't —" She stopped and examined the pinafore. It was filthy. Maybe if she washed it in the stream, it would be nearly dry in the heat by the time she got home.

She knelt on the bank and wished she could jump into the cool, still pool at the bend in the stream. She stared down at her face, twisting her tangled hair into a rough braid. "No wonder Claudia's practically a famous violinist, instead of someone who's just won a dumb English Prize!" she scowled at her reflection. "Who cares about the prize, anyway?" Nobody knew about it but Theo, Miss Schroeder, and Mr. Bernard. She hadn't had time to tell Maud before her mother had announced the unexpected news of Claudia's debut.

Theo sat on the bank and wrung out the dripping pinafore. After all, it wasn't Claudia's fault — how was she to know her chance to perform would come this soon? She was the youngest alternate violinist with the orchestra and a woman besides. . . . Even though Claudia rehearsed with them, and took her lessons, Theo knew her sister had not expected this chance to play before an audience so soon. But two violinists had gotten sick at the same time, and the telegram with the "wonderful news" had been sent to Number Eight, Cargyll Street in Savage, where Maud read it only an hour before Theo came home from school. Maud was still glowing with pride and excitement. "I'm sorry about your graduation, Theodora," she'd said almost as an afterthought. "But it's only ninth grade, after all — you'll have your big high school one in a few years."

"But there's the picnic, Mama — at the horse farm. . ."

Annoyance had flashed momentarily in Maud's eyes. "Theodora, can't you think about anything but those horses? For goodness' sakes, this is Claudia's *debut!* You can go to that silly farm anytime."

And after that, how was she to say anything about the English Prize? Let Mr. Bernard tell them! Papa would have to go to the school to inform them she would not be there the last day . . . let him find out that way.

She wrung the pinafore savagely and scrambled to her feet. She moved so abruptly the nearest yearling almost knocked her as he shied away in mock fear. Theo grabbed at the bushes but her foot lost a grip on the slippery bank and she plunged into the stream up to her knee.

The water stopped squishing from her boot by the time she reached the road, but the dust turned to mud on the leather and on the hem of her dress. She walked slowly, her head down. It was near dinnertime, so almost no one was on the streets or coming in from the fields. But before she turned down the elm-shaded avenue of Cargyll Street, she heard the rumble of a farm cart behind her and turned to see old Daws Grimer driving the mule his son Gyp sometimes rode to school.

"Howdy, Theodora," called Daws Grimer. Theo mumbled in reply. It seemed to her she caught a smirk on old Daws's face, just the same smirk Gyp had. She lowered her head again, too tired even to be angry. Of all the people to come along, it had to be Daws Grimer, she thought — now I'll never hear the end of it in school. Two weeks ago Daws Grimer had caught her trotting along the road with her neck arched and her feet prancing like a pacer ready to start a race, her hands holding the imaginary reins. The next day in school Gyp sneered at her. "What do you think you are, Theo*dora?*" he'd taunted. "A horse?" And everyone had laughed. "You think you can run faster'n Dan Patch?"

The stupidity of Gyp nauseated her, and she'd hated how all the rest of the idiots laughed at him as if he were the funniest thing in the world. Hot with shame, she'd snapped back: "Dan Patch doesn't *run*, stupid. He's a *pacer*. You don't know anything." And Gyp had held his arms out in front of him in mincing imitation of her imaginary driving, and everyone except Carl Johansson had choked with laughter.

Theo paused in the dusty yard and then sidled along the front of the house by the porch. The paint on the gaunt old house was peeling under the severe winters. Stevenson Harris had come as close to complaining as he ever did only two days ago, staring up at the big house. "I don't know when I'll get to this place," he'd said mildly, shaking his head. "Starting a new law practice all over again in this little town is as bad as it was way back when I was just out of law school. Sometimes I do miss the city. . ." Maud had grimaced a little in agreement, but there was no question of going back. Claudia was in Minneapolis, and this was as close as they could get where Stevenson could open his own legal office. But his time was spent entirely on his work, and the house and yard were left almost as they'd been when they bought the place.

Theo wondered if her father was home yet, and strained her ears trying to discover where Maud might be. If she could just get up to her own room, maybe she'd be able to mend her stockings and wash out the dress in the basin on her bureau. She opened the front door cautiously and crept up the stairs. Little dabs of mud marked each place her feet

11

touched the polished wooden floor, but she ran tiptoed down the hall and shut her door quietly behind her. She pulled off her clothes until she stood in her thin cotton shift, and stared at herself in the mirror. She was wiry and lanky, her arms brown from the sun where she pushed up the sleeves of her dresses, her long hair hanging in clumps around her shoulders. She frowned and turned sideways. I might as well be a boy, she thought. If I could only wear pants, like boys, and decent boots that didn't fall apart when I ran . . .

She sighed and flopped into the chair in front of her little desk, kicking away the pile of clothing on the floor. Maud would not be fooled by her efforts to clean them. Theo leaned on her elbows and poked at the papers lying on the desk. She was sure it was the story that had won her the English Prize. "Wild and Free," she had titled it after much thought; she'd been worried, because Miss Schroeder only liked stories with happy endings. But in "Wild and Free," the wild horse jumped off a cliff in the end rather than let himself be captured by ranchers . . . and Miss Schroeder, in front of the whole class, had confessed it brought tears to her eyes. She'd read it aloud from start to finish instead of continuing the unit on pronouns. No one else had cried. Gyp had giggled throughout, of course. Only Carl Johansson had appeared to listen.

She picked up the story — fifteen pages long, she thought proudly — and leafed through it listlessly. Underneath lay another story, this one unfinished . . . "To Drive A Dream." She studied the title. It wasn't right, somehow, but she hadn't thought of a better one yet. The story was about a boy who had a special way with horses, and could handle the wildest, craziest animal until it calmed completely. The boy was discovered by the owner of some famous harness horses, and . . . Theo shuffled the pages impatiently and stared up at the posters she had pinned to the walls of her room.

Was this as close as she would ever get to seeing the world-famous horses that lived in the barns hardly more than two miles outside of Savage? One poster showed Dan Patch hitched to a sulky, the famous Harry Hersey driving. The lean brown horse stood relaxed and attentive, his fine large head turned toward the camera, his ears pricked forward, his eyes deep and knowing. Theo slipped from her chair and studied the way the driver's hands held the reins, and curled her own hands to mimic them. She sat on the chair again and propped her feet up against the bed. She closed her eyes and held her hands out in front of her. In a moment she sighed again. "Girls can't drive harness horses," she muttered. "Stupid."

She twisted around on the chair. On a shelf above the desk, Claudia's picture seemed to stare down at her from within the delicate silver frame. Maud had given it to her last Christmas. Theo took it down and held it carefully in both hands. Girls can't play in symphony orchestras, she thought. But Claudia does. She ran her finger over the glass. The sepia-toned photograph was a perfect likeness, and Claudia seemed to sparkle out of the frame. Theo could almost hear the high, sweet notes of the violin that Claudia had played since childhood with such amazing skill, determination, and passion. She swallowed. It wasn't the same, now Claudia was gone. She remembered her as she had last seen her, at Christmas. Claudia had stepped down from the train just as a great billow of steam rose up around her; she seemed to float like a laughing angel. Claudia had filled the new home with such heady energy that Theo sometimes felt exhausted being in the same room with her. There had been mornings during Claudia's visit when Theo had paused in her bedroom doorway before going downstairs, gathering strength to meet the onslaught of her sister's dominating presence. Yet to stay alone in her room was even more unbearable, since she could not stand to miss a single moment of her sister's intoxicating attention.

Theo went to the mirror again and held the photograph up next to her own reflection. Yes, there was no doubt they were sisters. But somehow . . . somehow . . . where Theo was tall and narrow-boned, Claudia was graceful and willowy. Where Theo's hair hung unruly and coarse down her back, Claudia's was full and shining, pulled softly back from her face and piled in a grown woman's style on top of her head. And the eyes! Claudia's eyes sparkled with humor and vitality, while Theo thought her own glittered like a skittery horse about to bolt.

She put the photograph back on the shelf. No wonder Maud was proud! Claudia fulfilled every personal and political dream Maud Harris had ever had, while Theo was an enigma. Art was important to Maud, Art and Science and all Pursuits of the Mind. Theo screwed up her face and looked fiercely at the large poster of Dan Patch on the wall. Horses were . . . *silly*. It wasn't that her mother disapproved of horses in particular — she just considered it a frivolous waste of time to spend energy and thought on things that did not enlighten the world. And there were such important things to be done in the world, like winning the vote for women, like demanding the acceptance of women in all levels of life . . . like Claudia being accepted in the Minneapolis Symphony.

Maud Harris refused to let her sex confine her dreams, and toward that ideal she worked with untiring determination. She herself was a graduate of Smith College, one of the best women's colleges in the East. There she had learned about the women's suffrage movement. One cold January weekend in 1883, while visiting her sister Harriet in Boston, Maud had met Stevenson Harris, a promising law student at Harvard who cheered her work and ideas and shared her vision of a future world where men and women lived and worked together in equality. They determined that in their marriage and in the raising of their children they would allow no imposition of conditions designed to keep anyone from following their dreams.

And Claudia was the perfect answer to their determination. She fit into the family effortlessly and matched them all skill by skill — Stevenson, the brilliant lawyer; Uncle Franklin, a historian who translated ancient books from languages no one else understood into English; Maud, who was gaining national recognition for her brilliant articles and speeches within the National American Women's Suffrage Association; and of course, Aunt Harriet, Maud's revered older sister, one of only two hundred women doctors in the entire United States.

"I just want to drive horses," whispered Theo to the portrait of Dan Patch. It seemed to her for an instant that the great stallion's ears flickered in response. The huge dark eyes looked so alive and so knowing that she swallowed and turned away. She spread the stories idly on the desk. She had nothing to compare with Claudia.

By eighteen, Claudia played the violin with such skill she outgrew all her instructors and Stevenson and Maud sent her to a famous teacher in Minneapolis. She so impressed this man that he convinced the conductor of the newly formed City Symphony to grant her an audition. Despite the fact that almost no women musicians performed in large orchestras, Claudia was accepted as an alternate violinist and had moved to Minneapolis nine months ago.

Theo shoved the pile of dirty clothing farther into a corner. She flung her boots angrily under the sagging bed. Her face had gone hot and her chest felt as if it might explode. She hardly had *any* chances to make Maud as proud of her as she so obviously was of Claudia! And now she had won the English Prize, and . . . How she wished her mother would look at her and speak to her the way she did to Claudia. It was such a fierce longing at times, pushing at her heart so she could hardly breathe. If Maud spoke to her when she felt that longing it was as if she'd become an idiot and could only mumble a broken answer and her mother would turn away in irritation.

Theo heard her mother's footsteps coming down the hall, and the door to her bedroom was pushed open after a perfunctory knock.

"You've been at those horses again, Theodora," said Maud without preamble. "I can smell it from downstairs." She looked pointedly at the pile of dirty clothing on the floor, but did not say a word about them. She sat on the bed and lay the half-finished dress she'd been making for Theo's graduation on the faded quilt. Theo stared down at the papers on her desk until Maud sighed.

"Theodora, look at me," she said quietly. Reluctantly, Theo turned her eyes to her mother's. "I know you're angry about the graduation and your picnic," she said. "But slamming out of the house like that was a childish thing to do. Do you understand why this is so important to Claudia?"

Theo remained mute and glowering. Did she *understand?* Hadn't she lived in this family all her life? Hadn't Claudia always come first? Of course she understood! Reluctantly, her eyes caught the photograph of her sister smiling down from the shelf. It was hard to be really angry at Claudia . . . Claudia did what came naturally to her. And who could help but love her? Theo willed herself to relax, to nod her head, to blink away the burning in her eyes. She stood passively while her mother fit the long white folds of muslin around her and tucked them with pins. She heard the front door slam.

"Papa's home," she said in an attempt to talk. Maud only nodded. Theo hunted around for something else to say. She wanted so much to talk . . . the way she could talk with Claudia. It was never difficult to talk to Claudia, who laughed and teased her along, teased all her secrets from her . . . all except one. Claudia didn't know about the horses.

Stevenson Harris climbed the stairs tiredly and leaned in the doorway of Theo's room. She could see right away from his worried look at her that he knew about Claudia's debut. He still had his leather case bulging with papers tucked under his arm, and he'd taken off his jacket. There were dark stains of sweat under his suspenders.

"Papa," said Theo, "I know this is an important thing for Claudia, but she'll have other performances, won't she? Even more important than this one. And I can go to *all* of them . . . couldn't I just stay home this once? It's only three days, and Mrs. O'Leary could stay with me, I know she would. Because it's really important —"

"Theodora, stand still!" Maud interrupted. She jabbed a pin into a fold of the stiff muslin. "I knew I should have got Gertie Schmitt to make this dress," she muttered. Stevenson shot a quick glance at his wife and drew a tired hand through his hair.

"It's the picnic, isn't it?" he said slowly, and Theo watched the indecision cross his face. It bewildered her,

17

how he could think it was the *picnic* . . . did he think her only a child? It wasn't the picnic; who cared about a picnic! It was the International Stock Feed Farm — it was the chance, after so long, to see Dan Patch. But she nodded hopefully, seeing her father consider the request and turn to look again at Maud. But Maud set her mouth and stepped back from Theo to sit on the chair by her desk.

"This isn't just any performance, Theodora," she explained, trying to sound patient. "This is Claudia's *debut* with the symphony. This is an extraordinary breakthrough and a huge responsibility for your sister. She's not just playing her violin the best she possibly can — she's playing for all the women in the country! What do you think it would mean to her, if you weren't there?" Maud leaned her elbows on the desk and rubbed her face with her hands a moment. After a pause, she picked up Theo's story "Wild and Free," and leafed through it. Theo tensed. Maud raised her head and smiled at her, tapping the pages.

"I didn't know you were still writing stories, sweetheart!" She studied the first page carefully. Theo waited. "Why haven't you shown them to us to read?"

How could she explain? It was like the wild mustang in "Wild and Free." He'd leapt from a cliff to his death rather than allow himself to be captured. Somehow, giving Maud her stories would be allowing herself to be captured. For Maud would claim them for herself, the way she claimed Claudia's music . . . as if Claudia were merely playing out something Maud had thought up.

Maud skimmed a few pages of "Wild and Free" and riffled through the unfinished story. She smiled through an exasperated frown. "You're still writing about *horses*, Theodora! Isn't it about time you wrote about something besides horses?" Theo kept her face expressionless. Maud laughed and handed the story to Stevenson. "It won't be long before horses are obsolete, anyway, from all reports about those automobiles! Why don't you write about people, Theodora? They're much more interesting!"

Stevenson smoothed the pages of the story gently. "Oh, Maudie, let her be," he said grinning at Theo. "I know why she writes about horses. People are such flawed creatures. And no automobile will ever replace the horses in Theo's stories, endowed as they are with every noble virtue!"

He was teasing; he meant to be kind, she knew. But the stories were her secret. She'd stopped letting anyone read them a long time ago. They weren't just stories about horses — even her father couldn't see that. They were about dreams, about the longing for freedom, about power and perfection, speed, about breaking bonds with the earth and racing with those dreams. About magic.

Theo reached over and took the story from her father. Without a word she stacked it with the unfinished story and placed them both in the bottom drawer of her desk with all the others. Everything she could imagine, everything she could dream of, everything she dared to think of herself that she could never reveal to anyone — it all lay stacked in that drawer. She shut it carefully and turned back to her parents.

"I know it's only a horse story," she said quietly. "But it won me the school English Prize that I'm supposed to get at graduation."

She didn't stop to hear what Maud or Stevenson might say, but stalked from the room in the half-sewn dress and went to sit alone on the porch.

♋ Chapter Two ♋

ON THURSDAY MORNING the heat crawled along the dirt under the breathless elms and sagged down from the eaves of the porch. It hung limp and heavy in Theo's clothes and hair, wrapping itself like a fat lazy cat around her as she slowly walked to school for her last day. No one remembered a heat like this so early in the summer. In the stifling classroom, the nine students in Miss Schroeder's ninth grade gasped through their final exam in arithmetic. It was the last exam of the year; all their reports had been handed in, a reading list was handed out for summer, and Miss Schroeder stood wearily in front of her desk collecting the exams.

"Before I talk to you about next year, and what you can expect from your studies in the high school in Shakopee, I'd like to make an announcement," she told them. Her face was flushed from heat and agitation; she was not pleased to be denied the pleasure of handing out her top prize in front of the parents of the graduating class. Theo slumped down in her seat and fumed. She could hear Gyp whispering to Amelia behind her. Someone poked at Carl Johansson, but he only frowned and ignored them.

"I have some fine news to announce, as well as some disappointing news," continued Miss Schroeder, who enjoyed embellishing her announcements with long preambles. Theo tucked her hands under her to keep from fidgeting. Miss Schroeder smiled at her, but in the heat it seemed more of a grimace. "It is my pleasure each year to present the top academic student in the school with our prestigious English Prize. Usually this is done during the graduation ceremony, but due to outside circumstances, that will not be possible this year. It gives me the greatest pleasure to announce that Theodora Harris is this year's recipient of this outstanding award."

Miss Schroeder expected applause, and after a tense moment three or four of the more awake students clapped their hands listlessly. Theo's face burned and her stomach did a sudden lurch, so she wrapped her arms around herself. Miss Schroeder frowned briefly at her.

"Since Theodora's sister Claudia has unexpectedly learned that she will make her debut with the City Symphony of Minneapolis . . ."

Miss Schroeder's voice seemed to melt into a sodden drone, and Theo gazed beyond her out the open window. The heat shimmered in an oily haze over the hard dirt of the schoolyard and the rutted road. She stretched her arms out along the desk. Her fingers curled around imaginary reins. She leaned back and braced her feet on the rungs of the chair in front of her. She was on an open track, the fine dust in her nose. She closed her eyes.

The roaring inside her head swelled to an entire crowd yelling and applauding with a thunder of sound. She felt the power surge through the reins she held as the great stallion in front of her turned his head to acknowledge the crowd. And then Dan Patch began to pace. Faster and faster he flew, until the pounding filled her head and heart and muscles. The earth was swept away beneath her by the wind-eating hooves of the invincible horse. "Dan Patch! Dan Patch! Dan Patch!" The crowd chanted as if they, too, were caught by the immense power and speed. She held the reins tighter and called to the great horse . . .

"Theodora!"

Theo jerked to attention, bruising her elbow against the

back of the chair. Gyp snickered. Carl looked down at his desk. Miss Schroeder gave her a pained look.

"Theodora, don't you have anything to say?"

She couldn't think of what was expected of her. She could hardly remember what she'd been listening to, before . . . before . . . She looked dumbly at the teacher and felt herself go hot and then cold. She shivered.

"I think I might be sick, Miss Schroeder," she said at last in a voice she hardly recognized as her own. The teacher walked toward her, and Theo felt the eyes of the whole class. They were hoping she might throw up in front of everyone, she knew. That was the kind of kids they were. Amelia turned her head around to peer at her like a silly owl. Gyp made soft wretching noises under the cover of his perpetually filthy hand. Only Carl paid no attention, studying his reading list with an intent, worried frown.

Miss Schroeder put a damp, boney hand on Theo's forehead. "It's just the heat and excitement, dear," said the teacher.

"Can't I go home?" she begged.

"Theodora, you're already missing enough — this is a half day, you know. There are only forty minutes left, and what I have to say is important. I think you can manage to sit until lunchtime."

So she sat. The flies droned against the upraised windows and the dust sifted in from the road whenever a wagon or cart rumbled by, covering everything with a fine white powder. When Miss Schroeder rang the little bell she kept on her desk, the students made their way in an exhausted straggle down the stone steps to the yard. Miss Schroeder put out her hand to hold Theo back.

"I know you're disappointed, Theodora," she said softly.

"Would your parents agree to having you stay with me for three days, so you could attend the ceremony?"

Theo swallowed and looked reluctantly into Miss Schroeder's eager face. The teacher leaned closer and Theo could smell a stale sweet scent on her, as if the lilac water she'd used had gone sour in the heat.

"Thank you very much, Miss Schroeder," she answered carefully. "I don't think they would want me to do that. You see . . ." She paused. In her mind's eye she saw Claudia waiting for the train to stop, running joyfully along the platform, jumping to peer into the car windows . . . "You see, it is very important to my sister for me to be there. I'm her only sister, and this is . . ."

Miss Schroeder patted her shoulder and smiled sadly. "That's quite fine of you, Theodora. Of course, it is only right, and I do understand. Have a wonderful time."

She stumbled out into the deserted yard. By the gate she bent over and yanked her boots off, and without looking to see if anyone was around, she stripped her stockings off her hot legs and twisted them into a knot with the bootlaces. She felt the most profound relief as what little air there was cooled her skin.

She heard Gyp Grimer shout, and turned to see him shooing a rough-coated pony away from him as he led his mule over toward the gate. "Get away!" he whined. "G'wan — get away!" The pony threw its head up and shuffled away. Gyp gave Theo a taunting look. "You're gonna miss all the fun," he said. He yanked the mule's head. Theo ignored him, holding her hands tight against her sides. How she would love to pound in his stupid leering face and take that poor mule away from him!

Carl Johansson came around the corner of the school and

23

walked up to the pony. He smoothed its forelock down with his broad hand and gently slipped the bridle over its blunt head. The pony leaned against him and rubbed its head up and down on his worn shirt. Carl laughed, and Gyp shot him a suspicious look.

"What are you laughin' at?" he muttered, sawing at the mule's reins as he tried to mount. The mule sidestepped, leaving Gyp with one leg still on the ground and the other stuck over the animal's back. Gyp jerked the reins in a vicious snap.

"If you treated him nicer, he'd stand for you," said Carl mildly. Gyp glared at him. Theo swung her boots and stockings and watched. Carl reached over to hold the mule steady, but Gyp snarled at him.

"Aw, get away from me, you dumb Swede," he muttered. He pulled the mule around and clambered on its back, kicking it into an immediate jarring trot.

Theo traced a circle in the dust with her big toe and watched Carl from the corner of her eye. Was he disappointed that he hadn't won the English Prize? She remembered how hard he'd worked. But it occurred to her that Carl had never given any indication what he felt about school, one way or another. Carl rarely spoke more than a few words at a time, and never showed what he was feeling. She chewed her lip and watched him adjust the bridle carefully on the pony's head. Carl looked so big next to the little creature — he was the biggest student in the school . . . the biggest person, actually. She tilted her head, thinking. Whenever Mr. Bernard or the other two teachers needed something heavy lifted, they would take Carl from class and he would do it with ease. He always came back into the classroom and sat down to his work without a word.

Carl looked up and saw her watching. He nodded his head in the direction Gyp had gone. "He must have had porcupine for breakfast," he commented. As Theo walked away she thought: Did Carl make a *joke?*

She scuffled moodily down the road toward Cargyll Street. It was impossible to know what Carl was thinking about anything. Maybe he hadn't even thought about the English Prize. Strange, how he'd tried to help out Gyp Grimer, when stupid Gyp had never done anything but taunt him about his size, and about how his parents couldn't speak proper English . . . she grinned suddenly. As if Gyp could! He was such an idiot he wasn't even worth thinking about. But Carl, she mused, spoke English perfectly and he often got the highest marks on exams, although his writing was not as good as hers. And he was so gentle with his pony . . .

She was startled to hear the quick clop-clop of hooves behind her, and turned to see that Carl had followed her. His long legs almost reached the ground, and his strong body dwarfed the small pony. Carl lived with his family on a farm somewhere south of town, and always went straight home after school. Now he was heading in the opposite direction.

"Hey," he called to her. "Hey, Theo, wait a minute." She hesitated, half curious. Carl pulled the pony up beside her. Suddenly he flushed, as if he'd forgotten what he wanted to say, and he leaned forward to scratch the pony's ears. Theo fiddled with her boots. For a moment she almost reached out to scratch the pony as well, he was so soft-eyed and shaggy. But she kept her hands at her sides.

"I'm sorry . . . I'm sorry you can't be here for graduation to get your English Prize," he said in a rush. "I just wanted to say I was sorry, and —"

Theo watched him in amazement. She had never heard Carl say so much at one time. She narrowed her eyes.

"And, well, I'm real glad you got the English Prize." Carl finished with a short huff, as if speaking so many words had taken all the breath out of him. She would have smiled if she hadn't been so startled.

"Why?" she asked skeptically. He met her eyes. She couldn't believe how blue they were. She turned her face away quickly. The pony reached out to nose her with its bearded muzzle.

Carl took a deep breath. "Oh, because — you know. You're smart," he said. "That story you wrote — about the horse. I liked it a lot. It was real good. And anyway, I won't be back next year, so I didn't want Miss Schroeder to —"

"Why?" interrupted Theo. She immediately regretted how stupid her question sounded. She swung her boots and stockings back and forth in the dust.

"Why what?" asked Carl, but she could tell he was evading her question.

She shrugged. "Why aren't you coming back to school next year? Are your folks moving away or something?"

"No . . . my father needs me to work on the farm, that's all. I don't have to go to school now I'm fifteen," he said defiantly. But Theo saw his eyes were clouded over darkly. "My father says I don't need school anymore . . . and anyway, I have a good job now and I might get taken on as apprentice to a blacksmith."

The heat crept around them, weighing them down. Theo wiped the damp hair from her forehead and Carl shifted uncomfortably on the pony's back. She stole a quick look at him and wondered at the undefinable note of conflict in his voice.

"But you're really good in school," she said. "You could

have gotten the English Prize yourself. Doesn't your father care about that?" Carl shook his head abruptly and sat straight on the pony. He wanted to go now, Theo saw. She wished he would look at her once more with those incredible blue eyes . . .

"Is your father the man who drives the vegetable wagon?" she asked swiftly, to keep him from leaving. She knew who his father was. But it was the first time she'd ever had a conversation with anyone from school, and she didn't want it to end. She stepped closer to the pony to rub her hand through the tangled mane. The animal lipped at her with its soft mouth and Carl smiled.

"That is my father, ja," he answered, and this time she could smile back without looking away. Mrs. O'Leary always bought their vegetables from the big man who drove the old wooden wagon through town from early summer to late autumn. Norwegian, Stevenson had told Theo. Lots of Norwegians and Swedes moving to America now — hard-working, intensely religious, good farmers. Stevenson said immigrants were brave people, to come to a new land without knowing the language. They had to work twice, three times as hard as anyone else. Theo tilted her head up at Carl.

"You *want* to go to school?" she teased. "Sometimes I wish *I* didn't have to go sit around with idiots like that Gyp Grimer or listen to silly old Miss Schroeder all day long."

"Gyp doesn't matter," Carl answered shortly. "There's always going to be people like him in the world . . ."

Carl had seen the world, she thought curiously. She wished she found conversation easy, like Claudia did. She wished she could ask to hear the story of how he had come all the way from Norway . . . on a ship! And probably went to England first, and then New York, and then all the way

27

to Minnesota in a wagon or on the train . . . when she had only ever been from Indianapolis, Indiana, to here.

"Miss Schroeder isn't really silly," Carl said quietly. "I think she's just lonely and stuck here with her old mother."

Theo swallowed the sudden lump in her throat. Miss Schroeder *was* lonely . . . just like she was. And she really had cared about Theo, too, worrying about her missing graduation and offering to keep her for three days. And she'd seemed so proud as she made her announcement to the class. That prize meant a lot to Miss Schroeder.

"Maybe Miss Schroeder would give you the English Prize instead," Theo blurted. She flushed in astonishment at her own words, and Carl looked at her silently. "I'm not going to be at graduation, so what does it matter?" she mumbled quickly. What was she saying? But now she had started, she had to finish. "I mean, you deserve it as much as me . . . you know it's true, Carl! And then maybe your father would think you should stay in school, and that matters a lot more than —"

They stared away from each other, speechless now. The boots hung awkwardly from Theo's hand. The pony snorted at a fly. Carl suddenly turned and looked squarely at her.

"That's real nice of you," he said softly. "But it wouldn't matter to my father. And it *should* go to you — the prize, I mean. You write much better than I do. I don't mind. I have a good job . . ." He waved his hand vaguely in the direction of the river. "Mr. Savage's been real good to me."

"Mr. Savage?" she cried in a low voice. "Where do you work?"

"Why, over there — at that big horse farm. You know —

Mr. Savage's, with all the racehorses? I'm just a rag boy now — I clean brushes and haul water and keep the yard clean, but they've been having me help out at the blacksmith's." He grinned slightly. "It'll feel real strange to go there all dressed up on Saturday!" Carl pulled off his cap and stuck it in his pocket. "I wish you were going, Theo," he muttered, running his words together so she had to lean closer to hear him. She stared down at the dirty stockings and boots in her hand and didn't know how to answer. "Well, I'll see you around when you get back, I guess," Carl said. He turned the pony sharply and trotted off down the road. Without his cap, his blond hair seemed to glow under the afternoon sun. Everything about him seemed as bright and clear as a summer day. Theo ran a few steps after him.

"Carl!" she called. He twisted around to see her. "Thanks," she said. The words stuck in her throat and for a moment she wasn't sure if he'd heard her, but his face opened in a broad smile and he waved to her before turning back down the south road out of town.

She thought the heat had made her giddy. When she got home she went to the back yard and stuck her head under the pump, splashing water over her hair and face. Mrs. O'Leary stuck her head out the kitchen door.

"I've made you a pitcher of lemonade, love," she called, shaking her head at the mess Theo was making. "Your mum was thinking you'd be fair washed out with this heat." Theo shook the water from her hair and followed Mrs. O'Leary into the kitchen. She drank straight from the pitcher in gulps, until the liquid sloshed in her stomach and for a moment she thought she might really be sick after all. She sat at the well-scrubbed wooden table and lay her head on her arms. What a stupid thing to do, to offer her prize — the top prize in the school — to Carl! What had come over her? She sat for a long time listening to the quiet sounds of the afternoon house. Mrs. O'Leary called a cheery good-bye to Maud in the other room and Theo heard the front door slam. She heard the low drone of Maud's voice as she rehearsed a speech she'd written for a meeting of the Shakopee Women's Club, urging them to join in the national suffrage movement to fight for women's right to vote. She remembered Maud's depression after they'd been in the little town of Savage a few weeks.

"It's a good name for the place — Savage!" she'd joked morosely. "It's full of savages! These women, some of them, haven't even *heard* of the suffrage movement, Stevenson! They just waste their lives away in their awful kitchens."

"And it's a great thing for us that you don't, my love," said Stevenson solemnly in reply. He lifted a forkful of Maud's casserole and sniffed it dubiously. "Thank heavens Mrs. O'Leary only has one evening off a week! Just you tend to writing those speeches!"

Theo sighed and brushed the damp hair from her eyes. If she were a boy, she'd be able to think about driving harness horses seriously . . . she frowned. She *did* think about it seriously! But she was a woman — well, a young woman. Who had decided what things women could and could not do? Who had made the decision not to let women vote? And why? She squeezed her eyes shut and tried to imagine whether it would make a difference to her or not, if she could vote for the president of the United States. The president seemed very far away, and it was hard to understand what he had to do with her life.

And even though it was difficult, there did seem to be

women who went right ahead doing what they wanted with their lives. Claudia . . . Claudia did what she wanted. Claudia had always wanted to play the violin, and it never occurred to her not to be the best. No one had ever told her she couldn't. And what about Aunt Harriet, whom Maud always talked about? Maud's older sister had always wanted to be a doctor, and she was a good one — very good, well respected. Had it been a struggle for her? Somehow, when Maud talked about it, struggles sounded more like grand adventures. And what about Maud? Her mother always said women should do more than marry and have children — but wasn't that what she had done?

Theo sat up cautiously and the lemonade stayed quiet in her stomach. Strange, to think about marriage and children. She wondered if Claudia would ever get married. Inexplicably, she thought suddenly of Carl, of how the sun seemed to settle deep in his eyes and how his rare smile grew straight from that warmth. She stood abruptly just as Maud came into the kitchen.

"There you are!" she greeted Theo happily. It must be a good speech, thought Theo. "I need to hem that dress before it gets dark. Have you packed your case yet?"

"You asked me that twice already, Mama," said Theo. She shed her school clothes slowly and let Maud drape the new dress over her head. She twisted her head to look at the papers on the table. "Is that your new speech, Mama?"

Maud pulled her around. "For goodness' sakes, Theodora, don't twist! I'm trying to get the hemline straight."

If Claudia had been there Maud would have chattered happily about her article through the hemming session. Theo struggled to think what Claudia would ask about the speech, so that the talk would swirl around like a bright stream bubbling over rocks.

"Are the women in the Shakopee Women's Club savages, too?" she asked, and Maud paused a moment and looked at her in surprise. A faint smile crossed her mouth but she bent her head to the dress again. "I think I can bring them into the twentieth century!" Maud answered. "After all — it's inevitable."

Theo twisted her mouth. What was inevitable? Maud always talked like that, as if her thoughts raced on ahead of her, faster than her spoken words could keep up. She slumped her shoulders. It wasn't any use trying to be as bright and knowledgeable as Claudia. The sweat had begun to trickle down her back and her skin itched under the stiff material. The lemonade sat like an iceberg in her stomach. Maybe she should really get sick, and then no one could go see Claudia. See how Claudia felt about *that*. But no, Maud probably *would* leave her with Mrs. O'Leary after all. Maud wouldn't miss seeing Claudia for anything.

"Theodora, if you don't stand up straight . . ." Maud yanked the dress so sharply it hurt. "Do you want this done or not!"

But this was supposed to be my graduation dress! Theo screamed silently to herself. Now I have to wear it to Claudia's debut. The lemonade seemed to have turned to bile in her. She wished she didn't have a sister at all. She wished Claudia would just disappear. If Claudia didn't exist, Maud would talk and laugh with *her*, see the things in *her* she would be proud of, instead of being blinded by a brighter light. If Claudia wasn't always commanding everyone's attention then maybe *she*, Theo, would have a chance to show everyone who she really was.

ᶜᵛᵛ Chapter Three ᶜᵛᵛ

A FEW DAYS LATER when Theo remembered her angry wish, she knew that everything changed from that moment on. Only a few days later, the trip to Minneapolis would seem as long ago as a half-remembered dream from childhood.

But on Friday morning Theo waited on the porch, clutching her leather case and sniffing the heavy scorched air. There was no morning sun through the acrid haze. Joe Watson, who drove his fat white milk-wagon horse through Savage early every morning, appeared at the far end of Cargyll Street. He'd built long seats down both sides of his cart so he could act as taxi for people catching the first train.

"This weather sure ain't natural," said Joe, leaning with his elbows on his knees to look at Theo when he pulled to a stop by the gate. "Couldn't hardly get ol' Bess up this morning . . . didn't want to leave her stall." He peered down the street toward the tracks and the rolling grasslands that opened into prairie a few miles out of town. "Tornado weather," he nodded, squinting at Theo.

"Papa said this isn't tornado weather yet," she answered flatly. Old Mr. Watson assumed that all girls were as easily frightened as Amelia McCarthy, who squealed at everything. Joe draped the reins over the front of the wagon and climbed stiffly down. "Maybe not," he said laconically, "but it's fixing to storm, anyhow. Where's yer Ma and Pa?"

Maud ignored Joe's offer of assistance and hopped into the wagon, settling herself with her bag on one side of Theo, while Stevenson sat on the other. When the wagon lurched off, Stevenson smiled down at Theo. "Excited?" he asked.

She made herself smile back. There was nothing more to be discussed about her own disappointment, but she couldn't dismiss the sharp pang as the train pulled away from the platform and raced north past the Savage farm.

She looked over at the dim blur of the buildings and could just make out the brilliant flags above the onion-domes hanging limp in the oppressive heat. There was such a sharp yearning in her, although she couldn't define it; it was as if she wanted to jump from the rushing train into . . . what? What pressed against her heart so insistently?

The dull suffocating haze stayed with her for the whole trip, and she struggled against the sadness that kept clutching in her throat. What was the matter with her? Even as Claudia ran to meet them, catching Theo as she stumbled down the steep train steps, she could not shake the heavy stillness that seemed to have taken over her blood.

"You're still asleep, Thee!" cried Claudia, and her laugh had such a delightful ring that people turned briefly to smile as they passed. Even the horses pulling the hired cab to the hotel seemed under Claudia's joyful spell. They lifted their feet and fairly pranced through the crowded city streets. Around Claudia was a brightness that rivaled the wonderful new electric lights in the hotel suite.

"Aren't they amazing?" bubbled Claudia, rushing to turn them all on at once. The electric lights seemed too harsh to Theo; she felt exposed and stared out the window at the street four stories below. It was bustling with horse-cabs and streetcars, vendors and newsboys calling their wares, tides of men in bowler hats and the wider brims of ladies' bonnets. In and out among the throng moved the occasional automobile, the chrome and paint gleaming even in the haze. Claudia caught her hand and stared out the window with her.

34

"Isn't it an amazing place, Thee!" she breathed, as if she, like Theo, were seeing it for the first time. "Imagine! Electric lights and running water in every room in the hotel! And wait 'til you see the Symphony Hall! Oh, Thee! Chandeliers and velvet curtains, and everything painted white and gold . . . you'll love it!"

All through the long afternoon and evening, Theo forced herself to look for the enchantment Claudia so obviously felt. But the heavy yearning persisted and grew so strong that by dinner she sat silent and hardly touched her food. Maud was so caught within the animated conversation she and Claudia were having she didn't notice, but Stevenson glanced at her several times. "Are you all right, Theo?" he asked. Theo hastily pushed a potato into her mouth. "I'm fine, Papa," she mumbled. "I'm just thinking."

The storm broke after dinner. Curtains of rain slashed the street and pelted against the windows of the hotel. From the lobby, Theo watched cabdrivers rushing to shut the windows of the closed carriages. The electric lights flickered at every crash of thunder.

"You'll stay here tonight, sweetheart," said Maud. "There's no sense in your going all the way back to the Pretsky's in this weather." So Claudia shared a room with Theo instead of going back to the house where she boarded with a musician's family. Claudia sat curled in a huge velvet armchair. Her face was flushed and her eyes sparkled as she smiled down at Theo.

"You're awfully quiet," she remarked. "You haven't said two words since you got here." Theo felt her sister's slender fingers in her hair and for a moment she relaxed, sitting on the soft rug and leaning against Claudia's knee. Almost like before, when Claudia still lived at home. The design on the carpet reminded her of the opulent patterns painted on the barns at the Savage farm, and she looked sharply up at her sister. Was it possible Claudia did not know that this weekend was Theo's graduation? Maybe Maud and Stevenson had not told her, so she wouldn't feel badly . . .

"I'm just tired," she answered at last. Claudia continued to stroke her hair idly. Theo was startled at how hot the fingers felt against her skin.

"Are you afraid?" she asked, because it was the only thing she could imagine that would make Claudia seem so feverish. "About tomorrow night, I mean?" Claudia let her hand drop limply over the arm of the chair.

"Tomorrow night," she repeated slowly. "It's all I've ever wanted." The flush in her face suddenly paled and she put her hands to her cheeks. "Yes," she whispered. "Yes, I'm scared." She held her hands out and turned them over, flexing her fingers. "Dreams are strange things, Thee," she breathed. "You dream and dream . . . and the dream is so big and so perfect, and then — then it comes down to something very small, so small you hardly think of it . . ." She opened her hands wide. "It's all here," she continued. "Here, in my fingers. That's all it is now, my dream. I've got to where I want to be, and now it's just these fingers — either they work, or they don't. That's all. Funny, isn't it?"

Claudia slipped from the chair and sat close to Theo. For a moment they sat silent, and Theo could feel the heat from Claudia through her clothing. She took her sister's hand and held it in her own. These fingers could hold a bow and move it with utter grace over the resined strings of the violin. They could fly from string to string pressing, releasing, commanding, caressing, as if they had a life of their own and Claudia simply followed.

"I'm scared of the others, too," said Claudia after a few minutes. "All those men in the orchestra. They don't think

I can do this, Thee. They think women can't take the strain, that I'll break under the pressure."

"You'd never break under any pressure!" cried Theo indignantly.

Claudia smiled, something of the joy creeping back into her eyes. "I need you to believe in me, Thee," she said softly. "I think you understand about dreams better than anyone."

Theo looked at her, astonished. What did she know about dreams that Claudia didn't know ten times better? What dreams did she have, after all, but daydreams? Silly ideas about driving horses around a track. Was that a real dream? How could it be real, if she never even came close to doing it? The closest she could come was when she wrote about it. Then she could describe the rush of speed through her blood, the heart of the great horse singing down the long reins into her hands and into her heart until it became her own, lifting her, taking her beyond all the bonds of earth . . . But how could she *know* that was real, just by writing words?

"I don't know . . . I don't think I know," she replied in a low voice. Claudia hugged her close. "You just haven't found a way to follow your dreams, Thee. But they're there — I can see them. When you go off in your head alone, like you did at dinner, thinking and thinking . . . see? You do understand."

Claudia swayed unsteadily to her feet and leaned against the back of the chair. She held her long skirts bunched in her hand. Her eyes flamed from her pale face. "I have the worst case of stage fright I've ever had!" she laughed weakly. "I've never felt it this much. I think I better go to bed."

The performance the next night was everything Claudia promised. The gilt-painted balconies were thronged with

37

men and women dressed in their finest clothes, and the chandeliers glittered brilliantly off the shining instruments in the orchestra. The musicians were dressed in velvet black-tailed coats and shirts so white they blinded the eye. Claudia wore a gown made of the softest white, like thousands of pure-spun webs draped over her graceful body. Her hair gleamed as rich and dark as the polished wood of her violin. Even from where Theo sat, she could see how flushed Claudia's face was, and the color only made her indescribably lovely. Theo thought she had never seen anything so magnificent and so beautiful.

"Let her be perfect," she whispered so low no one around her would hear. "Let her be perfect."

The music burst forth and swelled up around the audience like waves. Theo listened, transfixed from the first sweet notes of the violins. Claudia's eyes burned more intensely than even the thousand lights of the chandeliers, and the music streaming from the violins seemed to transform into a shimmering satin ribbon of sound that flew high over the listening audience.

Theo closed her eyes and let the music lift her free from the earth, until she was a horse racing on a ray of light. The music was like the wind against her skin. It seemed to Theo that Claudia played alone and just for her, until there was only the two of them in the great swirl of sound. And for that instant, the terrible yearning sadness in her disappeared.

Then the ribbon of music ripped apart and the broken applause fluttered to a terrible silence that tumbled down around her. She clutched the arms of her seat and gasped, "What is it? What happened?"

Maud threw herself toward the aisle and pushed with Stevenson through the dismayed crowd. Theo was alone among hundreds of people. They closed in around her so she could not see or hear, and no one could hear her cry out. She fought her way through the crowds but lost her sense of direction, and no one seemed able to tell her what was happening.

The next afternoon, Stevenson explained as he took her home to Savage on the train. "Polio," he said shortly. "She played right to the very last note, but it was too much for her."

Theo imagined what she had not seen . . . the slow body folding up on itself like a gossamer web blown apart by a storm, the flash of polished wood as the violin crashed to the floor.

"Her body was burning up," said Stevenson in a daze. "It burned my hands right through her clothes."

"Will she get better, Papa?" Theo could hardly make her numb lips form the question.

Stevenson smiled sadly. "No one can ever tell, with polio. You just have to wait. But Claudia's like her mother — just like you, sweetheart. Strong blood. Remember how your grandmother drove a covered wagon all the way from Rhode Island to Indiana alone?" Theo nodded. She knew the story. "That's the kind of blood you women have," he said, something of the old teasing tone in his voice.

And so Theo stayed with Miss Schroeder and her old mother after all, in a house that smelled like musty dried roses. Stevenson returned to the hospital in Minneapolis where Maud had never left Claudia's bedside. There were countless days of nothingness then, as if the bottom had fallen out from a speeding train and all there was under Theo was darkness.

∾ Chapter Four ᴄ∾

Stevenson had been gone five days and Theo had not heard anything from Minneapolis. Claudia could be dead and she wouldn't know it. Theo hardly moved from the house those days, waiting for a telegram, concentrating on feeling if Claudia was still alive. Miss Schroeder didn't know much about polio. She lived with old Mrs. Schroeder in a creaky house with shades always drawn and clocks that ticked so loudly in the stuffy stillness Theo had a dull headache all day. Miss Schroeder spoke in whispers to Theo, as if Claudia had died and the funeral were taking place in her drawing room.

There was nothing to do. Theo spent hours on Miss Schroeder's front porch swing, staring at the wilted peony bushes and watching for the thin yellow cat that lived under the steps. The porch swing creaked, and by now the sound was so much a part of Theo's existence she felt uneasy when she stood up and the creaking stopped.

One day Gustav Johansson drove his vegetable wagon into town with the first summer harvest piled in willow baskets on the back. Fat damp lettuces spilled from one basket, and from another tiny carrots bright as jewels. He had turnips and potatoes as usual, the last of the winter's storage, and some sweet spring onions no bigger than marbles.

Carl sat dangling his bare feet over the end of the wagon. He wore the same brown cap and the same patched shirt he'd worn all year to school, tucked into his trousers with a single suspender running over a broad shoulder. He slid off the wagon when he saw Theo on Miss Schroeder's porch swing. He held a small basket of strawberries, tiny and red and beaded with dew.

"My mother said these are for you," he said without greeting, as if he had seen her only the day before. He stuck the basket out to her, stiff-armed, and she took it equally stiffly. He looked down at his bare feet. "We are all very sorry about your sister, Theo." Carl scuffed the dust and the thin cat ran out from under the steps. "When will she be back?"

"I don't know."

"When will you be back at your house?"

She gave the swing a vicious shove with her foot, and it banged against the post behind it. "I don't know anything!" she snapped at Carl. Miss Schroeder closed the door softly behind her as she came out onto the porch. "Carl was only being concerned, Theodora," she chided. "Don't kick the swing so hard, child! Why, Gus — you have carrots already!"

Gustav Johansson was a tall powerful man with hair as yellow as ripe autumn wheat. He smiled the same slow smile his son had, and jumped lightly to the ground. He heaved the basket of carrots from the wagon and waited courteously as Miss Schroeder picked through them. She shook the dirt from a large bunch and held them up to inspect them. "What are you selling them for, Gus?"

"For dot — twelve cents," he smiled. Miss Schroeder paused as if deciding, and Theo hoped she was not going to dicker with Gus over the price. All of a sudden, she became acutely aware of Carl standing silently to the side of the wooden steps. On his face was the hard stillness of embarrassment.

"I love carrots, Miss Schroeder," called Theo, and

without a word the woman reached into her apron pocket for the coins. Gustav nodded at her politely, and Miss Schroeder elbowed open the door with her hands full of carrots, and disappeared inside the house. Theo felt Carl relax.

Gustav Johansson spoke to Carl in a lilting language and together they lifted the heavy basket up onto the wagon bed. His father turned to lead the horse on, but Carl hesitated, looking back at Theo. Gustav led his horse and wagon out onto the road.

Theo jumped off the swing and ran down the steps. "Wait," she said. "Thank you for the strawberries." She hunted around desperately for something else to say. "Hey, Carl — you want to come over to my house and see my father's books?" Her eyes went wide in surprise at her unexpected words. Carl's eyes widened, too, with a startled hunger. He glanced uneasily toward his father, waiting for him on the road. Theo stammered in her hurry. "I don't have to stay at Miss Schroeder's all day," she said. "I can go back to the house whenever I need anything. I just . . . I didn't want . . . it's so *empty*." She swallowed hard. "But if you wanted, I'd show you Papa's books."

Her voice had dropped to a whisper so she could keep herself from crying. The long hollow days in which she could not cry or think or move had been broken by the appearance of Carl. She could not bear him to go now, and leave her alone again in the silent musty house with the dying peonies and the frightened yellow cat. She watched the uncertain eagerness in his eyes and remembered him at school, how his broad slow finger would trace the lines of text in the primers and how his lips would move carefully as he formed each word. He had read steadily through every ragged book in the school's meager library, sometimes three times over, as if each word kept him from starvation. At recess he always sat apart from the others and refused to join in the bickering games, preferring instead to sit under a tree and read. She was suddenly certain that she had said the one sure thing that would keep Carl with her.

Gustav Johansson called from the road and Carl ran to him. Theo could not hear what Carl said, but she saw Gustav shake his head slowly from side to side, peer up at the sun, and shake it more decisively. She went to the road and stood at the front of the wagon, looking up at the big man. "Couldn't Carl stay awhile?" she asked. "It's been five days since Papa . . . since my father went back to the city and I'm . . ." She'd hoped he would feel sorry for her enough to let Carl stay, but with a rush of shame she realized she might cry — that she was speaking the truth. The unspoken word "lonely" was the truest of all, but she could not say it aloud. Gustav Johansson shifted on the wagon seat and smiled kindly at her.

"Five o'clock," he said to Carl. "You come home by den. No later. Der's all dot milking." He flicked the reins over the horse and the cart rumbled off down the road. Carl slipped from the back and they walked halfway down Cargyll Street before either spoke.

"I like your father," said Theo. "He has a nice smile." Carl nodded abruptly but did not answer. "Did you tell him I was going to show you my father's books?" she asked. He shook his head. She walked silently next to him a few more steps, then turned to face him. "It makes me feel stupid, talking to you and you not talking back," she remarked. He shrugged sheepishly.

"I was just thinking," he said, twisting his cap in his hands. Theo laughed; it was the first time she'd laughed in days. To her horror, the laughter loosened the tears that

43

had been blocked up in her throat and she jerked her face away from him. Carl didn't say anything for a few moments, then: "Why did you laugh?" She took a deep breath.

"Because that's what *I* always say . . . 'I'm thinking.' " She imitated her own voice as she spoke, and Carl laughed out loud. "I always say that, even if I don't really know what I was thinking. Because sometimes my mother looks at me like —"

"Like she can't figure out where you came from?"

"Yes!" she grinned. "Like I suddenly showed up at her house — a stranger — and she can't figure out how I got there." She sniffed loudly and drew her arm roughly over her face, but she felt better than she had in days. "You know, Mama never looks at Claudia that way. Claudia's really her daughter . . . anyone could see that. They think alike, and Claudia . . ."

Her voice trailed off. They had arrived in front of the old house, and the sound of the gate swinging shut behind her as she walked into the still yard made her want to cry again. The house hunched under the elms like a stranger hiding from her. She hesitated, and Carl came to stand beside her.

"Let's sit here for a while," he said. He sat on the step and stretched his long legs comfortably out in front of him. Still shaken, she sat gingerly next to him. When he leaned back and shook his head to let the faint breeze from the leaves stir through his hair, she felt overwhelmed, suddenly, with comfort — Carl was so solid, so gentle, it made the house seem to soften into a welcome. She lifted her face to taste the slight breeze, and when she spoke her voice was hardly louder than a whisper.

"Can I tell you something?" she asked, and Carl nodded. He draped his brown arms over his knees and didn't look at her, but studied the house across the street. It made it easier for Theo to speak.

"I was so angry . . . you know, that I couldn't go to the graduation and the picnic, all because Claudia was performing with the symphony, and I wanted . . . I mean, I hoped all along I was going to get the English Prize, but I thought Miss Schroeder was going to give it to you, and . . ." She paused miserably, but Carl flicked his eyes across her own and half-smiled, shaking his head. "And then Miss Schroeder told me *I* was going to get it, and I could hardly wait for Mama to see . . . but really, it was the horses more than anything —" She stumbled and knew she wasn't making sense. Carl waited quizzically.

"It was the horses!" she cried in a low voice. "I wanted to go to the farm — the Dan Patch farm . . . where you work." Carl was looking at her steadily now with his serious eyes. "I always wanted to go there, ever since we moved here. And I hated so much being here. But my parents . . . Mama . . . thinks anything about horses is a waste of time. They want me to do something useful with my life. Like Claudia. I'm supposed to be a doctor like Aunt Harriet, or a lawyer or a scientist, or . . . I don't *know*. Something *important*. Not just a person who loves horses. But Carl . . . I'm not . . . I mean, I only want . . ." She ran out of words and flushed, overcome with confusion. Why on earth was she telling all this to Carl?

He leaned back on his elbows. "But you're a girl," he said. She tossed her head in scorn.

"I know I'm a girl," she snapped. "That's not the point. I'm going to do whatever I want, and it doesn't matter if I'm a girl. It's just that I can't think *what* I want . . . at least, I can't think of anything Mama would think was important."

45

"Well, don't worry about them, then," Carl said reasonably. "What do *you* want to do?" He had never heard of girls wanting to be doctors or lawyers or scientists, but he supposed they could be.

Theo sat straight up on the step and looked at him. "I want to drive harness horses!" she said passionately. "There! I want to drive the fastest horses in the world and win races." If he laughs, she thought fiercely, I'll walk in the house right now and slam the door in his face.

"Well, for that," Carl answered calmly, without hesitation, "if you want that, you have to go to the Dan Patch farm. That's where the fastest horses in the world are."

Her wish seemed simple enough to him. The farm held no mystique for him; he worked there every week. If she wanted to drive harness horses, she had to go there. He'd never seen a woman driving those horses but he supposed, if they could be doctors and lawyers and whatever else she'd just told him, that they could drive harness horses too. He himself had no desire for that . . . he sighed. Maybe girls could drive horses — but could the son of a poor immigrant Norwegian farmer go to university? Could *he* be a doctor or a lawyer or a scientist? He turned his head and gazed at Theo. He had never seen such a fierce expression on a girl's face, and the determination in her eyes sent a thrill down his arms. Yes! he thought. I want something as much as that! But before his eyes, Theo's face fell and dissolved into sadness.

"Oh, Carl! I wished she was *dead!*" she cried in a stifled voice. "I did, Carl. When I couldn't go to graduation and the picnic . . . when I knew I wouldn't get to the horse farm . . . oh! I *hated* her. Claudia. Because I wanted so much to go . . . and she's always first, so I couldn't, and she always knows what she wants and I never . . . and now . . ."

"But you were angry," Carl said. "You were just angry. You didn't know she'd get sick like that."

Theo wrapped her arms around her knees and rocked back and forth on the step. "But I wished she was *dead!*" she wailed. "And now she might die . . ."

"Lots of people get better from polio," he pointed out.

She shook her head violently. "But she plays the violin, Carl! Don't you see — if her arms are paralyzed, even a little . . . it's all she knows how to do!"

Carl studied the flushed face of the girl beside him. Her hair was always falling out of its ribbon, he thought. He brushed the dust off his pants. He'd never met Claudia. He wondered if Theo looked like her. He'd never seen anyone play a violin, either, and he wasn't sure what one looked like, unless it was like a fiddle. He gazed at Theo. She lived in a home where things like this were *known* and thought about and discussed. These people, this girl, knew about the world . . . they read books and went to universities . . .

In his own home, there was only the big leather-bound Bible his mother had carefully brought on the ship from Norway wrapped in a scrap of oilcloth and kept at the bottom of her marriage trunk. But here in this house — and he looked longingly past the girl at the closed door — this house was full of books, books of every kind, more than he'd ever imagined, and if he could just *see* them . . . if he could just hold them in his hands and look at the words on the pages, then he would have everything he'd ever dreamed of. But the girl beside him was not thinking of all those wonderful books. She was staring sadly at her dirty feet in the dust.

"You didn't make her sick, Theo," said Carl softly. "That's what you think, don't you? I get angry, too . . . I get angry at my father. Sometimes I wish he wasn't there, too. Sometimes I wish he'd just go away! Then I could go to school. Ma wouldn't mind. I could do anything I wanted."

They stared at each other without shyness for a moment. Hungry. They each had something of the other's dream. Theo lived in a house full of books, with a father who knew about law and science and a mother who thought girls should be doctors. And Carl went every day to the great horse farm by the Minnesota River, and every day he saw Dan Patch. Something they wanted and could not touch hung in the air around both of them.

"I don't know what to do," whispered Theo at last. She drew her arms tighter around her knees. "If I could just think of something to *do* . . . maybe it would help her. I guess that doesn't make sense . . ."

"It makes sense to me," Carl said slowly. He examined a fallen elm leaf and pulled it apart along the veins. "It makes sense. If you don't do anything, you just sit around thinking bad thoughts and making yourself sick. But if you could do *something* that would help you imagine her getting better, you know . . . well, maybe that's sort of like praying."

Theo tossed a twig sharply and frowned. Praying is for people who can't think for themselves, Maud had always told her. And Stevenson had always shrugged and said science was the new religion. Savage, Minnesota, was a staunchly religious town, the bells on the big Catholic church pealing for an hour on Sunday mornings, but the Harris family never went to church. All year in school she had endured the nagging of the others. How come you ain't in church, Theo*dora?* I heard Theo's Mama wears man's pants! Don't your Daddy believe in God, Theodora? Theo narrowed her eyes. "Praying is stupid," she said.

Carl shrugged. "Maybe it is," he said mildly. "I didn't mean you had to pray. I just meant that it might help your sister if you could imagine her strong and well and playing her violin, instead of making yourself sick thinking it's all your fault."

All at once, Theo felt calm, as if Carl's words had spread a soothing balm over her heart. Who would have ever imagined Carl Johansson could put that many words together at one time! She watched him with some wonder. He carefully pulled apart another leaf and studied it, as if determined to discover how the green life pulsed in the slender veins. It reminded her of the bright color-plates illustrating Stevenson's botany encyclopedia. She jumped up.

"We better go in," she said. "Your father said you have to be home by five." Carl followed her eagerly into the dim house. It felt to Theo as if it had been years since she had been there, and she fought down another bout of grief.

She pushed open the door to her father's study and Carl stepped past her into the room. He stood very still with his hands held at his sides. The hush in him was deeper than the silence of not speaking. He stood there in his rough farm clothes, with his bare feet and his wool cap shoved into his pocket. Yet he was not ill at ease. He seemed to Theo completely natural standing there, and she thought he looked at the shelves of books as if he were meeting at last with the most important part of himself.

She did not mind the silence now. It was different from the stifling hush of Miss Schroeder's house. She knew that if she were to find herself inside the huge barns on the Savage farm she would stand in wonder as Carl was doing now. But finally Carl did move, stepping close to the shelves to read the titles. Theo pulled back the curtains so he would have more light.

"You can take them out to look at, if you like," she said. "My father wouldn't mind. He likes me to read them."

Carl glanced at her. "Have you read all these?" he asked. She laughed. "I couldn't read them all!" she said. "Look — all these law books, and the science ones. But here's a whole shelf of story ones . . . I've read these. You want to read one?" She pulled a book swiftly from the shelf. If he took one home to read, he'd have to bring it back to her. She didn't worry about lending it, because she'd seen Carl handle even the ragged primers at school as if they were the rarest treasures. But Carl stepped abruptly back from the bookcases and shook his head.

"I couldn't . . . I mean, I wouldn't even know which one to take," he muttered bitterly. "And my father would be angry. He thinks any book but the Bible is a waste of time. I told you — he doesn't believe much in school. Anyway, when could I read it? If I'm not working with my father, I have my job at the horse farm."

"You could read it at night before you go to bed," she said. He gritted his teeth and shook his head again.

"We can't waste candles."

"I'll give you some candles," she persisted. "We have plenty. What about Sundays? You could read on Sundays."

An incredulous look passed over his face. "Sunday!"

She was silent. He went to the window and looked out, but after a moment he turned back to her. "What's the use, anyway?" he said. "Even if I do manage to read one, I'll just want another, and another . . . and where would that get me? I'm only going to be a farmer, or else a blacksmith." He bit the last words off like a curse.

Theo selected another book and ran her finger over the thick embossed spine. One of her favorites . . . *Gulliver's Travels*, by Jonathan Swift. She put it into Carl's hands.

"When you're done with it, you can get another," she said. "And when Papa comes back . . . when he comes back, you could talk to him about what you read. He loves that. He's always trying to get me to talk about his books with him, but I like to read them and . . . you know, just *think* about them by myself. Anyway, I know he'd want you to read as many as you can."

She was bewildered at her insistence. She hardly knew Carl. It struck her how she was here with him like this, with this same boy who only a week before she'd dismissed as too "stuck-up" to bother with. But maybe if she'd tried to talk to him before . . . She watched him now as he cradled the book she'd given him, his big work-roughened hands holding it as gently as if it had been a newborn creature. He traced the gold lettering on the cover with his finger.

"You can open it," she laughed. "It won't fall apart."

He reddened. "I've just never seen a book as fine as this . . . like these," he murmured, his eyes sweeping eagerly over the shelves. "I've only seen the ones at school. Farmers don't have books. My father can hardly read English, Theo. Just a little of the newspaper . . . and the Bible, in Norwegian."

She wished he were not so embarrassed about his father. She liked Gustav Johansson, liked how he rubbed his carthorse's nose and gave him carrots. The big farmer always had a kind smile and quiet manner; and when children followed along beside his wagon, he would toss them apples and laugh when they caught them. "Your father seems like a good man," she said slowly. "I like how he treats his horse.

51

Maybe it doesn't matter so much to him that he can't read."

Carl chuckled unexpectedly. "As long as someone's good to their horse, they're a good person?" he teased. "You really do love horses, don't you?" he asked seriously. "When you were telling me how you were going to drive harness horses, you looked so —"

He stopped and she was overcome with self-consciousness. She'd looked silly, that was what. The whole thing was a crazy idea, and she'd been crazy to tell Carl about it.

"You looked beautiful," he finished softly. Theo flushed. *Beautiful?* She glared at him but he appeared not to notice, and was holding the book close to his nose, sniffing at it. He smiled at her happily, as if he'd never said a word. "I love everything about books," he grinned. "I even love the way they smell. I love how heavy they feel, and how thick the pages are." He clasped the book against his chest. "I have to go now, Theo. There's the milking."

The air was still hot when they stepped out onto the porch, but the shadows under the elms were longer and held an early evening cool. Theo wrapped the book in a piece of newspaper and ran back into the kitchen for some candles. He hesitated taking them.

"We have plenty," she said roughly, still unnerved by his earlier remark. She wished her hair was not so mussed around her face. "Keep the book under your shirt when you get home, so your father won't see."

He shoved the candles into his pocket. "Thank you," he said. "I'll see you soon, Theo. When I bring the book back. I hope your sister is all right." They walked to the yard gate and stood, both unwilling to turn away first. The dust smelled hot and flies droned in the grasses. At the far end of the street a tall woman dressed in black was walking toward them. Theo watched her a moment. A stranger, probably just off the afternoon train from Chicago. Carl ran a stick tap-tapping along the wooden fence.

"Hey, Theo," he said, frowning thoughtfully. "Would your mother and father let you have a summer job?"

"I don't know . . . maybe," she said. "Baby-sitting or something . . . why?"

"Well, I just thought . . . I don't know, but maybe you could get a little job at Mr. Savage's farm. You know, like I have."

She stared at him. "A job at the farm!" She twisted her mouth in disgust. "Mama would never let me. She wouldn't want me spending all that time around *horse people*."

"What's wrong with horse people?"

"Oh, she thinks they aren't *educated* or something. She'd think it was a waste of time, Carl."

"Even for the summer?" he insisted. "A couple days a week?"

Theo shook her head harshly. "They wouldn't hire me anyway," she said. "I'm a *girl*."

Carl tossed his stick over the fence and studied her with a critical eye. "You could pass for a boy," he mused. "You could wear some of my old clothes, and pin your hair under a cap, and no one would ever guess. They always need rag boys over there, Theo! Mr. Savage likes the place kept so clean you could eat off the ground."

Excitement made her words catch in her throat. "But what about Mama? Maybe my father would, but Mama would never — " But her mind was already racing ahead, turning over the idea wildly. She clasped her hands together in front of her. Was it possible? Imagine working at the International Stock Feed Farm! She wouldn't just *see* the place then — she'd actually work in those amazing barns! And the horses . . . she hardly dared to think. Would she actually touch them . . . touch Dan Patch? Her eyes were shining and Carl caught her excitement.

"Look, Theo, couldn't you just tell your parents you were baby-sitting?" he cried. "You know those new houses they built down near the landing? You could say you were baby-sitting there!"

"And Mama's so busy . . . she never checks on me, really — "

"And it would take your mind off your sister," said Carl, as if that settled it. He leaned toward her. "It's what you really want to do, as much as me wanting books!" He tapped the book he held. "See? And *you* convinced *me* —"

They smiled broadly at each other in delight. Yes! she thought. Yes! It could work! She was sure of it. And the money she earned . . . why, it could help with Claudia's medical bills! There was really nothing wrong with getting a job with the horses, she thought. It's just a silly problem that Mama has.

While they were talking, the woman in black had been slowly approaching, and now she stopped a few feet from the gate and studied a slip of paper in her hand. She set two expensive-looking traveling cases on the ground by her feet with a deliberate air, and tucked her long man's umbrella more securely under her arm. Over her thick mass of hair she wore a small flat black hat, and despite the heat, her black dress was buttoned to the neck.

Theo stared at the woman. She had never seen this person before in her life, and yet . . . and yet, she might have been looking straight into her sister Claudia's face! She saw immediately that this woman was years older, as old as Maud, but it was the same face — the same high graceful bone in the cheeks, the same dark, vital eyes, the same sweep of forehead up into the thick hair. Theo was speechless, but Carl took a step toward the woman with a manner as naturally courteous as his father's.

"Are you lost?" he asked. "Can we help you find someone?" The woman looked up and smiled, and Theo gasped. With the smile the years fell away from her face and it *was* Claudia after all, Claudia well and strong and full of life. Theo stumbled over a root of a tree as she peered from behind Carl. The woman's smile crinkled the corners of her eyes.

"Well, thank you," she nodded at Carl. But her eyes went past him to Theo. "But I think I have found who I was looking for." She stepped nearer. "This is Number Eight, Cargyll Street? But of course it is! You must be Theodora — you look just like your mother!" The woman took Theo's hands warmly in her own, but still Theo could not speak. "Didn't Maud tell you I was coming?" the woman asked in surprise. Her voice was deeper than Claudia's, smoother, not so bubbly. "I'm Harriet — your Aunt Harriet, Theodora. But how could you possibly remember me? You only met me once, when you were two!" She laughed, and included Carl in her glance as she spoke. "Your parents wired me about Claudia, and I caught the train out of New York as soon as I was able." She looked swiftly past them at the house. "Where *is* Maud? And is your . . . is Stevenson here?" Theo shook her head.

"They're both still in Minneapolis . . . with my sister," she faltered. "She's still in the hospital. I think." She sidled closer to Carl and hoped he would not leave. This woman dressed so severely in black seemed set to stay. So this was her Aunt Harriet, Maud's older sister, the famous doctor in the East. Of course, it must be her — she looked so much like Claudia! All her life, Theo had heard stories about this amazing woman. She swallowed. Did she really mean to stay? In the house? But then, there were her bags . . .

"We'll just send off a telegram straight away, to tell them I've got here," announced Harriet. "And you and I can get the house ready for your sister's return." Theo looked nervously at Carl, who was scuffing his foot in the dust.

"I really have to go, Theo," he said, apologizing with his eyes. "If I'm late, my father . . ." He wrapped his arms around the book. When he smiled at Theo she felt reassured and the woman next to her did not seem so daunting. Carl nodded his head at Aunt Harriet. "It was nice meeting you, Ma'am," he said. "I'm glad Theo will be able to go back to her house now." He put his cap on. "I'll be back in town in a few days. I'll come by then, all right?" And he walked quickly off down Cargyll Street toward the road out of town.

Her aunt made no mention of Carl, and Theo was grateful for that. She wished she could go up to her room to be alone, so she could think. But Harriet was already bustling around the house, drawing back curtains, plumping the sofa cushions against her knee with a snap, as if she'd lived there all her life. Theo followed her from room to room.

"I left some things at Miss Schroeder's," said Theo at last, hesitant. "And if my father sent a telegram, it would go there. Maybe one came this afternoon." She paused. "I didn't know Claudia was . . . coming home. I thought she might have to stay in the hospital for . . ." She felt the tears stinging her eyes and squeezed them tight. "Is she . . . do you think she's going to be all right?"

Harriet shook her head slowly. "I only had the one telegram your mother sent," she said gently. "Polio is an unpredictable disease, Theodora. Sometimes nothing happens after the fever leaves; sometimes it seems the person gets better for a while before getting worse. We don't know much yet — but a few of us in the East are working on some new techniques." She frowned. "I'm sure those methods have not reached this far west yet, and I'm not going to let my sister's oldest daughter waste away under some primitive doctor's care!" The vehemence in her words made Theo back away, but Harriet smoothed the folds of her dress and smiled. "Let's go find your Miss Schroeder, shall we?" she said. "And then we'll walk to the telegraph office. I've been on the train for days! I need to stretch my legs."

There was much of Maud in the woman's decisive manner, and much of Claudia's graceful movement in her walk. As she followed her, Theo felt the terrible days of waiting break to pieces inside her. Loneliness sat thick in the back of her throat. When would Maud and Stevenson come home? And Claudia . . . Claudia was coming home, too. But everything was changed now . . . changed forever. Misery caught her in the pit of her stomach and her legs shook. She felt she was losing all her strength, as if she'd been holding herself in for days, weeks. Now everything she'd tried not to feel came screaming down around her.

Claudia! Claudia! She forgot everything Carl had said to her, and felt only a sickening plague of remorse. You wished she was dead! she chanted over and over to herself. You wished she was dead! She wrapped her arms around herself to stop the nausea from overwhelming her and then, unexpectedly, there were other arms around her as well. Strong, steady arms. She let herself be pulled against the tall woman and held firmly. Harriet did not say a word. Theo felt the warmth returning to her. Her stomach relaxed. She wished she could stay like this forever, wrapped within the strength of the woman who was at once her mother, her sister, and a total stranger.

∾ Chapter Five ∾

ON A MONDAY MORNING Otto Brunner's Mercantile and Dry Goods Store was as busy a place as there ever was in the town of Savage. There was a potbelly stove in the back with crates placed around it, and this was the gathering place during the long winters for the local businessmen, the farmers, wagon drivers and barge men who lived and worked between Shakopee and Savage. When the weather turned warm, the meeting place became the low sagging porch that ran the length of the store.

Besides the social advantages his store offered, Otto Brunner prided himself on being able to procure any product sold on the market. If it could be found, he would get it; one had only to inquire. On this particular hot morning in the first week of June there were, as usual, several people gossiping and loafing in the crowded aisles of Brunner's Mercantile. A brand-new Sears and Roebuck catalogue lay open in tantalizing invitation on the counter. But Otto Brunner was not having one of his better mornings as he talked with Dr. Harriet Kerr.

Theo loitered near the bolts of calico and muslin and watched her aunt describe in detail what she wanted to buy from Otto. Theo loved watching Harriet, especially today as she towered over the small round man and looked directly into his worried, spectacled eyes.

"I know I can't expect the range of choices I'd find in the East," Harriet was saying firmly, "but surely you could find something for me. I don't want those moth-eaten brown things you showed me, Mr. Brunner. I want *white* sheepskins . . . thick winter pelts, not those weedy things." Otto Brunner nodded his head vigorously and shuffled through his catalogues under the counter, painfully aware that a number of people were watching his discomfort with interest.

"And I want full pelts, perfectly cured," continued Harriet relentlessly, leaning her chin on her hand as she bent over the counter, level with Otto's face. Otto lifted his shoulders in defeat.

"Trouble is, Dr. Kerr, I just don't know as anyone's got them, this time of year." The merchant hooked his thumbs in the straps of his suspenders. "Now, I could prob'ly find a local farmer who'd have a few cured pelts lyin' around," he said. "But truthfully, Dr. Kerr, I just don't think that'd be what you're after. Now let me just check one more place . . ." Harriet straightened and put her hand against the small of her back, and Theo realized she was exhausted.

All during the last two weeks since Claudia had been brought home to lie on a bed set up in the front parlor, Harriet had worked from early morning until late evening, taking turns with Maud and Stevenson several times each night. Theo shook her head and tried to dismiss the image of her sister that continually haunted her. Claudia lay limp and white, propped up amid cushions and pillows on the makeshift bed. Ever since Stevenson carried her from the buggy up the porch steps to the house, Claudia had lain virtually silent, her eyes huge and shadowed in her pinched face, staring out the parlor window. Sometimes she did not say a word all day, and other days she whimpered for hours from pain. She could move nothing more than her head; from the neck down, Claudia was paralyzed.

Theo blinked her eyes rapidly and forced the image from her mind. So quickly and uncontrollably would her tears come at any time, she had grown afraid of herself. All day she hung around the edges of her family, until she felt herself fading away. Harriet had absolutely forbidden her anywhere near Claudia. "We're not certain, but there is evidence to suggest polio is contagious," she cautioned firmly. "The less time Theodora spends in the house the better." But where else was she to go? All day she watched her mother and Harriet work like machines. They cooked special food, cleaned and changed the bedclothes several times each day, and turned Claudia in the bed every hour. They washed her sheets and softened them by rubbing the cloth between their hands so nothing rough tore at Claudia's fragile skin. From the start, Harriet insisted on a regular program of massage. Hour after hour she worked a special pungent oil into the shrinking muscles. Hour after hour she moved the inert limbs one at a time, back and forth, up and down. Harriet's dress would be soaked with sweat and still she would not stop. Despite Claudia's pathetic crying and Maud's horror at the pain, Harriet proceeded with the backbreaking work. "It's worked on some," she said. "It's worked before."

So Theo was shuffled to the outskirts of her family, growing quieter with each passing day. Even Mrs. O'Leary, normally cheerful, snapped at her to "go somewhere" out of her way. It was as if the illness had mushroomed until the entire house and yard was hidden by a sickening shroud. Even the mockingbirds which sang in the upper limbs of the elms had disappeared. The few flowers and shrubs in the front yard withered and died from lack of attention.

Theo sat for numb hours on the bottom step of the hall staircase or rocked listlessly in the porch swing. From the porch she could see the slow passage of life beyond her in the town, but it felt utterly untouchable. Stevenson would walk away into it in the morning and return at dinner, and in between there was nothing. Through the window on the porch, she watched the adults in constant movement between the parlor and kitchen. The relentless rhythm of massage, the endless cycle of turning and changing, marked the passage of time until time came to mean nothing. Theo could not hear anyone speak from her swing on the porch, could not hear Maud reading for hours to her daughter, could not hear Harriet's decisive doctor's commands, could not hear the consultations between Stevenson and Maud and Harriet in the long summer evenings. So she began to notice another communication, one that happened without words. She watched her mother's body stiffen when she deferred to a wish of Harriet's, watched Stevenson grow alert whenever Harriet came into the room, watched the sense of helplessness grow between them all. When she was in the house, Theo heard them speak to each other but their words did not match that other silent communication hanging in the air around them. It seemed to Theo these unspoken things grew and grew until she wanted to clap her hands over her ears . . . even though there was nothing but silence. And in the center of the silence lay Claudia.

Now, as she stood in Brunner's Mercantile with the ordinary everyday ebb and flow of chattering life around her, she could relax and let it soak through her like a cool, refreshing rain. She sniffed the delicious vinegar scent of the pickles coming from the barrel she leaned against, and squinted at the sunlight streaming through the doorway into the dim store. Outside, mules and horses were tethered to the hitching rail that ran the length of the porch. People went to and fro with sacks and boxes, loading buggies or wagons harnessed behind the horses. At the far end of the hitching rail, Theo noticed a shaggy blunt-nosed pony — Carl's! She scooted behind the dry goods counter to get a better look.

Gustav Johansson stood on the porch and with his slow gentle manner joined in the idle conversation of the men, but Carl stepped into the store, blinking his eyes in the dimness. Theo tried to catch his glance, but Mrs. O'Hearne and Mrs. McCarthy, who considered themselves the most important wives in town, huddled right in front of her to exchange gossip. Theo sidestepped and knocked against a bolt of calico. She could hear Harriet coming to an arrangement with Otto Brunner.

"Well, then, I suppose they'll have to do. How long will it take to get them, Mr. Brunner?" The tiredness had crept up into her voice. "Sheepskins are the only thing my niece can lie on to prevent bedsores. The wool helps her circulation. I need them as soon as possible."

Mrs. O'Hearne frowned as Theo struggled with the unrolled bolt of calico, and Otto's reply was lost in the loud rustle of her skirts as she pushed past. Theo thrust the disheveled roll under the counter and slipped closer to Harriet. There was a sudden attentive stir among the men loitering on the porch. Theo couldn't see much, but she felt the change in the murmur of voices. The men seemed to pull back, to lower their voices. Another man was coming up the steps.

She could just see him through the open door. He was dressed in an immaculate white linen suit and seemed unaffected by the heat. Waiting in the street were two perfectly matched glossy horses hitched to a shining black gig. On the padded red-leather seat a driver sat, straight and unmoving in the sun.

The men eagerly greeted the man as he paused among them to shake hands. Inside the store, Mrs. O'Hearne and Mrs. McCarthy fluttered in excitement. When they moved closer to the door, Carl caught sight of Theo and came to join her next to Harriet. The man stepped into the store and Theo could see him more clearly now. Except for the fine cut of his clothing and his extraordinarily cool appearance, he was a pleasant, ordinary-looking man with thick dark hair and a neat mustache over his friendly smile. But the man's eyes caught Theo's attention and held her riveted. There was nothing ordinary about them. Deep-set and black, they snapped with energy. His movements and his voice were quiet and modulated, but nothing could contain the blaze of his eager eyes, so full were they with the exhilarating business of being alive. The man held out his hand to Otto Brunner, including Mrs. O'Hearne and Mrs. McCarthy in his greeting.

"Good morning, Otto!" said the man. "As usual, the busiest little store south of the city! How's the business?"

"I can't complain, sir," said Otto as he vigorously shook the man's hand. "It sure is fine to see you again, Mr. Savage! We don't see enough of you in town."

Theo's eyes widened and she looked at Carl. He nodded, smiling. "That's him — that's Mr. Savage," he told her, as usual speaking to her as if he'd seen her a few hours earlier instead of over a week ago. "He's a real nice man, for all he's a millionaire. Everyone likes him over at the farm. He gets in and works with the rest of them, and they like that."

This was the man who owned Dan Patch! She stared at

63

him hungrily. This was the man who had built the fantastic barns, who lived in the great mansion on the bluffs across the Minnesota River and came across to his farm in his own private ferry. This was the man after whom the town was named. Marion Willis Savage made his untold wealth from the secret mixture of his famous stock feed, manufactured in a gigantic plant in Minneapolis. All over the walls of Brunner's Mercantile were the colorful posters advertising "Three Feeds for One Cent" and guaranteeing the miraculous results that would come from feeding farm animals on this amazing diet.

Hidden behind her aunt, Theo ran her eyes over Marion Willis Savage, over the intense open face, over the white suit and small neat hands. Had those hands that very day stroked the great mahogany-bay stallion and fed him treats of apples and carrots? With those hands he had held the reins as he drove Dan Patch around his private track! The presence of the horse shimmered like an aura around the man who stood so near her in the store. Then, to her astonishment, Mr. Savage turned from Otto and held out his hand in greeting to Harriet.

"Permit me to offer my sympathies about your talented niece, Dr. Kerr, and please send her my wishes for a speedy recovery," Mr. Savage said. "I know we have never met, but your brother-in-law, Stevenson Harris, has been a generous attorney to one or two of my employees when they have needed one. I heard about his daughter last week. If there is anything I might do to help . . ." It was a polite gesture and Harriet accepted it as such, nodding her thanks. Already Mr. Savage had turned back to Otto Brunner. The men on the porch had resumed their conversation and Mrs. O'Hearne and Mrs. McCarthy had left the store.

But Theo still stared at the man who owned Dan Patch.

Harriet was moving toward the door and Carl leafed through a magazine at her side. Through the doorway Theo saw the two-horse gig shining in the sun. The harness on the horses was as supple as glove-leather. The chest-straps and girths were lined with thick, fleecy sheepskin. It reminded Theo of the harness horses she'd seen at the county fairs around Indianapolis. The chest-straps and leg-protectors of those pacers and trotters were lined with the same thick sheepskin. Surely then, the most valuable horses in the world would also have harnesses lined with sheepskin . . .

She took one step closer to Mr. Savage. "Please, sir — maybe you can help us," she said. She didn't think before she spoke. She was aware of nothing but the kindly eyes of Marion Willis Savage. He turned to her attentively. "I'm Claudia's sister . . . Stevenson Harris is my father," Theo continued. "We have to find good sheepskins for her to lie on — so she won't get bedsores. We need the best sheepskins . . ." Everyone was watching her, and her voice began to falter. But Mr. Savage listened seriously as if there was no one else there. "Mr. Brunner doesn't know where to get us any," she finished in a rush.

Mr. Savage nodded his head thoughtfully. She could smell the faint, sweet scent of horses about him, of hay and oiled leather. He smiled. "That was smart thinking, young lady," he said. He addressed her directly and did not take his eyes from her own. "I think I *can* help with that. We line all our pastern boots with the best sheepskin available . . . that was what you were thinking of, wasn't it?" Theo nodded.

Harriet had come back to the counter. She waited for Mr. Savage to finish speaking. "I order our sheepskins from a place in Virginia," he continued, in the brisk efficient tone he would use doing business with an adult. "If you describe exactly what you need, I can have a delivery made here within the week." He turned to Otto Brunner. "I'll do the ordering through your store, of course, Otto," he smiled. "And I noticed you were a bit low on the hog and chicken feed out back, so I'll get you stocked up on that, all right? And now, young lady, tell me exactly what kind and how many sheepskins you need."

"I don't know exactly," said Theo, looking at Harriet. "But my aunt is a doctor. She can tell you."

She hardly heard the rest of the conversation that took place around her. She was entranced by the quiet man who spoke to her like an equal. When Mr. Savage turned from Harriet and went back out on the porch, he spoke easily with everyone, asking after families by name and commiserating with the farmers over the dry summer. To any questions about Dan Patch he responded with almost boyish pleasure.

"Can he do it again, Mr. Savage?" asked the men eagerly. "Can Dan break his own record again? Can he go faster than he did in Lexington?"

In answer to all the questions Mr. Savage grinned with joy. Around the store among the stock-feed posters hung framed photographs of his treasured horse. "Feed Your Stock on the Food of Champions" proclaimed the colorful posters. Dan Patch was the only horse in the world to pace a mile in under two minutes — why, it was doubtful those stinking, cumbersome automobiles city folk made such a fuss about could ever match Dan Patch for speed! No indeed. There wasn't a thing that could touch him in all the world.

"Of course he can do it!" chuckled Mr. Savage. His eyes sparkled. "There isn't anything Dan can't do — you know that! He never lets anyone down." And the men on the porch grinned with him. It was certainly an amazing time to be alive, in this brand-new twentieth century, and they all thought so. There was no end of incredible wonders. Why, look at those telephones now — you could talk to someone clear across the country like you were standing in the same room! And what about those men and their flying machines . . . only last year, wasn't it? Men could fly! And look at the automobile, whatever you might think of the confounded machine. And electric lights, and . . . well, there was no limit to anything anymore, and Dan Patch could prove that better than anyone. He carried the promise and excitement of a new century on hooves of perfect speed around the racetracks of the country. Anyone could go see Dan Patch . . . anyone, rich or poor, man or woman, black or white. It didn't matter. He was everyone's horse and everyone's dream.

As they walked past the gig with its team of glossy horses, Theo tried to shake herself out of the spell. The hard-packed dirt of Savage's main street sent up a fine clay-white dust that paled the peeling paint of the buildings and clung to the folds of women's dresses. She tried to pay attention to what Carl was saying.

"I told you he was a nice man," he said. "That's why everyone likes him so much. He's always doing things like that."

"It was very good of him," Harriet said simply. She turned to Theo. "You have a picture of Dan Patch in your room, don't you? I should have known you'd love horses." She chuckled to herself. "When I was your age I couldn't get enough of them myself. I used to sneak off down to the livery stables just to be around them, although your grandmother hated that." Harriet raised her eyebrows at Theo's surprised expression. "Is it so hard to believe?" she teased. "I wanted to be a veterinarian once, you know. Being a doctor was really just a compromise."

Theo wasn't sure if she was joking. Carl spoke before she could ask anything else.

"I think *I* could be a doctor," he said, his low voice forceful. He seemed to want Harriet to reply, and it struck Theo how seriously Carl listened to everything her aunt said.

Harriet studied him now. "Do you *want* to be a doctor?"

"I'm not sure," Carl replied, thoughtful. "But I know I want to be *something* . . . I mean, I want to find one thing and learn everything there is to know about it. I want to discover things no one ever knew about before, like medicines . . . or invent things . . ." He burst out passionately to Harriet, "I hate it, that everyone thinks I should just be strong and work hard!" he cried. "It's like I was some big dumb workhorse or something! Even over at the farm — they think I'd be a good blacksmith, and my father's already talked to Mr. Savage about apprenticing me." Theo was shocked at the intense bitterness in his voice, but Harriet waited calmly for him to finish and only said: "Blacksmithing is a fine trade."

"But I don't want it!" he cried. "How could I be a blacksmith forever? What am I supposed to do with everything I *think* about? Just forget it? Blacksmith's don't have to *think!* They just pound pound pound all day. I want to . . ."

"You want to what?" Harriet urged quietly. Carl narrowed his eyes and a muscle in his jaw twitched.

"I have to do something where I can *think* . . . where I can use my mind," he said stubbornly. He squared his shoulders. "Maybe a doctor. Maybe an inventor, or a scientist . . . a botanist, like in that book Mr. Harris has. I think I'd like to find out new things you can do with plants, like medicines, or new kinds of fruit. But I have to under-stand them first . . . you know. How they grow, what makes them green . . ."

Harriet put both hands on Carl's shoulders and turned him so he faced her. Their eyes were on the same level.

"Then you must refuse anything else," she said. "If you know this about yourself, you must refuse to do anything else *no matter what.*"

Harriet held Carl's eyes a moment longer, then dropped her hands from his shoulders and smiled. "I saw Dan Patch race once," she said.

"You did!"

"I did," said Harriet with the familiar crinkle at the corner of her eyes. "In New York. I went with a friend to the fair. I had just begun working my first year at the hospital, and it was very hard, so hard I didn't know if I would make it. I went away for a weekend to think." There were times Harriet looked so much like Claudia, Theo felt her breath catch. "When I went to that race, I thought Dan Patch was the most magnificent creature I'd ever seen, human or an-imal. I don't understand it exactly, but . . . when I saw that horse race his heart out, it made me *believe* I could make it. Who knows. Maybe all it takes is to *believe.*"

They had come to Cargyll Street, and Carl suddenly stopped and exclaimed, "I forgot! I left your father's book under the wagon seat! I have to go get it!" He called the last words over his shoulder, already running back in the direction they'd walked.

"You're a quiet little bird," observed Harriet. "But you sure spoke up when you needed to, back in the store."

"It was all right, wasn't it?" asked Theo, dismayed. There, in front of the entire town, to approach Mr. Savage, to ask him a favor! What had she been thinking of! And yet, and yet . . . There had been that smell about him of horses, that aura of something mysteriously *familiar* . . . something she had recognized immediately, as if she and Mr. Savage shared something she was unable to explain.

"Of course it was all right," laughed Harriet. "He offered to do whatever he could to help, didn't he? A person must be taken at their word."

"Mama always says women shouldn't act in awe of men," Theo giggled suddenly. "I guess she would've been pleased."

"But you *were* in awe of him."

Theo looked at her aunt. "Yes," she said carefully. "But not because he's a man. It's because . . . well, I think Mr. Savage can do anything he dreams of. . . ." They were halfway down Cargyll Street and in a minute Harriet would go in the house to Claudia and would be swallowed up the way Maud and Stevenson were swallowed up by the still, white body of her sister. Theo would fade into the shadowed corners of the house. She thought of Harriet's words to Carl: "You must refuse anything else *no matter what*." If she did not finish what she was trying to say, she would burst.

"It was the *horses* . . . that's why I spoke to him!" she cried fiercely. "It *wasn't* because of Claudia . . . it wasn't because she needed sheepskins for her bed. I wasn't even thinking of her!"

"Go on," said Harriet gently.

"I'm tired of thinking about Claudia!" Theo took hold of her words as if they were reins, and felt them gather force within her. She had to let these words run! "Even before . . . before she got sick, everyone always thought of Claudia. And now we *have* to! Oh, Aunt Harriet. I can hardly stand it . . . she just lies there, and nobody really talks — I don't know what will happen if she doesn't get

better. If she can't play her violin . . . and it's not just Claudia, either, it's Mama, and —" Theo touched the whip to
the horse and her words sprang forward with the strength
of courage. "And sometimes I just *don't care!*" she exploded.
"Because Claudia swallows me up. There isn't anything
that's really *mine* when she's around, except —"

"Except the horses," said Harriet. Theo nodded. She
knew she could finish what she had to say now, and felt
calmer.

"Yes, the horses," she said. "But it's more than that,
really. They mean something else to me, something bigger.
The only time I really understand what I feel is when I
write stories about them." She paused. She hadn't meant
to tell Harriet about her stories. But her aunt only nodded
briefly, saying: "So you write stories."

"Mama thinks it's time I grew out of writing about
horses," Theo continued. "And Papa just thinks my stories
are . . . cute, or something. I don't let anyone read them
anymore, except the one I had to write for school. Mama
told me I should write about people . . . she said they were
more important. But I —" She stopped and frowned. "Oh,
I guess Mama just wants me to be more like Claudia. She
thinks girls should do something *important* with their lives,
and I guess I'm not. I mean, real writers don't write about
horses, do they, Aunt Harriet? They write about people,
and ideas, and —"

"But you aren't really writing about horses," Harriet reminded her softly.

"Well — I am and I'm not," said Theo. "It's hard to
explain. I guess I don't really know . . . that's the thing. I
mean, I know what I *feel*, but I don't know what to do with
it. It's like what Carl said . . ." Her eyes shone as she looked
up at her aunt. "There *is* something about horses," she

71

explained eagerly. "They're so *perfect*. And the horses on Mr. Savage's farm — they're the fastest horses in the world. You know what I mean! You said you did! Those horses . . . all they want to do is race, and they put their whole *heart* into it."

Aunt Harriet was looking at her steadily with her clear eyes, and Theo remembered how strong her aunt's arms had felt around her on the first day they'd met. Like she could understand anything. She took a deep breath. "So that's why I went up to Mr. Savage in the store," she said. "Because he had that feeling all around him. He *knows* what it is. He lives it every day! *He* understands it's more than just horses . . . and *I* need to understand what he knows. So I had to speak to him. The sheepskins were just an excuse."

It seemed so simple once she had finally spoken all the words aloud; she wondered why it had been so difficult, and why she felt so exhausted. Now, Harriet knew everything she'd always kept hidden. Knew how twisted up she was over Claudia and her mother, and knew about her stories . . . she knew it all. Theo didn't look at her aunt now, but watched Carl in the distance returning with the book held carefully under his arm.

"You are a brave person, Theodora," said Harriet at last. She spoke it as a statement of fact without praise. She put her hands on Theo's shoulders just as she had done with Carl. "You might not know it yet, but you understand something most people don't learn in their entire life," she said. "You understand about freedom. Because that's all freedom is — putting your whole heart into something you love. That's all that matters. And you aren't going to do anything important unless you decide to put your whole heart into it . . . no matter what your Mama and Papa think you should do. When you discover what that important thing is, you will know it."

Carl had stopped politely a few feet away from them. He smoothed the cover of *Gulliver's Travels* so lovingly Theo had to smile. Harriet pulled Theo against her in a quick embrace.

"Keep those horses inside you," she said. "It's your own heart you're feeling . . . and when the time comes, you'll know where to race that heart of yours, and you'll *win!*"

Theo was sure she could never fade into the shadows of the house again. When they reached the house, Carl sat with her on the bottom step of the porch and they took turns aiming twigs at a leaf on the ground. Harriet disappeared immediately inside, and Theo heard the squeak-thunk of the pump handle being raised in the back yard as Maud, relieved of her work for the moment, ran cool water over her hands and face. Mrs. O'Leary stuck her head out the door and told Theo her lunch was ready. Carl threw a twig that landed perfectly in the middle of the leaf.

"Did you like *Gulliver's Travels?*" asked Theo, patting the book.

"I liked it very much," said Carl. "It's strange — even though they're all make-believe people in the book, they seem like a lot of people I know. I'm sure Gyp Grimer was in that book."

Theo giggled. "I know which one I want you to read next," she told him. "*Robinson Crusoe.* About a man shipwrecked on an island. Aunt Harriet said it was one of her favorites, too." She aimed carefully and threw the last of her twigs, but Carl had beat her six times out of ten tries. She sighed and leaned back on the steps.

"I wish Aunt Harriet was my aunt too," said Carl. "She's the smartest person I ever knew."

"If she was, we'd be cousins," giggled Theo. "Or brother and sister."

Suddenly they were both flustered. Carl drew a line in the dirt with a stick. "Well, then, I'm glad that she's not," he muttered, but he half-grinned at her. He gazed up into the broad canopy of the elms. "She's right — your aunt — about refusing to do anything that isn't *right*," he said slowly. "I was thinking about it when I went back to get the book. It's almost like being dishonest, doing something that you know isn't *right* for you, you know? I'm going to tell my father that I'll only work at Mr. Savage's until the end of the summer. I don't *want* to be a blacksmith!" He jabbed at the hard dirt with his stick. "I'm just going to go back to school, that's all. And if he says I can't, then I'll just . . . I'll run away!" His voice trembled with bravado, but Theo heard the hard edge of determination. He turned to her suddenly and caught her hand in his own. She was so startled she didn't pull away.

"Theo, I asked Mr. Savage if he needed another rag boy, and he said he did!" he cried. "You want to go there as much as I want to go to school . . . I know you do! If you were there, it wouldn't seem so boring and awful." He leaned closer to whisper, his rough, brown hand dwarfing her own, and frowned impatiently at the doubt on her face. "Nobody'll ever know it's you," he insisted. "You can wear my old pants and my other cap . . . listen, Theo! You're just moping around here! You're not even supposed to get too close to Claudia."

"But sometimes I can talk to her through the window . . ." she faltered.

He gripped her hand. "You still think this is your fault, don't you?" he challenged, and she pulled back, stung.

"I know it's not my *fault!*" she mumbled. "But she might need me."

"If you don't take this chance, you'll always wish you had," he stated, and she knew he was right. But she could not look at him while he held her hand. He leaned toward her again. "You love those horses! You know it feels right — and you have to refuse anything else!" She had to smile at the passion with which he repeated Aunt Harriet's words, and she looked at him shyly.

"I know," she said. "All right. I'll tell Mama I got a baby-sitting job in one of those new houses down by the landing. There's a whole bunch of new families — she won't know them, anyway. She'll probably be glad I'm out of the house. She's always complaining how she trips on me every time she turns around." Her enthusiasm mounted as she spoke. "I'll tell them tonight! So I could go tomorrow!"

Carl laughed. "It'll take a little planning, idiot," he said. "I have to get the clothes together without my ma finding out. And Mr. Savage told me to speak to the foreman to-morrow to find out when you can start. So it won't be until next week, anyway."

Theo jumped up, pulling Carl with her. He still held her hand. "Come with me now!" she urged him. "Not far — just to the edge of the farm, that field across the bridge by the tracks. I want to show you something!"

They ran through the high summer meadows, through fields popping with grasshoppers and singing with larks. Next week, she chanted to herself as they ran. Next week, next week. They stopped, panting, at the fence that reached across the fields from the distant barns to link with her everyday world. Carl followed as she climbed up on the fence-rails and leaned out over the sloping meadow.

75

The yearlings grazing along the shadowed stream raised their heads. Theo felt their stirring, felt their eyes watching her. She held her breath. She heard the flutter of curious nostrils and the stamping of long legs in the grass.

"What is it?" Carl asked.

"Watch," she breathed.

The earth began to rise up and beat under them, and the shadows broke apart into a herd of horses sweeping up the slope. Theo leaned far out from the fence and called as they came to her, their necks tossing and their tails streaming. She leaped into their midst and ran with them, and Carl saw that she was both horse and master in the swirling dust. He leaned spellbound on the fence and did not feel a single moment of fear for her. She was in her natural element.

And Theo, as she ran, thought how strange it was that she had told all her secrets in one day.

⁓ Chapter Six ⁓

CARL'S OLD WOOL CAP was hot on her head as Theo stood in the busy stable yards and looked around. Her scalp was pinched where she had jammed in pins to hold up her hair. She waited for Carl to come out of the main building with Dennis O'Connor, the farm foreman. The activity around her was overwhelming. I'm here, I'm here, she repeated to herself. I'm here at the International Stock Feed Farm, and Dan Patch is somewhere inside that building. But she only heard the words in her head, and felt nothing but anxiety and the discomfort of the unfamiliar clothing.

It had taken her two days to broach the subject of a summer job to Maud and Stevenson. She spent hours fabricating details in her head, only to discard them all. Finally, at the dinner table the family had set up in the small room off the parlor, to be near Claudia, Theo blurted out her request.

"Papa, I can have a summer job, can't I?" she'd pleaded, hoping for his approval before Maud had a chance to object. "This girl from school . . . her aunt knows a woman who just had a baby and she already has four children and she needs a little extra help just for a couple of months and —"

"Whoa!" Stevenson laughed, folding the newspaper he always read before Mrs. O'Leary brought in the food. Theo could see Harriet through the open door, setting Claudia up to be fed. "You want to become financially independent?" She wished Stevenson would not tease her when she was being serious. She took a huge bite of bread, flustered.

"I just want a job for the summer," she mumbled through the food. "I just want something to do . . ."

"I wish you would wait until everyone is seated before beginning to eat, Theodora," said Maud as she came from her study. She still had a pencil stuck behind her ear. "And where is this family, did you say?"

"They live in one of those new houses by the landing, Mama." She hoped fervently Mrs. O'Leary wouldn't know any of them and that Maud would not inquire further. She glanced at Harriet in the parlor. "Aunt Harriet even said I shouldn't be spending so much time in the house."

"Oh, let her go, Maudie," said Stevenson, rattling his paper. "She's almost sixteen, after all, and there's no harm in a little baby-sitting job." Harriet came into the room and added: "It really might be safer, Maud. You know we aren't sure if polio's contagious." Theo watched gratefully as Maud gave in with only a slight frown before the subject was dropped.

"I have to leave very early," Theo mentioned, as if an afterthought. "The lady gets up early and that's when she needs the most help with the children."

She stood in the yard now and resisted the urge to tug and pull at Carl's rough clothes. She tried to remember everything he'd told her. "Don't have so much expression on your face," he instructed as he stood by the stream and surveyed her. "I don't think boys move their faces around so much." Then he grinned. "But you don't have to look like you're going to a funeral! Don't worry — you have a pretty serious face, anyway. You'll pass." She'd walked back and forth in the field with his boots, trying not to trip. A page from the Savage newspaper was stuffed in each toe. It terrified her that her hair might tumble down from the pins. She stood in the stable yard and forced herself to relax.

The place was in a whirl of activity. The long wings that radiated out from the central building formed separate yards with dozens of stalls opening out onto them. It was just before six in the morning, but it seemed the horses and men had been awake and active for hours.

A wide boulevard, busy as a street in Minneapolis, led from the barn to the mile-long oval track near the river. Horses pulling sulkies were being led on and off along the boulevard. The horses going to the track pulled at their grooms impatiently, but the horses returning walked slowly, lathered in sweat and steaming in the cool morning air. Grooms ran up to them and unhooked a strap so the horses could drop their foam-flecked heads and blow loudly in relief. Drivers paused to confer with grooms, trainers had long animated discussions with drivers, and around them moved countless other men unharnessing horses, wheeling sulkies away, raking the yards, hauling water, shaking out horse blankets, walking horses back and forth to cool them down, examining legs and picking hooves, wheeling barrows of straw . . .

Everywhere there was a good-natured hubbub of sound. The men joked and bantered with each other, or kept up a running commentary to their horses. Theo never heard a raised voice. If a nervous filly skittered at the sight of an overturned bucket or a temperamental stallion challenged its handler, the stablehands and grooms spoke in low, soothing tones. Horses were never struck or yanked around. Theo realized that all these people were here for one reason: they loved the horses they worked with. A thrill ran through her, and at that moment, a door in the main building opened and Carl followed a burly red-haired man into the yard.

Dennis O'Connor shook her hand brusquely. "Carl here tells me your daddy's a friend of his daddy's, from way past Shakopee — that so?" he asked her. His voice was amiable but his quick eyes measured her from head to toe. She stood as straight as she could.

"I'm staying with Carl for a while," she answered, determined to keep her voice even. She avoided looking at Carl. Don't let anyone speak to Gustav! she wished. She was sure Gustav didn't come as far as the farm with his vegetable wagon. But what about Gustav's speaking to Mr. Savage about Carl's job! She clenched her teeth and willed herself to be calm. Mr. O'Connor dusted his hands on his pants.

"Well, we sure got plenty of work for another boy here,"

he said. He interrupted himself to call out instructions to a passing groom. "We run a tight ship," he explained, turning back to Theo. "Now, I know you're just a young'un, but you should understand we don't allow no drinking, smoking, gambling, an' no bad language around here. That clear? The horses always come first. Always. That's our most important rule, son. You won't be working directly with the horses, of course, but — what did you say your name was?"

"Theo, sir," she said, her voice cracking.

"Good name — after our president, Theodore Roosevelt, eh?" He snapped his fingers at Carl. "Listen, sonny. Bob down at the blacksmith's tells me he can spare you for a day or two so you can teach your friend the ropes — but he needs you back soon as possible, that clear? You quick, son?" The burly foreman swung back to Theo. She hesitated.

"He's real quick, sir," Carl assured him. "I can teach him everything he needs in two days, and he'll pick the rest up easy."

Dennis O'Connor nodded and checked his watch. He clapped Theo on the shoulder, not unkindly. "You work good these two days, we'll see how it goes," he told her. "We got enough work for three, maybe four days a week." He turned away, and Theo twisted her hands together.

"Won't I . . . won't I be able to work with the horses, sir?" she asked. O'Connor swung back to her, a rough grin breaking out over his face.

"A real horse lover, eh?" he chuckled. "I can always hear it in the voice." He became suddenly serious. "Let me tell you something, son. These here horses are the most valuable animals in the world. No one but the best works with them, that clear? You stick around, Mr. Savage might let you walk a quiet one once in a while, to cool them down after work-outs. But until then — you don't go near them. Clear?" Theo nodded and took a deep breath.

"But could I see Dan Patch?" she whispered. The fore-man gave her a measured stare, but gradually another grin grew across his face. He raised his bushy eyebrows at Carl.

"You sure got a persistent friend," he said. "He's got the itch, that's for sure. We'll not get a lick of work out of him 'til he's seen Dan, eh, son?" Mr. O'Connor shook his head and shrugged. "Okay, kid," he said, indicating the huge barn with his head. "Carl can take you down — Dan's still in his stall, the lazy brute. Eating like a pig. Now get goin' . . . I haven't got all day. Don't worry" — he reas-sured Theo with a wink — "Grown men get silly about that big old horse, so why shouldn't you? It's awful hard not to love Dan."

When the big foreman strode off with a groom, Theo let out her breath and Carl whispered, "You were great, Theo! You sounded just like a boy!"

She followed him through the yard to the door of the opulent barn. On the doors, as on the white sides of the building, bold dark-green geometric designs were painted. The towering onion-dome on the central building and the smaller domes at the end of each wing gleamed in the morn-ing sun. The rows of polished windows that ran along the wings seemed made of pure gold. When Carl opened the door, she stepped at last over the threshold into the cool cavernous interior.

It took her eyes a moment to adjust. Everything felt hushed, and the air smelled sweetly of hay and warm horses. She thought she might be in a dream. *Was* she dreaming? Had she never really woken this morning in the silent pre-dawn house, nor slipped in her bare feet down the stairs?

But then, she had seen Claudia asleep on her bed, her pale face seeming to float in the milky half-light against the dark cushions. Theo had heard Claudia's shallow breathing, and somehow, she wasn't sure why, she thought her sister was awake and listening to her leave. And surely the walk through the dewy hayfields in the lavender mist had been real? But how like a dream! She had crouched behind some thickets along the stream to pull on Carl's old clothes, had rolled up her own dress and boots and shoved them in a hole in a cottonwood tree. And how dreamlike was the walk down through all the pastures, coming closer and closer to the place she had only seen from a distance for so long!

Theo lifted her head in the barn, and the air felt silky against her face. They stood on a thick carpet of shredded bark. She gazed around the huge round room. A gleaming brass railing ran around the wall to protect the glass display cases filled with trophies. She had never seen so much silver and polished wood in her life. On the walls hung dozens of photographs, lithographs, and the colorful "Three Feeds for One Cent" posters, all in gilt frames. A massive system of pipes ran high into the vaulted ceiling, part of the innovative steam-heating conductors that kept the stables warm in winter.

She could not stop gazing around her. Down the long, dim corridors she heard the constant stirrings of the horses as they moved through the deep straw in their stalls. There was an occasional whicker or snort, the knock of an impatient hoof against a door, the rattle of a feed bucket . . . she was surrounded by horses! Carl watched her wistfully.

"I wish I could feel the way you do," he said. "It wouldn't be a problem for me then. It's a good place, really . . . I just don't want to get stuck here."

The sun had not quite reached the high banks of windows, but the lamps had all been turned off for the day. In the low light, Carl's blue eyes were as deep as a night sky. They stood close together. Suddenly Theo wished Carl would take her hand again, the way he had done last week. He seemed so calm standing near her, compared with the way her own thoughts and heart tumbled around inside her. But under his quiet expression, she sensed he was as anxious as she.

"Do you really hate it here so much?" she asked softly. He rubbed his face with his broad hand and shook his head. He stared around him moodily. "I'm *afraid* of being here," he muttered. "The longer I'm here, the more everyone just takes it for granted . . . until even *I* begin to accept it!"

"You mean, about being a blacksmith?"

"Well, not only that . . . it's just that all anyone expects a strong Norwegian boy to do is hard work." Theo heard the bitterness thicken his voice. "Anyway, what should I expect? My own parents can't even speak English properly."

"But you speak English perfectly!" She felt uncomfortable with him now; his frown was like a stranger's and his bitterness hurt her.

"Of course I can — I worked at it," he said. "I practiced and listened, and anyway, I came here when I was only six, and I guess it's easier when you're young." He suddenly challenged her: "Why do you think I was always reading and working so hard at school? Why I didn't play with everyone at recess?"

He stepped away from her in his agitation, and she missed the warmth of him standing so close. Her cheeks flushed with shame. "I thought you didn't like anyone at school," she said in a low voice. "I thought you were . . . stuck-up."

Hc looked away from her and his mouth tightened in a straight line. "My father will always be a farmer," he said in his hard stranger's voice. "A big strong farmer who can't speak good English and hardly reads anything but the Bible. And my mother will spend her whole life working hard and being poor with him. The most any of my older sisters can expect is a job cooking or cleaning in someone's house . . . and my brother, Lars, he's already hired out as a farmhand." He shrugged again. "See? That's what's expected. Norwegians, Swedes, they're big and strong and don't complain. *Dumb!*" he burst out. "Imagine people like Gyp Grimer calling you *dumb!*"

"Gyp calls everyone dumb," she said in a small voice, but as suddenly as the mood came on him it was gone, and Carl's face brightened like the sun coming out after a rain. "I'm sorry," Theo said, but he smiled at her and shook his head, pointing down the corridor.

"We better get going. I'll show you Dan, and then we have to get to work."

They walked down one of the long corridors. The thick oakwood walls muffled the sounds of horses and stablehands. Through the bars of the stall doors Theo caught glimpses of dark forms moving quietly in clouds of fresh straw. Once or twice a curious horse poked its long face through the bars as they passed. Men were mucking stalls with long-tined pitchforks or rubbing cloths over horses, checking water buckets, talking among themselves. In one of the stalls a man was humming a lilting tune. The sun began to stream in through the windows.

"Hey, Carl!" called one man. "Just tell Bob I'll be down with Peppermill after lunch, okay? And don't forget to tell him it's a shoe for the right *hind*, now. It's gotta be just a tad bigger."

Theo followed Carl toward an immense box stall at the far end of the wing. It was bigger than any room in her house. Light streamed in through the windows and hay dust hung in shafts of sun like golden stars. They were still several yards away when Theo felt a tingling in her fingertips.

She no longer moved of her own free will, but knew that something was drawing her down the dark corridor toward the flood of light. So powerful was the sensation she had the urge to fight against it, to pull away and go back. Her throat was tight. No picture she had ever seen of Dan Patch conveyed the immense power she now sensed waiting behind that high oak door. She took another step and hesitated.

She could hear the breathing of the horse on the other side of the door. The tingling in her fingers spread up her arms and down into her stomach. There was something bigger here than she had ever imagined, something much more than a famous horse. Suddenly, Theo was afraid.

Carl looked back, and his smile reassured her. They were only a few feet from the stall when Theo was startled to see the dark figure of an old man sitting on a crate against the wall. At his feet lay seven or eight small sharp-faced dogs who watched her with bright black eyes. She stopped in amazement. The old man peered up at her with eyes that seemed as animal-like as the dogs'.

"That's Amon Szabo, the rat killer," whispered Carl in her ear. "No one knows where he's from — they all think he's a bit odd in the head, but I'm not so sure." He put his hand on her arm. "See the dogs? Those are his terriers. He hunts them in a pack around the barns at night to keep the rats out. He sits down here a lot. Dan Patch likes the dogs, that's why. Funny horse, really. He likes a lot of things, really *likes* them, and you can always tell by —"

There was an impatient thump against the boards on the

stall door and the terriers jumped up with eager yips. Their stiff tails stuck straight up and wagged energetically. The old man stirred on his upturned crate and beckoned to Theo. In a daze, she stepped closer to the stall. Carl stood back and watched. He let her go alone to meet Dan Patch.

The great stallion moved through the sunlight and looked at her from the stall door. The terriers danced around her feet. In the streaming light the horse seemed to float in a golden pool. She stared transfixed into his huge dark eyes. His ears flicked sharply forward and he whickered in curiosity. He bobbed his head and snuffled against the bars of the door.

The old man scrutinized her with his glittery eyes. The horse snorted and pawed the deep straw with his front hoof. The old man stood up and murmured something to him with a rasping voice in words Theo could not understand. Dan Patch turned in a circle and pricked his ears again when Amon Szabo spoke. Then the old man hunkered down on his crate, speaking sharply to the terriers, which lay down again at his feet.

"Good morning, Mr. Szabo," said Carl. Dan Patch shook his head and snorted, and Theo glanced at the old man. He was dressed in layers of raggedy clothes. Everything from his boots to his squashed old hat was full of holes.

"So, boy-Carl," rasped the old rat killer. He poked a finger at Carl. "So. They make you blacksmith. This is good?" Carl looked away and did not answer. Amon Szabo leaned down to take a tick off a terrier's ear, crushing it between his fingers. He swung his head around to Theo and narrowed his eyes. "So," he hissed. "Here is a girl, dressed as a boy. There is a reason?"

Theo looked at Carl in shock, but Carl could only shrug helplessly. She flushed and turned away from the stall door.

The old man watched her slyly, and something like a smile passed over his face. "Of course there is reason," he chuckled, as if he'd made a joke. "Reason for everything. No matter. Everyone has to hide sometimes, yes?"

"Please don't tell anyone," Theo managed to whisper. Her mouth had gone dry and it felt as if a huge chasm had opened up between her and the great horse. But already the rat killer seemed to have forgotten her and busily searched for ticks on his dogs. Behind her, Dan Patch threw up his head and whinnied. He turned sharply in a circle and came back to the door, pushing at it with his muzzle. Again he trumpeted a loud whinny, banging the door with his hoof and staring down the long corridor past Theo.

Marion Savage was walking toward them. He was dressed in a fawn-colored linen suit much as when she'd first seen him, but wore no tie or hat. In his hands he carried a few small apples which he polished on the cloth of his jacket, his eager eyes fixed on the horse. The horse quieted suddenly and stood very still.

Something passed between them as surely as if words had been spoken. There was a greeting, each to the other, but it was far more than the affectionate greeting of a human being to a favorite animal. This was a greeting between equals . . . between partners, between two creatures who acknowledged they needed each other to achieve what was of utmost importance to them on this earth. The man and the horse each had a job to do and when they greeted each other, it was a confirmation of their pact.

Marion Savage turned his eyes from the horse to Theo. At the same moment, she felt a soft bump against her shoulder and a warm breathing through her hair. She stood motionless. Through the bars of the door, Dan Patch pushed his velvet muzzle and explored the back of her neck. His hay-sweet breath washed over her. He tugged playfully at her cap and snorted. She gasped, turning to face him. Under the cap, her pinned-up hair shifted. She couldn't bear it if it all came tumbling down, not now! Not when everything was just beginning!

Dan Patch pushed gently at her again. She lifted her face and met the silken touch of his nose. He blew softly and she breathed that living breath from the great hidden lungs, pumped by the heart that carried him as fast as a dream around the tracks. She was filled with such a strength that she thought whoever she touched would feel it, too. If only he could breathe like this into Claudia! she thought. If only this breath could flood through those wasted thin arms and legs so they would move and glow with life again! With her face against Dan Patch, Theo closed her eyes and imagined Claudia's thin legs kicking off the confining quilts, imagined the beautiful hands reaching for her violin . . . "Oh!" she said, in a small startled voice, and her eyes flew open. The image dissolved. Mr. Savage laughed kindly.

"I can see Dan has another friend," he said, and although he smiled, Theo could see he was perfectly serious and did not use the word "friend" lightly. The man put an apple into her hand. "Here, son," said Mr. Savage. "Dan doesn't need apples to be your friend, but he loves them just the same." Theo held the apple flat on the palm of her hand and the horse snuffled happily through the door, picking it up with a feather-light touch. He bobbed his head and crunched, and flecks of apple dribbled from his lips. Mr. Savage grinned.

"For someone with so much dignity, you sure make a mess of an apple, Dan-boy," he said. He held out another apple and it was taken in the same manner and chewed as vigorously as before.

Marion Savage turned to the old man. Theo tensed. She watched him warily, and the rat killer's eyes seemed to pierce her own.

"How's the rat business, Amon?" inquired Mr. Savage, reaching down to scratch a terrier's ear. "Not good, I trust?" It was evidently an old joke between them, for Amon Szabo rolled his eyes in a caricature of chagrin.

"Very, very good, boss, I'm afraid," he rasped mournfully. "I think I never seen it such good, in fact. Eight big fat ones last night, right here . . ." He gestured with his long arm down the corridor. "You know, boss, they come up from the river in spring, hungry as wolves." For a moment an undefinable look scurried over the old man's face and his eyes went flat. He sighed and repeated, "Yup . . . so bad, like the wolf. But you not worry — these dogs, they fight like anything, boss! All those rats dead on the ashheap now!" Mr. Savage gave the terriers a final pat and turned to Carl.

"Well, young man — you haven't introduced me to your friend yet . . . although Dan has certainly made his acquaintance!" Carl stepped closer to Theo, but she hardly looked up for fear of meeting the black eyes of the rat killer.

"This is my friend I was telling you about, sir," said Carl, trying not to speak too quickly. "You said you needed another rag boy, now I'm down working with Bob McAlistar."

"Well, it's fine with me if it suits Mr. O'Connor — I leave him in charge of the hiring at the barns," said Mr. Savage thoughtfully. He studied Theo. "So you want to be part of the International Stock Feed Farm, do you, son?" he asked. Theo nodded. "Well, I must say Dan sure thinks you're suited . . ." In his vital eyes Theo saw the kind smile she was coming to recognize. He looked at her so intently, she was sure he would remember her as the girl who had approached him so boldly at Brunner's Mercantile. She forced herself to smile in return. "Well, do you have a name, son?" Mr. Savage chided gently.

"Theo, sir . . . um, Theodore Stevens," she said.

"Stevens?" he said, cocking his head. "Don't recall any Stevens around these parts . . . but then Carl did say your father is a family friend, from Shakopee way?" She nodded, and suddenly she hated this deception. She wished she had the courage to pull the cap from her head, shake her hair free, and speak honestly with this man.

But she could not. The grizzled old Amon Szabo shuffled over to her with his terriers milling around his feet. He reached out a dirty hand and pinched her arm. "This is good strong boy," he said. She couldn't tell if he was grinning or grimacing. A terrier jumped up and pawed at her leg. "Look, boss!" hissed Amon. "All the animals like this boy, yes? Good. Animals, they know everything. Lucky they not talk. Ha!" Gold teeth flashed in his mouth. Savage laughed with him.

"Amon Szabo, I know just like everyone else around here that you understand perfectly what all the animals are saying," he said. "And I also know you've been up half the night. You better go get some rest if the rat business is as good as you say. I need you in fighting form!"

Amon Szabo turned, and Theo could see him more clearly. He was surprisingly powerful under all his layers of clothing. He was short, with broad shoulders, his arms were long, and he walked soundlessly, rolling on the balls of his feet. The terriers trotted close but he never stepped on one. They watched him constantly with sharp, ready eyes. The old man sidled past Mr. Savage and looked swiftly into Carl's face.

"So poundpoundpound all day, not good for head, yes?"
He tapped one finger against Carl's temple. "Head hurt?"
Carl nodded. The old man shook his own head slowly back
and forth. With a movement like a slinking rat, he turned
swiftly to Theo. "These big old horses, they can break your
heart," he whispered so only she could hear. He flashed
another gold-toothed grin and scuttled off down the corridor with the terriers prancing at his heels.

Marion Savage, too, seemed anxious to leave. He looked
distracted and preoccupied, as if his restless mind had already passed on to bigger things. He clapped Carl on the
shoulder and instructed him to show Theo all the details
of the job, wished her luck, and then disappeared after the
rat killer.

As she followed Carl, Theo turned to look back once.
Dan Patch was standing very still in his stall, his head up,
ears alert, watching her go.

ᕙ Chapter Seven ᕗ

THE REST OF THE DAY was such a flurry of bewildering
activity that Theo was sure she would never get any of it
straight. The main barn was immense, each of the five wings
housing stalls, tack rooms, groom's quarters, storerooms,
and closets. There were stairs leading to living quarters,
huge grain rooms, and supply closets full of tools and
equipment.

"You have to do a lot of running around here," said Carl

as they were sent from wing to wing, from yard to black-smith to track with messages and errands. The rag boy's chores consisted of endlessly cleaning brushes and combs, keeping the scrapers and hoof picks and currycombs for each horse in order and ready for the groom to use, hauling buckets of clean water, emptying buckets of dirty water, lugging heavy wool blankets, picking up litter and keeping the hard-packed earth of the yards raked and clean. Theo struggled to lift the heavy baskets of dirty rags and groom-ing supplies. She repeated messages to herself as she ran to give them, and tried to keep three errands straight in her head at one time.

The men were busy, never impatient, but rarely able to stop and explain anything twice. Several times Carl was called away, leaving her floundering in a sea of instructions. She set her mouth and willed her aching arms to lift another box, shake out another blanket, pump another bucket of water. Her legs trembled with exhaustion by the middle of the afternoon, and she could no longer run from one wing to another, but walked. She had to be on the lookout for anything a horse might shy at — a rake lying on the ground, a dropped rag that looked like a snake, a blanket shaken out with a loud snap.

By three in the afternoon, the sky had burned to a hazy white in the sun and the heat danced against the walls of the barns. The yard was quieter now; the horses were not worked in the midday heat. Theo dropped a basket of heavy wet rags on the ground with a thump, and paused to wipe the sweat from her neck. Carl had been gone twenty min-utes, helping to load hay into a cart. A groom led a black stallion into the yard to sluice him down with buckets of water.

"Hey, sonny, I need some more water here," the groom

called over to Theo. "Take them empty buckets there . . . that'll be plenty."

She looked at the four buckets stacked against the wall and wasn't sure she could command her arms to lift the pump handle one more time. She watched the stallion as she struggled to fill each bucket. He skittered nervously and surveyed the yard with rolling eyes. The groom spoke to him gently, and grinned at an older groom nearby. "Look at ol' Arion today!" he laughed. "Ain't he a fine sight? He thinks we're gonna let him in with those mares today again . . . too bad, fella." He turned again to the stallion, trying to calm him.

The older groom shook out a tangled lead rope and snorted. "He's a clown, he is," he said good-naturedly. "Spoiled, I say. Give me good ol' Cresceus any day!" He gave the rope a swift snap at the same moment Theo set her first full water bucket carefully on the ground by Arion's groom. The stallion started at the sound, squealed, and knocked the bucket. The groom called out to him, but the horse reared back and fought the lead. His haunches swung around so close to Theo she had to spring back, and without thinking she reached her hand up to his gleaming neck.

She had only a momentary glimpse of the wild white-rimmed eye and a tangle of long black mane. Through her fingers she could feel the beating pulse of the frightened stallion, but instead of veering away at her touch, he swung his head around. She kept her hand on his neck and murmured to him. His sweating coat quivered and the horse lowered his head to blow loudly, standing splay-legged but calmed. Theo ran her hand down his withers and down the powerful shoulder, and then turned to go for her other bucket.

"Hey, kid . . ." She looked back, and saw both grooms

studying her. The old groom came toward her and she suddenly remembered Dennis O'Connor's admonishment to never go near the horses. Her face burned, but the old groom smiled at her and shook his head. More to the other groom than to her, he said, "My dad used to tell me about that — and you know, Bill, he was a great one with horses — some folks got magic in their hands, he'd tell me." He studied Theo again. "And them horses always know, too . . . take care of them hands, sonny."

She ducked her head and sloshed some of the water from the bucket in her nervousness. Where was Carl! She plunked the bucket on the ground and almost ran to the edge of the yard, looking for him. Instead, she saw the hunched figure of Amon Szabo hidden in the shadows where he lay half-propped against the barn wall. At first he seemed to be asleep, but as she went past, she saw his strange black eyes fixed on her and realized he'd seen the whole incident. His eyes narrowed when he caught her staring, and he cackled under his breath. "You feel heart," he said, tapping his chest. "Heart." Theo stumbled away, and to her relief saw Carl approaching across the yard.

"Mr. O'Connor wants to see you," he said.

"Why?" She realized her voice had cracked, almost hysterical with exhaustion and worry. She hadn't *hurt* that stallion, had she? She glanced anxiously over at the groom, but Arion was standing calmly, his coat jet-black with water.

Carl looked puzzled. "It's the end of the day," he said. "He just needs to sign you on and talk to you about your wages, I guess."

Wearily, she stood in front of the battered old desk in

94

Mr. O'Connor's office. "Well, you're a good worker, no doubt about it," he said gruffly. "How d'you feel?"

She was too exhausted to pretend. "I'm real tired."

The burly foreman wrote her name down in a ledger. "You'll get used to it, son. There isn't a better place to work. Now, here's your name . . . you gotta sign here, see? Now — your wage'll be a dollar fifty cents a day. Pretty good, for your first job." He leaned back in his chair and put his hands behind his head. "Okay, sonny — you be here at six tomorrow." And she was dismissed.

A dollar fifty a day! And she could work here at least three days a week — just enough money to pay for the special medicinal oil Aunt Harriet massaged into Claudia's muscles. She drew a ragged breath as she waited in the quiet yard for Carl. But could she keep up this backbreaking work? And then manage the two-mile walk home across the fields? She rubbed her arm across her face and squeezed her eyes shut. She imagined everyone at home today, except for her. Even Stevenson had stayed to work in his own study. They were all home, going about their day without her. And they thought she was at one of the new houses by the landing!

Sweat trickled in cold threads down her back. What if something happened to Claudia? What if she *died?* And Theo wouldn't know, and no one would know where to find her, and she would walk in the door of the house to find . . .

She stood frozen with anxiety. She should never have done this! Nobody knew where she was, and anything could happen any day to Claudia. And Claudia *needed* her! She'd even said so, in her small, weak voice. "I love watching Theo out the window," she'd told Maud. "I love watching

her climb the tree . . . I'm going to do that one day, Mama!"
Tears were mixing now with the sweat on Theo's face. She
looked around the dusty yard and thought about the backbreaking work she'd done all day when she should have
been home near Claudia. The onion-dome roofs blinded
her in the low afternoon sun. The flags hung limp. The
dust choked her. There was nothing special about this place;
it was just a farm like any other — maybe more prosperous,
but a farm just the same. The wonderful promise had
dissolved.

Theo scuffed slowly across the yard. Her hands tingled
uncomfortably and she shook them. Suddenly she stopped
and lifted her head. A horse walked toward her, seeming
to come straight out of the sun. The heat from his body
shimmered around him, and his supple muscles slid under
his mahogany-brown coat like a perfect machine. He turned
slightly and Theo saw the alert eyes looking at her. She
stood absolutely still when the horse came to stop in front
of her. Behind him trailed the sulky, and the man sitting
with his legs dangling in the seat peered around to see her.

"Well, Dan sure does seem to have taken to you," said
Mr. Savage. Gone was the impeccable summer suit and
starched white shirt. His once-neat hair was tousled and
dusty, and he looked happier in his dirty work clothes than
she'd seen him before. Dan Patch blew loudly through his
nostrils and butted her gently with his head. His ears flickered back and forth between the man behind him and the
girl standing so still in front of him.

She could not move, and hardly dared to breathe. The
stallion nibbled the laces of Carl's old boots. He rubbed his
forehead up and down against her until she almost lost her
balance. Slowly she reached up both her hands and put
them on his head. She scratched the hollow over his eyes.

She leaned her cheek against his hot neck and put both her arms around him. The horse's eyes half-closed in contentment. Mr. Savage shook his head merrily.

"I always knew Dan could charm the shirt off a person's back, but this time it looks like *he's* been charmed," he said, slipping from the woven sulky seat and walking around to the horse's head. He, too, leaned his face against the other side of Dan Patch's neck, and for a moment they all three stood quietly. Then Mr. Savage straightened and ran his hand under the black mane. "C'mon, Dan, old boy — we can't stand here all day. We've got work to do, you and I." Theo stepped quickly back and caught Marion Savage's look. The dark eyes smiled as usual, but behind the smile was an expression of intense interest.

At the cottonwood trees along the stream, Theo knelt and splashed water on her hot face. She could not shake the enchantment of the horse's touch. Slowly she pulled the pins from her hair and shook it loose down her back. Carl leaned against the tree watching her.

"I think I like you best as a girl," he teased softly. She stood up and smoothed the wrinkled cloth of her muslin dress.

"Does it look all right?" she asked.

"You better tell your mother those kids you were baby-sitting have ponies," he drawled, still with a grin in his eyes. "I can smell horse three feet away."

"Carl!" she cried, anxious. "Don't laugh! Do I look all right, *really?*" He cocked his head and frowned.

"Well, you better say the kids were wild ones," he said. "You look a little mussed up." He paused. "But I think you look fine." He flashed her a quick look and then sprinted up the slope toward the last fence, while Theo followed more slowly. She tried to smooth her hair as she walked, and tugged anxiously at her dress. At the head of Cargyll

Street her unease was so acute she could hardly mumble a reply to Carl as they parted.

"Tomorrow, by the tree. At five-thirty!" he said, and she could only nod, already staring down the street to her house. *Had* anything awful happened? Was Claudia all right?

When she walked in the door, Maud met Theo with a strained expression and high color in her face; for a moment Theo was sure her worst fears had come true.

"I had no idea you'd be gone this long, Theodora," said Maud. "And *look* at you . . . are those children civilized, for goodness' sakes?" But she was so distracted she cut her scolding short, and took Theo's hand in a rare touch.

"What is it, Mama?" whispered Theo. "Mama, is Claudia all right? Is she?" Her voice rose, and Maud almost pushed her to the doorway of the parlor.

"Just look!" Maud smiled. "Look — she's been waiting all day to show you!"

Theo stared across the room at Claudia. She lay as she had been for weeks, but today there was a wan smile on her face. Claudia said weakly: "Hello, Thee!" Her dark eyes sparkled in a way Theo had not seen for a long time. "I want to show you something, Thee. Watch!"

Claudia slowly lifted her hand from the quilt. She lifted it almost a foot from the bed, wiggled her fingers slightly, and then let it drop. She stared at Theo with shining eyes.

"Oh, Claudia!" gasped Theo.

"It happened this morning, isn't it amazing? All of a sudden, I just felt it . . . I just knew I could move it! And I *did*, Thee!"

Again she lifted the thin forearm and this time she playfully wiggled her fingers at her sister, waving her hand back and forth in the air. Theo went to her bed before Maud could stop her.

"When did it happen, Claudia?" she cried in a low voice. "Do you remember — *exactly?*"

"Why, I think it was early morning . . ." said Claudia, faintly puzzled. "Yes, it must have been . . . I know, because Mama had just brought me some toast, so it had to be around seven, I think. Why?"

Seven! Yes, that was almost exactly the same time! Theo could only shake her head wordlessly. She took Claudia's hand and when the thin fingers curled around her own, alive and warm, she began to cry.

She squeezed her eyes shut and felt again the sweet warm breath of the great stallion. She took a deep breath as if she were pulling into herself again that powerful strength, and felt as she had early that morning the same certainty . . . the certainty that whoever touched Dan Patch would be filled with that same indomitable strength. Somehow . . . somehow . . . Dan Patch had reached past Theo to race along her wishes as surely as he raced along a track, and had filled Claudia with the same vital strength. Yes! She was sure of it. She took Claudia's hand and raised it in a victory salute.

ᕮᘁ Chapter Eight ᘁᕭ

THE TENACIOUS HEAT hung over Savage. No breeze sifted up from the Minnesota River, and the cottonwoods along the meadow streams panted in a dry whisper. Sluggish brown clouds drifted up into the white-hot sky on the horizon west of town, where the vast grassland plains were breaking into spontaneous wildfires.

Claudia lay day after day on the special sheepskins on her bed in the parlor. By midmorning Maud drew the shades down to keep out the sun. Flies droned in the murky air and settled on Claudia's motionless arms and face. She lay awake for hours staring at the wallpaper. Sometimes she did not speak from morning until evening. Theo made a fan for her out of folded newspaper and Harriet directed Claudia to hold it.

"Even moving one hand will help with the circulation," she said, showing her how to work the fan. "Try to move your wrist more — like that. Try to push the movement up into your muscles."

Theo stood at the end of the bed and watched. Lately she could think of nothing to say to Claudia. After the initial elation caused by Claudia's moving her hand, the whole family seemed to Theo to have slid into a gorge of despair. Even Harriet, whose manner was always so calm and efficient, moved heavily and rarely spoke. The shroud of lethargy resettled itself around the old house and Theo was sure it would never change . . . she moved like a puppet, as if being alive did not belong to her but to the oppressive heat and monotony that wrapped them all.

Claudia flicked the fan feebly once or twice after Harriet left the room and then let her hand drop back onto the sheet. Theo watched her uneasily. The black flies, dislodged by the motion of the fan, crawled again on Claudia's skin, but she did not move and her eyes stared blankly at the wall.

"You have to swish at them," encouraged Theo. "Otherwise they'll just come back." Claudia turned her head imperceptibly away from her. The fan slipped out of her fingers.

"I don't care about the flies," she said. She licked her dry lips. Theo stumbled over a pile of dirty sheets on the floor as she reached for the pitcher of water on the dresser. She poured a little water into the special broad-handled cup Harriet had found at Brunner's Mercantile. Her hand trembled slightly and water spilled onto the dresser. She held the cup tight.

"Here," Theo said, placing the cup in her sister's good hand. She had watched Harriet instruct Claudia in holding it many times. The white fingers closed spasmodically around the handle and Theo lifted the thin arm toward her mouth. She forced herself to smile cheerfully as she raised Claudia's head from the pillows. But it shocked her that, in the two weeks since she had been allowed in the sickroom, Claudia's weight had dropped noticeably. She weighed no more than a wisp of hay. No, it's just that my arms are getting stronger, thought Theo wildly.

But she knew it wasn't that. Claudia was withering away. The light was shrinking from her eyes and her blood lay stiller and stiller in her veins like a stream drying up under a deadly sun. She lay unresisting against Theo's arms. The cup slipped.

"You have to hold it, Claudia!" Theo cried softly. "I know you can — Aunt Harriet said you have to do as much for yourself as you can. Come on, just hold the handle . . . it'll spill —" But Claudia turned her face even farther away and water spilled all over the front of her and over the clean sheets Maud had tucked on the bed earlier. The cup dropped from her hand and clattered onto the floor.

"Theodora, what are you *doing!*" Maud appeared from

the kitchen at the sound of the cup falling. She pushed Theo aside and lowered Claudia gently against the pillows. "You aren't to do any of this, Theodora," said Maud, and her voice cracked in a strange, high way. "I thought you knew better. It's too dangerous for her. You could pull something . . . strain her . . ."

"I was only . . . she was thirsty, Mama," whispered Theo, stricken. Claudia would not meet her eyes. Her sister's hair stuck in damp sweat against her skin, and Maud brushed it out of her face. Theo hid her tears by fumbling under the bed for the cup. She scrubbed at her eyes with the edge of the quilt. Harriet came into the room and watched a moment before speaking.

"Claudia's not made of glass," she said finally. Under the quiet voice Theo caught an unfamiliar sharpness. Harriet's long black skirt swept across the floor as she moved to the bed. She looked neither at Maud nor at Theo, but straight into Claudia's averted face. "Have you given up, Claudia?" she asked, her voice deceptively soft. "Is that it? I thought there was more spirit in you than that." She spoke matter-of-factly, with a shrug of her shoulders. She took the wet sheet from the bed and shook out a dry one. She tucked the edges deftly around the mattress and shifted Claudia's head so she lay straight on the pillows. Theo was shocked at how rough her aunt's movements were.

"Well, Claudia, I don't blame you," said Harriet, dropping the wet sheets into a pile on the floor. "I suppose you can't do anything else but give up. After all, what's the use? You can't do anything about anything, can you?" A faint flush appeared on Claudia's cheeks but she continued to stare at the wall and did not speak.

"Claudia can do anything she wants to!" Theo cried. She banged the cup down on the dresser with such force it

102

rattled. Harriet shrugged again, as if she did not care. Theo glared at her. How could she dare talk to Claudia like that! Claudia — *give up?* She didn't know the first thing about Claudia . . . how Claudia could practice for hours and hours without rest, how determined she'd been before the audition with the symphony . . .

"Not if she's given up, she can't," said Harriet brusquely. "But it doesn't matter, does it, Claudia? You can't play the violin — so what's the point of doing anything?" Maud, her face white, put her hand pleadingly on Harriet's arm, but Harriet ignored her.

"You don't know what you're talking about, Aunt Harriet!" Theo burst out, stinging with anger. "You think you know what you're doing, pushing her arms and legs around, but you don't know her *at all!* You don't live here! You didn't know her before —"

"Theodora!" Maud snapped. "You are not to speak to your aunt in that way. She's a doctor and she knows exactly what —" But her voice broke and she could not continue. The air quivered between them all, as if their anguish had got trapped between sound and silence. No one spoke. Then Claudia picked up the fan and with a flick of her weak wrist flung it across the room. It slithered over the floorboards and disappeared under the dresser.

"Just go *away*," she said dully. The sweat stood out on her forehead. "Go away. I want to think."

"Sweetheart . . ." murmured Maud.

"Please, Mama," Claudia pleaded. "It's so hot. I just want to be alone." Maud hesitated, and Theo ran from the room.

She sat hunched over on the porch step. Above her, the sun slanted down through the leaves and burned holes into the pale dust. In the dry grass along the fence, cicadas buzzed. The sound generated a throbbing heat of its own.

Theo stared out at the street and felt herself burning up inside. She couldn't think at all. All that afternoon and into the evening, the silence stuffed every crack of the dim house. Her father came home from his office and slunk away into his study. Mrs. O'Leary left a platter of sandwiches on the kitchen table and went home. Harriet stayed in her room with the door closed, and Maud wandered between the kitchen and parlor until Theo thought she would scream. When the lamps were lit, the summer dark wavered sluggishly around the pools of yellow light. The night was no cooler than the day.

Theo dragged the kitchen buckets into the back yard and pumped them full of water. She dipped her face into a bucket and blew softly, letting the coolness soak up through her hair. Coming to her on the night air was the sharp menace of prairie-fire smoke. After a few minutes she took the buckets in, gathered the last pile of dirty bed linen and dumped it into the big copper laundry pot that sat in the lean-to off the kitchen. Tomorrow, Mrs. O'Leary would pour boiling water in it to start the washing. Theo held the empty platter listlessly under the sink pump and cleaned it, leaving it to dry on a cotton rag. When she had done everything, she snuffed the lamp wick and sat in the still darkness at the kitchen table.

Harriet appeared in the doorway with a familiar swishing of skirts. Her aunt's tall body was backlit by the light from Stevenson's study and Theo could not see her face clearly.

"You know what I was doing, Theodora," Harriet said without preamble. Theo did not answer. "Claudia thrives on challenge," her aunt continued. "It's what moves her blood. If she gives up she'll die, you know." Theo clenched her hands together. Harriet came to stand behind her chair and put her hands on Theo's shoulders.

"Will she die, Aunt Harriet?" Theo asked. Her voice was so faint she was not sure if Harriet had heard. But the hands tightened and drew Theo back against her.

"I don't think so," said Harriet. "But she's starting to drift away. I've seen it happen with people before. They just stop trying. Sometimes all it takes is to make them angry, and they'll get all fired up to live again." Theo leaned her head against Harriet and felt the strong fingers stroking her hair. She closed her eyes. How could she have been angry at Harriet? She'd been angry at herself, at her own helplessness. Her aunt pulled out a chair and sat facing her. She smiled. "You have to fire yourself up a bit, too, Theo," she said, brushing a heavy strand of Theo's hair from her face, just as Maud had done to Claudia. "Aren't you enjoying your job? You're gone all day — you must work very hard with those children. Your shoulders feel as strong as a horse!"

"I give them piggyback rides a lot," said Theo quickly. Harriet smiled again, her thin shoulders drooping in the black dress, and Theo saw the exhaustion in the tight face. She leaned forward impulsively and hugged her. "I'm sorry," she whispered.

"There's nothing you have to be sorry about," Harriet said firmly. Theo followed her from the kitchen and peeked into the parlor.

"Are you asleep?" she called quietly. Claudia turned her head in the darkness.

"It's harder to sleep at night sometimes," she said. "Isn't that strange? I sleep in the morning and after lunch . . ."

"I'm sorry I got you all wet," Theo murmured. She slipped into the room so Maud would not hear her. Claudia sniffed slightly to show she was smiling in the darkness.

"It felt nice to get wet," she said. "I was so hot,

Thee . . . I wish I could go swimming. I want so much to go swimming!" Theo swallowed. "You haven't given up, have you, Claudia?" she begged. "Because Aunt Harriet said you —"

"Aunt Harriet's right," Claudia whispered. She drew in a deep breath. "But it's all right, Theo. I can fight it . . . I *can!* You believe me, don't you?" Theo knelt on the floor by the bed.

"I believe you," she answered.

Claudia's eyes shone at her. "It's really important that you believe me," she insisted. "Because sometimes I *do* feel like giving up. Sometimes I think about lying here like this for years . . . forever —" She reached for Theo's hand with her thin fingers. "But if I know that *you* believe I haven't given up . . . it just helps." She hesitated. "I know it's hard for you, Thee."

"It's hard for *me?*" cried Theo. "What about *you?* I keep thinking about the way you were . . . the way you've always been, and I can't *imagine* you giving up!" How could anyone believe Claudia would lie inert and helpless like this forever? No one believed that, or they would all give up! She *had* to believe that Claudia would glide again onto a stage and fill the world with music. But how long could Claudia go on like this?

Theo slept restlessly and woke while it was still dark, but by the time she had pulled on her loose muslin dress and stockings, the first light mist of dawn shone through the trees. She was stifled in the still-warm house, so she slipped out the door and made her way across the hayfields to the stream. The first hay was being cut, and the reapers loomed dark in the misty fields, ready for the teams of horses the men would hook to them. It would be an hour before Carl joined her, so she settled under a tree by the

106

stream and looked across at the International Stock Feed Farm.

Even in the gray predawn, the massive domes on the building shone as if infused with an inner light. The barns were no longer a mystery to her. She knew every tack room and equipment room, knew which horses lived in which stalls, knew their grooms and the stablehands for each wing. She was part of the pattern of days there — true, perhaps she was the most insignificant part of Mr. Savage's enterprises, but she was a part just the same. She was a good worker, learned quickly, and the grooms spoke fondly to her and called her by name. And most of all, she had touched the very heart of the place — Dan Patch himself. But to her dismay she realized that the magic had dissolved, and the promise seemed further away than ever.

Theo scratched her back against the rough bark of the tree. From the meadow grass tendrils of mist rose into the growing heat of the day. Far across the field, a herd of brood mares and foals moved like ghosts through the haze. The yearning within her seemed to press painfully on her heart.

What did she want? What was she looking for? Why did she feel more empty than ever, even though she was actually among the horses at the barns?

Nothing had changed — there was still the same restless sense of resisting something she didn't want, without knowing what she *did* want. I want to drive harness horses! she'd cried to Carl. I want to drive the fastest horses in the world! She pressed her cheek against the cool tree bark. Was that it? Was that what she wanted — just that? In between her busy errands, as she ran about with buckets and rags, she would often catch a glimpse of the horses warming up on the track beyond the barns. She could see no more than flashing dark shapes in a cloud of dust before they were

107

gone or she was called away. When the horses came off the track, she would see them exhausted and covered in lather, their drivers streaked with dust and sweat. The grooms would run up to uncheck the harness, remove the sulky, rub the dark bodies with the rags Theo brought and splash them with the cool water Theo pumped into buckets. That was as close as she ever got to the horses . . .

But there were times she felt closer. In the evenings, after she'd gone to her room for the night, after finishing her chores and reading to Claudia, she worked on her stories. She could feel the reins in her hands when she wrote, feel the wind flying out behind her and hear the powerful hooves beating against the earth. When she worked on the story about the boy who wanted to drive harness horses, she *was* the driver, she *was* the horse breaking his heart against the clock, she was even the wind!

She stretched her arms out in front of her and closed her eyes. But stories aren't *real*, she thought. How can I write stories about things I don't really *know?*

If she could just sit behind a real horse on a real sulky and hold the living reins in her hands . . . Her eyes flew open. All those drivers at the barns must have started sometime! They all had to have been apprenticed once, the way Carl would be apprenticed to the blacksmith. Surely even a rag boy on Mr. Savage's farm could be promoted to apprentice driver if he showed promise? Somehow, she had to convince Marion Willis Savage that she had the makings of a harness-horse driver. She *had* to. Surely, then, this awful empty longing would leave the pit of her stomach.

She watched Carl climb the fence and come down the sloping field toward her. He waved, but it took an effort to shake herself out of her solitude. But Carl only grunted hello to her after he jumped across the stream, and asked her nothing.

"Do we have to go yet?" she said, and he shook his head. "No, I'm early this morning, too."

Unexpectedly, the words came tumbling from her. "I had to get out of the house. It's hard for me to breathe there . . . I can't even *think!*" she cried. "It's hard to explain. I feel like there's layers and layers of things going on, but no one says much of anything and they all just go around doing the same chores over and over again."

Carl settled himself on the ground near her to listen, attentive and serious as always. "Well, families are funny," he said thoughtfully. "Everyone thinks a family is like a team of horses . . . you know, all working together the same. But I don't think it's like that at all. It's like —" He frowned and pushed a twig into the dirt. "It's like there's an *idea* the family believes in, about who they are, and that idea is like . . . well, like the sun," he said, glancing at Theo. "So then everyone in the family is like planets, all twirling around that idea . . . but they're really all separate. See — they're like whole different worlds, each one of them, all by themselves and all alone."

Carl looked up through the cottonwoods filled with flocks of blackbirds. A pheasant screeched in the thicket across the stream. The tips of the meadow grass glowed like jewels in the rising sun. Theo thought about the sun with all the planets whirling around in the vast emptiness of space.

She looked at Carl with wonder. How was it he could go for days without saying much at all, and then calmly say the truest, most solid words? She was never sure what Carl was thinking about, or even if he was thinking at all, until suddenly he would say something amazing in a perfectly ordinary voice. She thought about her family and the sun and planets for several minutes.

"The idea in my family is Claudia," she said slowly. "Claudia *is* like the sun. She's always been the idea in my family, at least for Mama and Papa. Mama always has lots of opinions about things . . . you know how she does, about women's rights and that sort of thing. But Claudia is the one who really *does* anything, you know what I mean?" Carl only nodded, and waited for her to continue. Theo wove a bracelet from the long grass as she talked.

"Claudia does everything Mama *talks* about," she explained. "It's like she *lives* Mama's ideas for her, so Mama can't do without her. And now it's even more strange with Aunt Harriet here . . . she's a lot like Claudia." She held the bracelet up and inspected it. "I mean, Claudia knows what she wants to do in her life, and she works really hard. I don't think she even cares much about all that women's rights stuff, even though I know she thinks women should have the vote. But she seems to *do* more of what Mama talks about than Mama does. Does that make sense?"

Carl nodded. "Yes," he said. "It's like religion, in my family. My father is very religious, and he always quotes the Bible whenever he wants to get his point across. But sometimes I don't think he really lives the whole idea of it . . . at least, not the way my mother does. And *she* never talks about religion."

"But your father seems like such a good person to me," Theo said. Carl shrugged and broke a twig into tiny pieces.

"I guess he's a good person," he said moodily. "It's just that he has an idea of what he wants me to be — what he *thinks* I should be — and he won't listen to me at all."

"Have you told him yet? About going back to

school . . . and borrowing books from Papa? Do you still have to hide them?"

Carl did not answer and from his stubborn expression she knew he would refuse to talk any more about it. The sun was up now and they would have to start across the fields to the farm. Carl looked troubled, as if he wanted to speak and didn't know where to begin.

"You know what you said . . . about layers and layers of things going on in your family?" he asked at last. She nodded. He pursed his mouth and frowned. "I feel it too," he told her. "I mean, about things not being said. I love coming over, and your father always asks me what I think about the books he lets me read . . . you know, my father never asks me what I think about anything! And I think your aunt is the most incredible person, like she can do *anything*, she's so smart. But —"

"But what?"

"Well, what you said . . . there's something *uneasy* with them all, with your father and your aunt." He looked at her uncertainly. "And your mother, too. I think that's the 'layers and layers' you feel. I hope you don't mind me saying all this, Theo!" She shook her head. "I just think what you feel is not all because of Claudia," he continued in a rush. "There's something else between the three of them . . . your mama and papa and your aunt. It feels funny to me, when they're all in a room together. So you aren't just imagining it, Theo . . . and I just wanted you to know." A faint red appeared under his sun-brown skin. "I just don't like it that you're so unhappy," he muttered. He jumped suddenly to his feet. "We have to go or we'll be late."

Theo didn't say a word until they stood at the gate into the yards. "I know you're right," she said in a low voice.

"You're right about Papa and . . . Aunt Harriet. It *is* like they're all separate planets whirling around. I just wish I could understand." She narrowed her eyes. "If Aunt Harriet's in the room when Papa comes in, he leaves in a little while. And then Mama goes out to find him. And if Papa is already there, Aunt Harriet won't come in at all . . . it's so stupid!" she burst out. "I hate it! I don't know what's the matter with them, but it's like they won't talk about it because Claudia's sick. And it's hard on Mama most of all, because she loves Aunt Harriet and admires her . . ."

"Like you love Claudia, even though you feel so small around her?"

"Yes, like that!" She nodded violently. "Aunt Harriet's the only one who can really do anything for Claudia. And Mama looks so helpless sometimes, Carl. It's awful. I think she sometimes wishes Aunt Harriet wasn't there! But she doesn't want her to leave, either, because Aunt Harriet knows about polio . . . if Claudia died I think Mama would die too. Oh, Carl, Claudia might die!"

Carl shut the gate behind them and stared at her. "What do you mean? I thought she was getting better."

"Well, Aunt Harriet's afraid she's sort of . . . given up," said Theo miserably. "She just lies there all day and hardly says a word. She was so happy when she moved her hand. I know everyone thought she'd be all better soon, but she's not. She told me she hasn't given up, but she seems so tired and weak —"

For a moment, she thought wildly that Carl was going to put his arms around her. She held the fence post and felt a little dizzy, and swayed away from him. What would she do if Carl *hugged* her? She said quickly: "Do you remember what you said once, about prayer? About imagining Claudia the way she was before . . . the way she really is — strong and beautiful?" She was sure Carl's eyes were bluer than the cornflowers growing along the fence. "Carl — Claudia moved her hand the same day I touched Dan Patch! He was butting me with his nose, remember? And I kept thinking how strong and perfect he was, and he made *me* feel strong and perfect too . . . and I was wishing that Claudia could feel the same thing. And that was when she moved her hand! So maybe it *is* like prayer! Carl, do you think if I just do that, she won't give up?"

Carl jammed his hands into his pockets and looked over at the blacksmith's barn. Already one of the grooms was calling to Theo. "I have to go," said Carl, and she heard his voice go dull with the anticipation of another endless day spent at the hot forge. He leaned toward her fiercely. "I wish you didn't feel like it was all up to you, Theo!" he blurted out. "Claudia has to decide for herself what to do. It's up to her if she gives up or not. And Dan Patch . . . the horses — they aren't really magic . . ." He smiled quickly. "The magic is what's inside *you*, that's all." As he turned to walk away, Theo pressed the woven grass bracelet into his hand. He shoved it in his pocket, but he was smiling as he left.

All that long day as she pumped water and beat out brushes and raked the yard, she thought about Carl's words. She imagined Carl in the terrible heat of the blacksmith's forge, stripped to the waist and pounding until he couldn't think straight. Once, after they sat silently eating their lunch together, she thought: But I can stop working here whenever I want to! It's not like Carl — he has to stay. I can go home right now, if I want. It's true — there isn't anything magic about horses . . .

Then the empty longing place inside her sucked all the strength from her in a rush of panic. I *can't* go! she thought.

There isn't anything else! What else would I want to do? She clutched a pile of dirty rags to herself and leaned against the side of the barn, thinking of the stifling days in the house on Cargyll Street.

Was this all it meant to be alive — always this constant yearning, this restless loneliness, this sense that there would always be more to people than she could ever understand? Carl was right about families. Theo felt herself whirling like a lonely planet way out in the cold darkness of space. She thought of the sun-bright Claudia, with her light dimming weaker every day. And there was Mama, another lonely bewildered planet bumping into Harriet and Stevenson, crashing against them and whirling apart, over and over. Mama, who loved her sister but wanted her *gone*, just like Theo had wanted Claudia *gone* . . .

She squatted down in the dust, stunned, and pretended to sort through the rags. *Was that true?* Was it true that in some part of her — some unspeakable part of Theodora Harris — she wanted Claudia *gone?* Didn't want her to get better? Didn't want Claudia's shriveled limbs healed and full of the energy that swept the family around her like planets around the sun? Didn't want it because she, Theo, felt herself to be the smallest and least significant planet on the furthest orbit from the sun? Oh, she would rather die than have this be true! She folded the rags into shapeless wads.

A movement caught the corner of her eye. Out of the turmoil of her thoughts, she saw the queer figure of the rat killer, Amon Szabo, sidling toward her along the wall of the barn.

ᑌᑎᘉ Chapter Nine ᑌᑎᘉ

THE TERRIERS PRANCED around the old man's feet, jumping up at the burlap sack that was slung over his shoulder. Amon Szabo stepped close to Theo and peered sharply at her. He dropped the sack on the ground with a dull thud and the terriers pawed at it. The old man grinned.

"See how they hate the awful rat!" he boasted. He pushed at the bag with his foot. "Full of rats. Yessir. You want to see?"

Theo shook her head violently and then caught herself. Boys weren't supposed to mind about dead rats. A groom passing close by looked over and laughed. "Hey, boy!" he called. "You can't get away without admiring Amon's rats!"

Theo held her breath and peeked into the bag. Inside were a dozen dead rats, their lean bodies mauled and chewed and their faces writhed into snarls. She stepped back quickly, but Amon Szabo leaned toward her and whispered, "A person has enough sorrows of their own without taking on the sadness of others," he said. His words were so clear and serious Theo was startled. The only speech she'd heard from the old man before had been so disjointed she'd privately concurred with the men that he "was not right in the head." But now he took hold of her arm and shouted over to the groom. "This boy-Theo, I need him help me now." He pulled her after him as he went. "I want this boy, yes? I take now."

The groom shrugged. "Okay by me . . . but Bill's gonna need a coupla buckets of water in about ten minutes, so you come right back. That ol' man'll keep you all afternoon. And son — bring the yard rake when you get back."

115

Theo followed Amon Szabo reluctantly. He frightened and fascinated her at once and she wasn't sure she wanted to go with him too far from the yards. He gestured with a jerk of his head toward the ash-heap that lay past the barns near the quarter-mile post on the track, and handed her the sack. She took it gingerly and held it as far from her body as she could, trying not to trip on the eager terriers. They leaped and snapped at the sack until the old man growled a command at them and they fell in behind him. It was a long walk to the ash-heap and Amon Szabo loped silently along for several minutes without looking back at her. She dragged the sack in the dirt and half-ran to keep up.

The old man unlatched a gate and held it open for her without a word. "Where are you from, Mr. Szabo?" she asked, because his silence made her nervous. She wanted to ask what he'd meant by "taking on the sorrows of others" but she was beginning to doubt she'd heard those words.

"Far away," he grunted. He pushed the lagging dogs through the gate with his foot and slammed it shut. "Ocean. Mountains. War."

"Why did you come here?" she persevered. The old man seemed to have a hundred untold stories hovering around him. He lowered his blunt head. "Everybody dead, girl-boy," he said. He paused and rubbed his face. "All dead now. Wife. Babies. You know . . . I was hunter, such best wolf-hunter in mountains. Lots snow. Cold all time. Then . . . war. Bad men in mountains. So everybody dead but me. Then I go away."

Theo tried to fill in the blanks around the old man's jumbled words. To her astonishment he began to shake with silent laughter. He pointed to the terriers and his eyes twinkled. "Once I have such big wolf-killer dogs. Now I have little teeny dogs and such different little teeny wolves!" He grabbed the sack and stumped swiftly toward the ash-heap. He chuckled again and gleefully whirled the sack around his head and let it fly to land with a thunk on the top. The terriers immediately dashed after it and he commanded them to stay. He turned to Theo and fixed her with his glittery eyes. "If you let yourself get lost in other people's sorrows, you will lose your courage," he said.

Theo was not sure how to respond. The old man seemed to stare right into her, as if to imprint his words on her mind. She looked away from him. They were standing on a narrow strip of field between the ash-heap and the track. The track itself was built up several feet higher than the ground and enclosed by a white fence. She could just make out, along the far side, a group of horses jogging through a warm-up. Farther down the track on her side was the gate leading from the boulevard. As usual, there was a cluster of men gathered along the fence with stopwatches in their hands. The drivers and trainers squinted their eyes in the glare as they watched the horses and discussed them among themselves.

Amon Szabo sidled closer to Theo. "You love those horses, girl-Theo?" he asked, and slipped past her until he stood by the fence. He looked back and grinned. "You think these horses . . . they magic? No. They just fast. They just strong. That's all." He leaned on the fence and Theo came to stand beside him.

The group of horses came pounding down the track toward them. Theo knew these horses were young and inexperienced because of the erratic manner in which they rounded the turns. They swung wide, uneven, and some of them broke stride and wavered all over the track. One colt careened so close to the outside rail Theo was spattered with dirt from his hooves. The driver shouted constant commands and the young horse, covered in nervous lather, rolled his eyes at Theo as he flashed past.

She answered Amon Szabo boldly. "I want to drive horses," she said, looking straight into his eyes. Somehow, she was sure he already knew. "I want to drive horses, but I don't even know how to start. I *have* to — it's all I want. I can feel myself driving down the track . . . I can *feel* it! Do you understand? If I could drive the horses, everything else would be . . ." As her words trailed off she saw a mist come down over the old man's grizzled face, like a delicate veil. Even though he held her eyes, she could see he was far, far away in that place of snow and mountains on the other side of the sea, and his face was full of beauty and sorrow.

"Ah," he said, speaking to her from that far-off place, "I know this. I know this *wanting*. *Wanting*. It is just dreams, inside here . . ." He tapped his broad chest. "It is just dreams, wanting to come out. That's all. Dreams have such many shapes, girl-boy. Dream the same, never change. But shape always changes, all the time . . . change, change, just when you think you got it!" He shook himself and shaded his eyes, looking at the sky. "Bad storm coming, real quick now," he commented.

Theo was startled to see the sky to the west had lowered into a black mass of clouds. She sniffed apprehensively. Smoke from the prairie fires hung in the still air. Amon Szabo laughed. "Look. Ha!" he cried, pointing toward the barns. "There is he — king-horse. See. He never afraid. He love storm."

At the back of the barns a big brown horse paced around a paddock. Theo scrambled up on the lower rail of the track fence. Dan Patch! She caught her breath. The stallion paused in the center of the paddock and seemed to stare straight at her. His neck was arched and his proud, alert head was raised, tasting the coming storm. Even from a distance Theo saw the knowing eyes and felt the energy that pulsed around the stallion. Her heart pounded.

A bolt of lightning shot through the clouds and cracked into the earth. The great stallion did not flinch. Another shattering crack of lightning split the sky, and with a blast of thunder a dry wind flattened the grasses. Now the thunder raced down the sky and rumbled along the ground like the hoof-beats of a hundred unearthly horses. Dan Patch screamed a wild challenge and met the storm head-on, pacing with the wind. Theo threw back her head into the wind.

Suddenly Amon Szabo gave a sharp grunt and leaned out over the track fence. Theo heard shouts from the men gathered at the entrance gate a quarter of a mile away, where the young horses were being led off the track. They skittered and threw themselves around in the shafts of the sulkies, squealing with fear. The trackhands and trainers ran among them to grasp their bridles as the drivers struggled to keep them under control. But one driver could not stop his rangy two-year-old colt. The horse sidestepped a trainer and broke into a rough gallop past the gate. The men on the track shouted instructions to the driver, and Theo watched him lean back in the seat and saw at the reins. Another tremendous streak of lightning broke through the sky, and the storm stirred the dust on the track into miniature tornados.

"That horse — he run away!" cried Amon Szabo. He climbed over the fence and watched the approaching horse and driver. A runaway horse was dangerous, capable of injuring himself and killing his driver. The old man snapped at the terriers, who slunk away to lie in the grass, and stepped farther out on the track. Theo followed.

The young horse dashed wildly from one side of the track

to the other. At every crack of thunder the horse leaped forward in a frenzy. His head was arched back sharply by the pressure of the reins, but still he bounded on like a jackrabbit. He veered against the fence and the sulky wheel screeched along the wood. The driver fought for control but the speed and force of the collision was too great. The sulky tipped sharply and the driver flipped out and tumbled over and over on the hard dirt.

The men at the gate not already engaged in holding frightened horses ran to help him, and Theo had just a glimpse of the driver's shaken white face before the panicked horse dashed toward her along the outside rail. The collision had slowed him to a ragged trot, but his wild eyes still rolled and his head was thrown back in an agony of terror.

Amon Szabo crouched. He called out to the horse in his guttural language. The horse's ears were plastered flat back against his head. Amon Szabo jumped to intercept him, but the horse shied violently and skittered toward the center track. The old man lunged again, grabbing for the reins. The horse squealed and half-reared, narrowly missing him with his hooves, and Amon Szabo leaped aside.

Theo stood pressed against the fence and looked straight into the terrified eye of the on-coming colt. The bloody foam streaming from his mouth spattered on her face, and she tasted his fear. The sulky flashed by her. She grabbed the shaft and lunged up onto the seat. The reins were tangled in the seat-struts and she yanked them free. The horse squealed again, bucked sideways and almost drove the sulky back into the fence. It tipped up on one wheel. Theo called to the horse.

She called the way she called to the yearlings who raced with her in the high summer grass. She called to the strength and power in the horse and her call sang down the reins into his heart. She answered the fear pumping through his blood by calling his name again and again. It was not his spoken name; she only knew him by his secret name, the name of the dream-promise deep in his heart and muscle.

The horse heard her call and his ears flew forward. His rolling eyes calmed. Amon Szabo darted quick as a rat and caught the reins at the horse's head. Theo spoke softly and the horse shuddered, his dark hide quivered, and he lowered his head and stood still. For a moment there was no sound but his loud labored breath.

Theo held the reins firmly. Her eyes met the old man's. Suddenly her arms began to tremble and she felt as if the storm was rushing through her head. "Sit up, girl!" hissed Amon Szabo. He dropped his hold on the horse's head and immediately she felt her strength return. The old man seemed to bore through her with his look. "Stay, girl! Hold on. *You drive horse.*"

And for the first time she realized what she was doing. She sat straight in the sulky. She held the reins of the runaway horse, kept him steady and calm. He walked toward the gate. Amon walked at his head but did not touch him. Theo drove alone.

"You all right, boy?" The men's voices clanged around her. "What'd you do such a fool thing . . . cripes! You coulda been killed!" A trackhand stepped alongside and grabbed the sulky. The horse tensed and skittered sideways. "Hold him, Jim! For the love of . . . get him there or he'll bolt again!" Another man grasped the reins at the head. The man holding the sulky reached out his hand to Theo. "C'mon, son. We gotta get you off of there," he said. "Don't know how you managed . . . it sure was amazing! You're a plucky kid —"

The horse snorted and threw back his head. The reins

began to slip from Theo's hands. She grasped them tighter. The horse was still listening to her. Something still connected them from his heaving frightened heart to her own restless longing heart. The storm wind slashed around them and she felt a shiver through the reins. The horse trusted her. She had to stay with him until he was safe. Because he listened to her, because she knew his name, and because *she* needed *him*.

"Let me be," she said to the man beside her. "Please." But before he could answer, another man came toward her from the gate. Theo looked up directly into his eyes.

"Let him be," Mr. Savage told the men. He did not take his eyes from Theo. He walked beside the sulky but did not touch it. He gestured to the men. They stepped back, puzzled, and the horse immediately calmed again.

"What did you do?" asked Mr. Savage at last, keeping his voice low enough for only her to hear.

"I called his name," she whispered. "He listened." Mr. Savage smiled slowly and she smiled back. He turned briskly to the men.

"Let the boy drive him to the barn," he instructed. "Then get him rubbed down well and put that liniment on his legs . . . the new oil I brought over yesterday, John. Don't leave him alone in his stall for a while. And Bert . . ." A wiry man limped closer to Mr. Savage. "Bert, make sure his mash is hot — you stay with him, all right? He's an awfully good colt — one of Dan's. He's got a lot of promise. Let's not lose him."

Theo drove slowly down the long boulevard toward the barns in the midst of the group of men. No one touched the sulky and no one held the horse. When they got to the yards the rain broke over them and the hot dust hissed under the cold torrent, but under Theo's hands the horse did not shudder or shy away. At the door to his stall, Theo slid from the sulky and a groom led the colt inside.

Immediately her legs buckled and Amon Szabo caught her. She leaned against him, her face buried in his ragged wet clothing that smelled of dog and hay and horse and of something indefinably sad. And suddenly Carl was holding her, too. He had run up from the blacksmith forge and was breathing hard. He took her arm anxiously and for a moment she forgot she was meant to be a boy. Held between Carl and the old man, she stumbled into the barn and sat on a hay bale in an empty stall. She was soaked and shivering. A stablehand poked his head in and threw Carl some rough towels.

"Your friend looks worse'n them rats Amon got this morning!" he chuckled. "Dry him off, there . . . I've put some coffee on to boil." He stepped gingerly out through the pack of terriers who had scampered on their own back through the storm. They shook themselves vigorously all over Amon's legs and settled at his feet. The old man lay back in the hay, sighed, and closed his eyes.

"You sure have guts, Theo," said Carl softly. The tension in her drained out in tears and she didn't even try to hide them as she looked up at him. He hadn't called her crazy or stupid . . . she hadn't thought herself brave.

"He . . . he was just so frightened, Carl," she whispered. "I couldn't bear it that he was afraid." He reached out his hand and drew it down her cheek. A strand of her long hair had come loose from under the cap and he tucked it back in place. His hand strayed over her face. She closed her eyes. She forgot the old rat killer stretched out in the hay across from them. She forgot her disguise. She leaned

123

against Carl's hand and was warmed with a jubilant strength. She lifted her head and let him hold her eyes with his own.

"I drove a horse," she breathed to him. She took his hand. "I drove, Carl! It was one of Dan Patch's colts . . . and Mr. Savage saw me!" The joy flooded through her. Carl smiled gently and his eyes seemed impossibly blue in the forge-darkened face. He wiped his hand on his pants. "Your face is dirty," he said. "I got soot on it."

All at once they were overcome with shyness. They shifted uneasily away from each other and neither could think of what to say next. Amon Szabo opened his eyes with a snort and the terriers jumped up, wagging their tails. The tension was broken and they sat quietly listening to the storm crashing around the barn.

"Sam should be here with the coffee soon," said Carl. "It's kind of late, but I guess we can't go home until the storm stops. Look at the lightning! My! I bet the stream will flood."

Theo gasped. "Carl!" she cried. "I forgot to put my clothes in the tree-hole! I was thinking about something when I changed, and then you came and I forgot!"

"Where'd you leave them?"

"In the bushes by the stream . . . how far could it flood, Carl?" she asked desperately. He ran his hand anxiously through his hair and listened to the rain pelting the roof. "I don't know," he answered her. "The ground's pretty dry — it might soak right in . . . but it's hard, too, so it could all just run off into the stream."

Theo wrapped her arms around her knees. The storm shook the barn and Amon Szabo hummed a tuneless song under his breath. Through the open stall door Theo watched the stablehands and grooms moving back and forth

124

as they checked on horses and commented on the unusual ferocity of the storm. The red-haired man brought them coffee, and grinned at Theo. "So, kid," he teased her. "Guess we better warn Harry Hersey, huh! He's got competition!" Theo blushed more at the respect underlying his teasing. Harry Hersey! Dan Patch's famous driver . . . She hid her face in the hot steam from the coffee.

Carl lay on his side in the hay and played with a terrier. The dog worried happily at a bit of rag Carl tugged away from him. He looked up at Amon Szabo. "This won't spoil him, will it, Mr. Szabo?" he asked. "My father says you can't play with animals if you want them to work for you . . . it'll spoil them."

"Love don't spoil nothing," grunted the old man. "You love a dog, you play . . . they only work more hard. People too."

Carl rolled on his back and the terrier curled next to him. The windows in the stall flashed with lightning. "I want to be an inventor," said Carl dreamily. He traced a piece of straw idly over the brown patches on the terrier's white coat. "Your father gave me a book by Benjamin Franklin," he told Theo. "He went out in a storm just like this, with a kite . . . that's how he discovered electricity. That was a hundred years ago! And now look what they can do . . . electric lights, automobiles, telephones . . ."

"Are all those electric?"

Carl shrugged. "I don't know," he said. "The lights are. But think of everything that's been invented in the last few years. We can talk to people on the other side of the world! They've made machines that will sew clothes! And men can *fly*, Theo! Just think of that! All over the country men are inventing things . . . amazing things! And that's what I want to do."

"I wonder if women ever invent things," said Theo. Carl sat up against the stall wall.

"Your mother gave me a book to read, too — did I tell you?" he asked her. She frowned and shook her head. She hadn't noticed Maud take much interest in Carl. "She did," he continued. "They were both beautiful books, Theo. I loved looking at them together. Your mother's book was plays . . . by a Norwegian writer. Henrik Ibsen. I didn't even know there were any writers in Norway." He leaned closer to Theo. "You know, you write like that," he said. "Yes . . . yes, you do, Theo. That story you wrote for English class, the one about freedom . . . And Henrik Ibsen has women in his plays that are like . . ." He paused and she felt uncomfortable again. "Well, they're like *you*, a little," he muttered. "I mean, they're brave . . . and they *do* things. They do what they believe they have to do, and it doesn't matter what other people tell them. He wrote a play called *A Doll's House* about a woman who gave up everything so she could do what was most important to her."

Theo looked over at the rat killer dozing in the hay. "Do you think women can do the same things as men, Mr. Szabo?" she asked. "I mean, do you think they're as smart and clever as men and can be inventors or lawyers or . . . writers, or whatever they want?"

Amon Szabo grunted and yawned. "Man. Woman. What matter? They people . . . all people. Just human beings. No better than other, yes? They not too different in here . . ." he said, running his finger from his forehead to his chest and tapping it against his jacket. "See? Dream is not man, not woman. Dream just *is* — you *do*. That's all. Just you *do*."

"Well, I invented something today," said Carl.

"What?" Theo asked.

"I made this thing that . . . sort of regulates the bellows at the forge so the air comes out a lot or a little, depending on how much flame you want. And you can work it with your foot so your hands are free. But I haven't worked that out yet . . ." He gave a pleased sigh. "Mr. McAlistar's real nice and he let me fool with it for half an hour today. He said he'd use it, if I got it up and running." Carl scrubbed the terrier's belly with his knuckles until the little tail wagged. He looked at Theo. "Have you written any other stories . . . like what you wrote for English class?"

"Some," she muttered. She wished Carl did not think she wrote stories like that man Ibsen. She remembered Maud talking excitedly for days about the plays when she first read them. She did not think her own stories were like that at all . . . they were silly, really — just about horses. She felt unhappy under Carl's gaze. She'd started a new story last week, and put "To Drive A Dream" away unfinished in her drawer. The new story was called "The Magic Land," about a boy who had come all alone across the sea to America. She blushed. The boy had eyes as blue as the sky and thick blond hair and came from Norway where there was always snow. He went west and was adopted by a tribe of Indians who taught him how to ride wild mustangs. She wasn't sure how she was going to write it, but in the end the boy rode a mustang in the Kentucky Derby and won.

"I would like to read another story you wrote," said Carl.

"They're stupid," she said shortly. Carl pushed the terrier away and sat up.

"If you don't want me to read them, that's all right," he said. "But don't tell me they're stupid. I don't believe that."

"It's just that they're not . . . *real*," she muttered. "They're only about horses anyway, and I have to make everything up I don't know about, and that's almost everything . . ."

"Your imagination is real!" said Carl in a low voice. "It *is*, Theo. I know because . . . what *I* imagine is real. At least, I'm going to *make* it real!"

Amon Szabo chuckled and Theo saw him wink at her. She poked some hay into a pile. "Well, I don't mind if you read them," she said slowly. "The one I wrote for English is the only one I've shown to anybody since I was really young. But I'll give you one to read next time you come, if you want."

The storm had died while they were talking and now only a patter of rain tapped against the glass in the windows. The thunder rumbled far off in the east. They got up stiffly and joined the men looking out at the sodden yards. From a stall at the end of one of the long corridors a stallion whinnied loudly. Theo threw up her head and listened. The stallion called again. One of the stablehands snorted with laughter. "That ol' Dan!" he grinned. "He's tellin' us the storm's over and he wants to get back out there so's he can watch them mares over in the next field!"

Amon Szabo's eyes glittered knowingly. "That king-horse, he just calling goodbye to such a storm," he said. "Him and that storm, they brothers — yes? Same strongness." The grooms and stablehands went back to their jobs and Carl ran to the forge to get his jacket. Theo followed Amon Szabo into the yard.

"How did you know I was sad . . . this afternoon?" she asked, as if nothing had happened since the time he'd found her miserable by the barn. She could not understand how she'd ever been uneasy around the old man. He seemed to care for her secrets as if they were his own, and she felt safe with him. He cocked his grizzled head at her.

"When dog sick, I know — yes?" said the rat killer. "He not talk . . . I just know. Hmmm? Words not only talking things. Other ways talk . . . you know this." She squinted at him, puzzled. "You know, yes," he insisted. "Horse frightened . . . he not talk. See? But you know. Like dog not talk. Like sad-girl not talk, and I *feel*. Feeling not need words." Without another word he disappeared around the end of a wing with his terriers prancing at his feet.

Theo followed Carl through the gate into the meadows. "The stream's real high, Theo," he said, looking worried. "See? It's way up over the banks. We'll have to wade across to get home." They struggled through the rain-laden hayfields and slipped on the muddy slopes until they came to the bend in the stream where the grove of cottonwoods grew.

The stream was unrecognizable. Gone was the sparkling clear water bubbling over pebbles. Gone were the three steppingstones they used to cross it. The dirty water swirled deep over the banks and lapped sluggishly around the tree trunks. The tree Theo had sat under to think that morning was surrounded by water. Debris washed down in the current was snagged in the thickets.

Theo splashed down the flooded bank. The bush where she had left her dress and pinafore was half-submerged. She found her boots caught in the roots of a tree. Her shift was tangled on a twig in the middle of the stream. She waded in and pulled it out.

The rest of her clothes were gone.

↜ Chapter Ten ↝

"IT's NOT SO MUCH what you were *doing*, Theodora — although a *horse farm*, of all things — it's not so much that, as that you have been deceiving us. Your father and me," said Maud.

Theo stood in the kitchen in Carl's old clothes, dripping muddy water onto the floor. The miserable walk through the storm-flooded pastures had chilled her and she hid her shivering through clenched teeth. Stevenson Harris had said very little. Maud sat straight-backed on a chair, and around their feet the pool of dirty water widened.

"You are starting high school in two months," continued Maud. She looked at her husband, but he was staring at a fixed spot on the wallpaper behind the stove. "Theodora, are you listening!" snapped Maud. Theo lifted her head with a jerk but evaded Maud's eyes. "You are an intelligent young woman! I had really hoped by now that you would have *some* idea of where you were going with yourself, instead of mooning around over a bunch of horses every day. By your age, Claudia had —" Stevenson gave Maud a quick warning glance, and she closed her mouth into a thin line. She took a deep breath. "Theodora, we've really *tried* — your father and I — to expose you to the fine things the world has to offer. You have books to read, and music . . . we get two newspapers in this house, so you know what is happening in the world. You are a young *woman*, Theodora! It's such an exciting time for women — there's so much to be done! So much more is opening up for us than ever before, but we *have* to take advantage of it. And we have encouraged you in every way we know . . . we haven't stood in your way."

Theo flashed a look of outrage at her mother. Could it be possible that Maud believed that? She tried to control the anger lashing through her. "But that's what I want to do, Mama!" she said. "Women should be harness-horse drivers, too, and jockeys, and . . ."

"Oh, for goodness' sakes!" cried Maud impatiently. "What *for?* How could you possibly want to waste your intelligence on that? What can you hope to contribute to the world by driving racehorses? A mindless indulgence . . . empty entertainment? Horse racing, for goodness' sakes!" She pushed herself sharply back from the table and went to stare out the window.

"You don't know anything about it!" cried Theo, the blood racing to her cheeks. "You just have this idea of what you think I should be — just so it fits into your political ideas, that's all! You just want me to be another Claudia!"

"Claudia *does* something with her life!" Maud shot back.

"Well, it's more than you ever do, isn't it!" screamed Theo. "All you do is *talk!* Claudia doesn't *talk* . . . she just does things. And Aunt Harriet, too. I never hear her talk, talk, talk . . . all that women's rights —" Her voice had risen to a wail. "You don't know anything about me, Mama! You don't even see what I'm doing . . ." At that moment she caught sight of her aunt standing silent at the kitchen door so she did not see the stricken look that passed over Maud's face. She could only see Harriet through a blur of tears.

Maud twisted away from Stevenson and with an agonized look at Harriet, she ran from the room. Harriet stepped quickly to Stevenson and put her hand on his arm. When he looked at her, it felt to Theo that a nerve was touched in the room. Stevenson seemed to stare into Harriet's eyes forever, and Theo felt something pass between them more clearly than words. "I think she's gone out on the porch," Harriet said softly at last. Stevenson glanced at Theo before leaving the kitchen.

"Come here, Theodora," said Harriet.

"But I'm all wet," Theo gulped. Her aunt held her firmly, and Theo leaned against the woman who was so much like Claudia, so much like Maud, and who treated her so differently than either of them.

"You're cold, too," said Harriet after a few seconds, when Theo's heart had slowed from its violent pounding. "You better go change right now. I'll take care of Carl's things . . . they *are* Carl's, aren't they?" For a moment, Theo caught a twinkle in Harriet's eyes.

"He didn't do anything wrong," whispered Theo. "He helped me, Aunt Harriet. He really believes I can —"

"Of course he believes," said Harriet. "He's your friend, and that's what friends do. They believe in you."

"Then you're my friend, too," sniffed Theo, with her face buried against her aunt's shoulder. She sensed Harriet's smile and felt her familiar hand brushing the hair coming loose from the pins.

"You must have bought every hairpin Otto Brunner had in stock," chuckled Harriet. She held Theo away from her so she could look into her eyes. "Of course I'm your friend," she said softly. "And so is your mother . . . and your father." Theo looked away stubbornly.

"Mama is Claudia's friend," she muttered. "And Papa just follows whatever Mama does." Harriet's hands shook her a little.

"You know that's not true, Theodora. Your papa . . ." She hesitated, and it seemed to Theo the dark eyes were far away. She shook her head. "Your mama is doing with Claudia what our mother did with me. It may seem strange to you, Theodora — but your mother was quite a bit like you when she was your age."

"Then you must have been like Claudia," said Theo slowly. "Does Mama feel the same way about you, as I feel about Claudia? Maybe she doesn't like me because I'm so much like she is . . ."

"Oh, Theodora!" Harriet laughed sadly. "Families are complicated, aren't they? There's so much to a person — their past, what they hoped for, what they were afraid of . . . what they have now. But it isn't right to think your mother doesn't like you. It isn't that, at all." She gave Theo a little push toward the door. "Go change your clothes," she commanded. "I don't want another patient on my hands."

Theo paused in the doorway. "I want to tell Mama about the things that are important to me," she said in a low voice. "I mean, my stories, and . . . everything. But, Aunt Harriet . . . if I show Mama my stories, she'll just want to *take over!* The way she does with Claudia. But Claudia never minded . . ."

"The way you do," Harriet finished for her. Theo nodded.

"It's just that — those stories are *mine*," she explained. "I want to do them by myself, but Mama would want to tell me how to do them. It's the same with the horses. When I'm at the barns, I feel *free!* And if I could drive the horses . . . when I *imagine* driving them, I'm going so fast and I can go *anywhere!*" She took Harriet's hand in a plead-

133

ing grasp. "Will Mama let me go back to the farm?" she cried. "Will she, Aunt Harriet? Because I have to go back! I *have* to!"

Because Mr. Savage had seen her drive. He had watched her calm a frightened horse by calling its unspoken name, and he had *understood*. She was sure he would give her a chance now! She couldn't think of anything else but that. She refused to think about her continued deception or about school starting in a few months. Harriet squeezed her hand.

"I'll talk to your mother," she said with a determined look, but would say no more about it. "Now, go get out of those awful clothes!"

Theo glanced in the parlor before she started up the stairs. Claudia hated storms and this one had filled her with anxiety. By the time Theo got home, the thunder had died away into the distance and Claudia had fallen into an exhausted sleep. Theo felt her own exhaustion and shivered uncontrollably. She dragged herself up the stairs. From her bedroom window she saw the clear watery sky deepen into dusk. The elms rustled lightly in the breeze. She stripped her sodden clothing off and kicked it in a heap on the floor.

"I have to go back," she whispered as she pulled a cotton nightdress on. "I have to go back." She climbed into bed and slept immediately.

Once during the night she half-woke in the summer dark, blinking at the soft light of a candle. Someone was tucking the quilt around her and she nestled into the arms that gently held her. "Aunt Harriet," she murmured, almost asleep. But the arms tightened slightly and she opened her eyes. In the wavering light she saw her mother's face bent close to her own. Beyond Maud in the doorway was her father holding a candle. For a moment Theo was held warm and tight in Maud's arms. "Mama . . ." she breathed. Her mother laid her cheek against her own. "Go back to sleep, sweetheart," she whispered, and was gone.

But the next morning at breakfast, Theo was sure it must have been a dream. Her mother had been speaking for several minutes and her face was set tight and closed. In the parlor Harriet fed Claudia. Stevenson read the newspaper at the table.

"It really is out of the question, Theodora," repeated Maud. "I don't see how we could possibly allow you to go back there and carry on with such a deception . . . dressed as a *boy* —"

"But it's the only way I can . . . I mean, girls aren't —"

"Of course, girls aren't!" snapped Maud, exasperated. "If you are going to do anything with your life, Theodora, you *must* do it honestly. You aren't doing anything to further the cause of women's rights if you go around pretending you're a boy."

"I don't *care* about women's rights!" flashed Theo. Maud slammed her fork down on the table. Stevenson sighed and closed his newspaper.

"Well, you should, Theodora. You should," said Maud grimly. "Because if you don't, you'll end up living a nothing life. You'll waste your life. You'll end up marrying a . . . a farmer, or something, like Carl, and then —"

"Maud!" Stevenson's outraged voice cut across her mother's words. But it was too late. Theo clenched her napkin in her lap and stared at the table with a roaring in her ears. She wished she could shrink into the chair. Maud calmly picked up her fork. "Theodora, you are starting high school in two months," she said in a firm voice. "You have ruined most of your clothes and we can't have Mrs. Schmitt make you many new ones. You're going to have to help with them yourself. And now Claudia's past any possible contagious stage I really do need some help with her."

Theo pushed violently away from the table and her chair fell over with a crash. She threw her napkin on the floor. At the same instant, a loud thump came from the parlor.

Claudia lay propped up on the pillows. She stared through the door at them, her eyes burning in her pale face. She lifted her arms and thumped them down in frustration onto the mattress. She thumped the bed again. Both her arms beat on the blankets.

Both her arms. Theo froze. Maud stumbled from the table and ran to the parlor. Suddenly, as if seeing them for the first time, Claudia stared down at her arms.

"Mama!" she cried. Tears ran down her face. "Mama! Wait — listen to me! Don't make Theo take care of me, Mama! Papa, tell her she can't! Let Theo go, Mama!" Maud fell on her knees beside the bed and grasped Claudia's arms. Harriet leaned over her. But Claudia looked past them both to Theo standing in the doorway. "It's so awful, Thee," she cried softly. "Lying here every day and watching you creep around the house, and knowing everything is different because of me . . ."

"Claudia . . ."

"No, let me finish," Claudia demanded. She pulled her thin arms from Maud's hands and looked at them with wonder. "I — I guessed you weren't baby-sitting, Theo. You never were that interested in children before. I'd hear you tiptoe out of here every morning and it was like listening to someone *escape!* I can't explain. It was like you had to get outside so you could breathe again, Thee!" Tears stained the sheets drawn up around Claudia's neck. "I tried to imagine where you were going every day, Thee . . . you'd come home looking so *happy*, and then after a little while you'd get quieter and quieter, like something was squashing you down . . ." She drew a deep breath. "And I'd wish you could come in and talk to me about things, like you used to before . . . but ever since I've been sick we don't talk."

"Oh, Claudia." Theo's throat closed and remorse coursed like a terrible pain all through her body. But Claudia smiled tearfully, a ghost of the old smile that could light a room. She lifted her arms in the air.

"Oh, Mama! Look!" Maud shifted against the bed and Claudia slipped her weak arms around her mother's neck. Maud's shoulders shook. Stevenson patted them both wordlessly. Harriet had left the room but now Theo heard her running down the stairs.

"Play something, Claudia," said Harriet, placing the violin in Claudia's arms. "Play us all something beautiful." Claudia ran her hands over the polished wood. Her eyes glowed feverishly. All the color had drained from her face. She opened her mouth. "No, Claudia," Harriet whispered. "Don't even think it. Don't say a word. Just *play*."

Claudia took the bow in her trembling hand and placed the violin under her chin. Maud pushed it firmly into place. Claudia lay the bow over the strings and drew it across . . . once . . . twice. A thin whine of sound came from the instrument. She looked terrified.

"Play," breathed Theo. Claudia closed her eyes and let the bow find the strings again. For a moment no one moved. Then a sweet, simple note lifted from the violin, and another and another, clear and perfect. Claudia played a child's tune, a simple exercise. But she played. And the music banished in an instant all the fear, all the waiting, all the shadows hunched in the corners of the house and in the hearts of the listeners.

"Oh!" cried Claudia. She rubbed her face along the polished wood. "Oh," she said again. She hugged the violin against her. "Yesterday," she murmured. "It was yesterday, Mama . . . Aunt Harriet. The storm began and I could feel it . . . a tingling down my arms. It felt awful, and I was afraid. But everyone was running around closing windows and bringing in laundry, and then the storm came, and after it I just wanted to sleep . . ." She kissed the gleaming instrument passionately and laughed. Theo went to the parlor window and stared out so her face would be hidden.

Yesterday! Yesterday, when the storm began! She cooled her face against the window glass. When the storm began she had been looking across the fields at the great stallion standing in his paddock. The first lightning struck and he had stared straight at her. "King-horse," old Amon Szabo called him. Dan Patch. "The horses aren't magic," Carl had told her. "The magic is in *you* . . ." But there *was* magic in that horse — there was! How was it Carl could not see that? Carl, who understood everything and said the truest things she ever heard?

And as she thought of Carl, she saw Gustav Johansson coming slowly down the street in his vegetable wagon. The wagon looked as it always did, but Gustav was dressed in a stiff dark suit and he sat somberly upright on the wagon seat. Beside him sat Carl. Gustav stopped the wagon near the fence and looped the reins around the gatepost. He walked up the path to the house and Carl followed. In Gustav's hands were two leather-bound books.

"Mr. Johansson's here," called Theo, puzzled. Stevenson went to answer the door. Theo hung uneasily back in the hallway. The way Carl held himself as he walked up the path frightened her. And as her father opened the door, it hit her with horror. The books! Gustav Johansson was carrying the autobiography of Benjamin Franklin and the plays of Ibsen!

"I am very sorry to bodder you," said Gustav. His voice was grave and Theo was sure he had rehearsed what he was going to say. His movements were as stiff as his words. He put his hand on Carl's shoulder and pushed him into the hallway ahead of him. "I see my son has stolen some books," Gustav said without preamble. "I see your name here in dis one, Mr. Harris. I know my son comes to visit. I t'ink he steals books den —"

"No, no, Mr. Johansson!" cried Stevenson, trying to shake Gustav's hand. "No — that's not it at all! You see, I know your son loves to read, and I have many books . . . I have been *lending* them to him." Stevenson frowned thoughtfully, looking first at Carl and then at Theo. "Didn't you know I was lending your son books, Mr. Johansson?" he asked. Gustav shook his head once, staring straight ahead of him. Carl did not look at Theo. His eyes were blank and hidden from her — they were not sky-colored now at all. Stevenson took the books gently from Gustav's hands. "Mr. Johansson, won't you come into the kitchen . . . I'm sorry, but our parlor is a sickroom just now," he said. "Let's sit down for a few minutes. Actually, I need your advice . . . about your neighbor, Nils Hanson? Mr. Hanson came to my office a few weeks ago about a small legal matter . . . trouble is, I haven't seen him since, and I'm a little worried. I know he's a friend of yours, so . . ."

Gustav Johansson allowed himself to be persuaded to stay. The pride in the man seemed to Theo like an immovable steel wedge. She watched her father shift the wedge. He wasn't really worried about Nils Hanson, she knew. Stevenson turned to her and gave her the books. She imagined Carl poring through every page of them over and over, so frantic to learn new ideas, so fearful of being caught . . . she hugged the books to her chest and at that moment, Carl's eyes met her own.

He was crying. Silently. His face was still, but his blue eyes were no longer hiding from her. She could not bear to think what had gone on between Carl and his father before they made the long trip to town. She remembered Carl just yesterday — could it be only yesterday? — sitting in the hay in the stall. "I want to be an inventor!" She could still hear his voice, and felt again his hand on her face. "You could write stories like that," he'd said, because he believed in her. Not in the horses. Not in magic. But in *her*.

She put the books down on the hallway table. She went up to Carl and put her arms around him. She leaned her head on his chest and heard his heart beating. She didn't say a word and they stood very still.

"Carl, come in here!" Gustav called from the kitchen. Carl put his arms around Theo and hugged her tightly. He lay his head against her own. Then he pushed away and went into the kitchen. Maud came out of the parlor with Harriet behind her. Harriet gave Theo a shove, and she, too, had to go into the kitchen.

"Mr. Harris," Gustav was saying, "my boy Carl, now he is almost sixteen years — almost a man. He doesn't need any more school. He need to work. Dat is how it is, in America."

"But people also go to *school* in America," Stevenson said, and Theo could see the puzzled line across his forehead. He couldn't possibly know that Carl was forbidden to "waste time" reading books, that he would have to quit school in order to take on a man's responsibilities. Stevenson couldn't know because Theo had never told him — just as she hadn't told him about her job at the barns. She slouched against the wall. In fact, the past few weeks had been one big lie . . . and in one day, everything was falling apart.

"Mr. Harris," said Gustav with his slow dignity, "I know wot law, it says Carl does not have to go to school anymore now. He is man — almost sixteen."

"Yes, yes," said Stevenson, nodding his head. He looked hopefully at Maud, but she busied herself making a pot of tea and slicing cake. "Mr. Johansson, I hope you will forgive me — it isn't any of my business, but your son loves reading so much . . . he is very intelligent and wants so much to learn, and it would be a shame to waste —"

"He t'ink he is smarter den his fadder, I know," nodded Gustav quietly. Theo heard the hurt in his voice. "I cannot speak good English, I know dis. But it is not a waste, Mr. Harris, for a man to have honest work." Stevenson sighed and placed his hands on the table. He did not answer for a moment but looked thoughtfully at Carl. Carl stood next to his father's chair and his face was impassive. No one but Theo could know he'd been crying.

"I don't think I'm smarter than you, Far," said Carl in a low voice. "I want to do honest work, too. It's just different work." Gustav shook his head wearily and looked at his son with such love and grief in his eyes Theo felt she was intruding, and turned away.

"Dis is very hard, hard country," Gustav said finally. "I come here, I don't know any English, don't know anyt'ing. Only t'ing, I can work. I work hard . . . and look —" He spread his broad hands in front of him and Theo remembered Carl telling her how his father had broken in the prairie and built his farm with those two hands. "I have

141

farm — good farm. I raise family. We not hungry. I only want same good t'ing for my son."

Maud sliced a fat piece from a raisin cake and passed it to Gustav. "There are so many wonderful things Carl could do, on a farm or anyplace, Mr. Johansson — if he could go on to university," said Maud, speaking for the first time. "Carl talks and talks about the books he borrows from us, as if he can't get enough of them. Sometimes . . ." Her voice slipped into a softness that Theo rarely heard, and she caught Theo's eyes. "Sometimes, Mr. Johansson, our children don't always fit into what we think is the right thing for them. Maybe we're just afraid for them. Or maybe we're afraid for *ourselves*, that they'll become strangers to us . . ."

Gustav chewed his cake as methodically as he did everything else. He held the china teacup awkwardly in his big hands, and looked again at his son. "I am sorry I t'ink you steal dose books," he said at last. "I just find dem hidden, in hay, in loft, and so . . ." He spread his hands helplessly and shrugged. "You do not want to work at dot farm . . . at blacksmit'? You only want to go to school? Dot Mr. Savage, he give you dot job. He t'ink you ungrateful . . ."

Theo remembered the look on Marion Savage's face the last time she had seen him. She did not think there was anyone in the world who would believe in following dreams as much as that man. She clasped her hands together and leaned forward. "Mr. Savage would be proud to know Carl went back to school!" she cried. "He would, Mr. Johansson!" She looked at Carl, standing very straight next to his father's chair. He had as much pride as Gustav and she didn't want to beg for him. He would never beg for himself.

"Going to school doesn't mean I won't help you on the

farm, Far," said Carl. "I love the farm, too. It's my home."

"But den, after, in two, t'ree years — den you will go away," said Gustav. Carl gazed out the window with the faraway look Theo knew. Hope and the swiftest of pains passed across his eyes. He nodded. "Yes, Far," he answered. "Then I would have to go away."

Gustav pushed himself carefully up from the table. He was a big man and seemed to dwarf Stevenson. But Theo thought her father stood just as tall and straight. She understood why the people who came to Stevenson for help loved him. He did not shame them by contradicting them. He knew they could speak and think for themselves, and he respected the way they saw things. This time Gustav put out his hand to shake her father's hand. He smiled for the first time when he looked at Theo. "I t'ink it is very good Carl have such good friends," he said. She smiled back. He was still the same Gustav Johansson who tossed apples to the children and who gave his old horse a scratch behind the ears.

In the hallway everyone stood awkwardly for a moment, and Stevenson cleared his throat. "I would like to lend Carl another book to take with him," he said firmly. Gustav shrugged and smiled again. Theo had seen the same gesture in Carl many times, and an emotion so sweet and terrifying shot through her that when Carl caught her eyes, her stomach flopped over inside her.

Stevenson handed a heavy book to Carl. The title showed clearly on the cover: *On the Origin of Species*, by Charles Darwin. She caught her breath. Of all the ones to choose! This was the book that had caused such bitter controversy among many religious people because of its theory of evolution . . . and Gustav Johansson was a deeply religious man. What was her father thinking of? But Gustav only took the book from his son to turn it over gently in his big hands. He nodded slowly.

"So many ideas," he said, as if to himself. "So many new t'ings — Dis book, dis is dot scientist, ja?" Stevenson nodded. "My son, he can read dis book . . . he understand?" Stevenson smiled and Carl flushed happily. "I can read this, Far," he said, and Theo saw a pride grow in Gustav's eyes.

Theo followed them out to the wagon. The morning sun shimmered in the clear sky like a disk of gold. Carl's hair seemed made of the same clear light and his eyes shone. Theo threw back her head to sniff the sweet air. When Gustav walked around the horse to adjust the harness, Carl stepped closer to her.

"Will you be able to work on the farm anymore?" he asked.

"I don't know . . ." she hesitated. "I think Mama might come around. We were all talking about it when Claudia . . . oh, Carl! Listen! Can you hear her? I forgot to tell you . . ." Through the porch window came the high, perfect notes of the violin. Singing with the notes came Claudia's laugh. Sometimes she missed a note and sometimes she played slowly, but her music never faltered. It flew high into the sky through the open window. Carl grinned. He thrust his hands deep into the pockets of his pants and lifted his shoulders with a breath of happiness.

"It's better now everyone knows everything, isn't it?" he said. He looked up at the trees. "Next week is the Fourth of July," he remarked. Theo squirmed her feet in the dust. Carl seemed intent on studying the trees. He opened his mouth to speak, shut it, and then rushed out lamely: "Mr. Savage is going to have four champions in the parade —

did you know that? Mr. O'Connor told me. Cresceus, Arion, Directum, and of course, Dan Patch."

Theo flushed and forced herself to smile and nod. But that wasn't what he'd been about to say, she knew. He'd changed his mind. Of course she was excited that Dan Patch and the others would be in the parade! Of course she was. But . . .

"There's the dance, after the parade and picnic," said Carl gruffly. "Are you going?" She scuffed her foot in the weeds. He tried again. "Will you go with me?" he asked. Her face lit with joy and embarrassment. "Yes," she said.

ᕙᑐ Chapter Eleven ᑐᕙ

THE DAY AFTER the storm, the meadows burst into a profusion of color. Wildflowers that had withered under pale dust broke free into the sun. The Minnesota River Valley was arched by a clear, high prairie sky.

Theo sat on the low step at the back door and let the fresh breeze run over her face. She closed her eyes happily and tilted her head toward the sun.

"You must be thinking of something awfully nice," commented Harriet as she came in from the garden. She shook dirt from the carrots and beets and surveyed them critically. "Not nearly as good as the ones Mrs. O'Leary gets from Gustav Johansson," she smiled. "Listen to her in there, singing away . . . you think she'll agree to cook with these scrawny things?" She sat on the step beside Theo. "So. That Carl is an unusual young man, isn't he? One day he'll recognize what a good man his father is."

"He already knows," mumbled Theo. Harriet's eyes twinkled. Theo ignored her and stretched her legs out, hitching up her dress and shoving her stockings down. When Harriet stirred to get up, Theo said suddenly: "He asked me if I wanted to go to the dance on the Fourth of July with him."

"And do you?"

Theo scowled. "I said I'd go . . ." she said. "But Aunt Harriet — Carl only knows me, you know, the way I am at the barn. If I go to the dance I'll have to wear a stupid fancy dress —"

"And put your hair up," laughed Harriet. She settled back on the step and appraised Theo with a thoughtful look. "Eventually, Theodora, you'll have to take off those boy's clothes," she said. "Your mother was right, you know — anything as important as what you're trying to do is worth doing honestly. Otherwise, it doesn't mean much."

"But, Aunt Harriet! You know Mr. Savage would never let me work at the farm if he knew I was a girl!" she cried.

"Maybe he wouldn't," agreed Harriet. "But someone has to make the first move, Theo. Some woman, somewhere, has to take a big risk and make the first attempt. It's no different than trying to be a doctor. I couldn't walk into medical school with men's clothing on."

"But if he doesn't let me . . ." Theo said in a low voice, "if Mr. Savage finds out I'm a girl and tells me girls can't drive harness horses . . . then what else is there? It's all I want to do! What happens if you have a dream, and it's the only thing that feels right — but you can't do it? Ever?"

Harriet seemed troubled, and frowned as if weighing her

words. "I don't really understand how that works," she said finally. "But I don't think you ever really *lose* a dream. Maybe there are different ways of going after it . . . lots of different ways. So if one way doesn't work, you have to find another."

"Well, if you couldn't have been a doctor, what would you have done?"

"I don't know," said Harriet simply. "I never had to face that particular obstacle. But there are other obstacles . . ." She hesitated and her eyes went very dark. "Sometimes dreams demand a high price," she continued. "I had to give something up that almost broke my heart, so I could be a doctor. I couldn't do both — or I *thought* I couldn't do both, at the time. Maybe I was wrong."

"What?" asked Theo. "What did you have to give up?"

Harriet played with the carrots and beets and didn't answer. Theo could hear Mrs. O'Leary singing her tuneless songs as she worked at the laundry in the lean-to shed. At last Harriet spoke. "I couldn't go to medical school and do everything that demanded, and be married at the same time," she said. "There was someone whom . . . I loved, and who loved me — but I knew I wouldn't be able to do both. Be a doctor and be a wife and a mother. A woman who wants to be a doctor has to devote her entire life to it. Maybe someday it will be different . . . when it's more acceptable and women don't have to prove themselves so much. But right now it takes every ounce of determination and strength. I knew I wouldn't have anything left over for a marriage or children. So I had to choose."

Aunt Harriet . . . in love! Theo gazed at her in amazement. She'd never imagined Aunt Harriet with anyone . . . Her aunt smiled at her expression, but Theo thought her smile was sad. "Your sister may have to face the same decision someday," said Harriet softly. "Because I really think she's going to recover, Theo — I really do! Polio is so unpredictable, but there's every sign . . . I think Claudia could be on the stage again within a year!"

Harriet gathered the vegetables in her apron and stood. "I told Mrs. O'Leary I'd help her with the stew for dinner so she can leave a bit early," she said, but paused in the doorway and looked down at Theo. "Theodora, school does start in two months," she continued seriously. "You *must* know you won't be able to keep working on Mr. Savage's farm after that. I hope you don't really think there's nothing else for you in the world besides harness horses. I don't believe that, and I don't think you do either. I do know it's important to you right now. But I also know it's important to speak to Mr. Savage as honestly as you can and exactly as you are." She paused again, then grinned. "And *I* am going to put your hair up for that dance, Theodora. It's high time Carl saw you as a young woman. No arguments."

Theo met Carl the next day as usual at the grove of cottonwoods by the stream. Carl's clothes had been cleaned and pressed by Harriet, and as she slipped into them, she worried they looked too neat for the barns. But it had been strange to leave the house with everyone knowing where she was going. She felt uncomfortable around Carl, too. She remembered the feeling of his heart beating as they'd held each other in the hallway. They did not speak until they reached the gate into the busy yards.

"It's bound to be real busy from now on," he said then. "Around the middle of July the racing season begins. The horses will be shipped all over the country . . . you wait and see. The place'll be as crazy as a circus from now on!"

Carl was right. Like the rest of the world, the farm had been refreshed by the rain, and it seemed to signal a new burst of energy. Stallions whinnied, mares and yearlings skittered and danced, and the glossy herd of brood mares and their foals streamed over the rolling pastures like a beautiful brown ribbon. A few weeks after the Fourth of July the summer and autumn fairs would take place all over the country. No state or county fair was complete without a wide oval racetrack at the center, and the stars of the fairs were the horses themselves. The biggest state fairs had the most famous champions of the harness-racing world, the jewels whose names were familiar to everyone. And no fairs were more blessed than the ones graced with the presence of Dan Patch himself.

But the races at the smaller fairs were exciting, too. On those unknown tracks a new star could be born, flying in from nowhere on hooves of pure speed. That was the lure of it all, the ever-bright promise. Every horse that stepped out on a track, no matter how small and insignificant the place, was watched as carefully as the champions — for who could know when some unknown brown horse from nowhere might suddenly lift himself free and race into the realm of greatness?

At the International Stock Feed Farm, the horses began to work out in earnest. The private boxcars that carried the champions by train from one coast of the United States to another were loaded with hay and supplies. Dan Patch's own boxcar, with his name painted on the gleaming white sides, was like a miniature mansion as it sat on the railroad siding that ran past the barns. The grooms and stablehands whistled as they rushed about their tasks, and the trainers and drivers spent hours huddled together at the fence on the track, checking their stopwatches and discussing endless speculations.

There was a festive atmosphere to the barns now, and everyone Theo watched seemed to glow with the pride of being a part of the most famous harness-racing stable in the world. The horses felt it most of all. Theo was sure they understood that they were the center of Mr. Savage's whole enterprise. They pranced and shimmied and danced. They trumpeted their challenges to the high prairie sky and the sun streamed over their invincible bodies.

Theo could not keep the smile off her face. Her heart was so full she couldn't help herself. The buckets of water and bundles of dirty rags seemed to weigh nothing today. That morning she'd overheard Mr. Savage talking about *her!* "Well, he seemed to have better hands than most any youngster I've ever seen," Mr. Savage had been saying to a trainer as Theo passed them on an errand. "How he got in that sulky seat I'll never figure out, but that colt was crazy by then — and he calmed him down. He drove as steady as . . ." And she slipped by unnoticed, her face burning and water slopping out against her leg. She could hardly wait for the lunch break so she could tell Carl.

She was annoyed to find Carl so caught up in his own thoughts that he hardly responded to her words. "What's the matter?" she asked at last, swallowing her disappointment. "Did you have more trouble with your father this morning?"

"No," he said shortly, fiddling with the buckles on a broken harness. He picked through the leather straps and wouldn't look at her.

She tried again. "Carl — maybe Mr. Savage will let me start learning to drive!"

He threw the harness in a heap and turned to her sharply. "Doesn't it bother you now?" he said. "After the other day? Doesn't it bother you, that you have to lie to Mr. Savage?"

Her mouth fell open in hurt and anger. Whose idea had it been in the first place, for her to dress as a boy and work on the farm! Who had encouraged her during those first difficult days, and who had believed in her dream to work with the horses? She couldn't answer him and at last he looked down, ashamed.

"I didn't mean it that way, Theo," he muttered. He yanked at a piece of strap. "But don't you see? I hated it so much when my father found those books . . . I hated *myself*, Theo! It didn't even matter that he thought I stole them — what was he supposed to think? I hid them and lied about what I was doing when I came to visit you. I wasn't honest with him at all, and I kept putting off telling him I wanted to go back to school . . ."

"But that wasn't easy for you —"

He threw the strap into the pile. "But Theo, nothing is easy, nothing that means anything! If dreams were easy, they wouldn't *be* dreams!"

She stepped close to him. "But, Carl! I thought you understood! I'm so *close* now — Mr. Savage saw me drive, and I heard him talking this morning . . . don't you see, Carl? Oh, I wish I could tell you how it felt, to hold those reins, and feel that horse . . . I have to try, Carl! And if Mr. Savage finds out I'm a girl now, I'll never even have a chance . . . you know I won't!"

He nodded unhappily. "I know," he said. "It isn't that I don't know, Theo. But I keep thinking about what'll happen to *you*." His voice softened and he took her hand. "I mean, what happens when school starts, Theo? So you drive a horse a few times — then what? I just don't want you to be unhappy." She looked nervously around the yard to see if anyone was watching. His hand on her own made her stomach jump like a nervous colt.

"I don't know . . . I have to go, Carl," she said miserably, pulling away from him. He held her hand a moment longer.

"I'm glad you're going to the dance with me," he said gruffly. Her eyes flew to a groom walking toward them. Old Amon Szabo scuttled around the corner of the barn. She pulled her hand from Carl's. "Me, too," she said over her shoulder as she ran off.

She avoided everyone that afternoon and sat against the wall in one of the wings, cleaning brushes and combs. She jabbed a hoof pick into the floor. It was true, she thought fiercely. Everyone was right — Aunt Harriet, her mother and father, Carl. How could she keep up this deception, anyway? She pounded the pick against the floor. It wasn't fair! Had Claudia ever had so much against her? Of course not! Of course Claudia worked hard — but had anyone told her she couldn't do it? No!

Amon Szabo came silently down the wing toward her. She didn't want to see him, and scowled down at her work. He stood in front of her until she felt she had to look up.

"Again unhappy, girl-Theo?" he said. She didn't answer. It almost seemed as if the old rat killer was laughing.

"You have fight with boy, I know," he nodded to himself.

"Go away!" she mumbled rudely. The old man crouched suddenly so he could look into her eyes.

"Boss looking for you, boy-girl Theo," he said. "You go."

She walked slowly down the corridor and found Mr. Savage standing with the foreman, Dennis O'Connor, in the main room. He beckoned to her when he saw her. "So," he smiled. "What are we going to do with you, young man?"

"I don't know, sir," she mumbled. She wasn't sure what he wanted. To her astonishment, Mr. Savage took her hands and turned them over in his own, studying them. He nodded at the foreman.

"You never can tell, can you — just by looking?" he smiled. "But you have the hands, son. And I hear the other

152

day wasn't the only time — although that was impressive enough. I'm told you calmed that rapscallion Arion down, first day you were here."

She could not trust her voice to reply, but Dennis O'Connor spoke for her in his brusque manner. "Sure, first day he was here . . . taggin' after Carl. Wouldn't start work 'til he'd seen Dan Patch, and pestered me about workin' with the horses. I told Carl then — he's a real horse lover, I said. I can always tell."

Mr. Savage looked at Theo thoughtfully. "Well, son," he said. "Do you still want to work with the horses?"

Now was the time. If she had any courage at all, if she was honest, she would take off her cap and shake loose her long dark hair, look this kind man in the face and say, "I'm a girl, Mr. Savage. I know girls don't drive horses . . . but I'm still the same person I was dressed as a boy! I still have magic in my hands. I can still drive horses . . ."

But Mr. Savage was already thinking ahead, and his words broke into her hesitation and the moment passed. "I'll try you out under Bill Turner," he mused. "Yes, he'd be the best one for you . . . you know who he is? I'll speak to him this evening. He's started countless boys out as apprentices, so he'll give you a try and tell me what he thinks. You don't have much muscle yet, but that will come with time and hard work — No sense your talent going to waste, is there, son? But we'll wait until after the Fourth. You report to Mr. Turner next day."

She stammered her thanks and ran from the barn. How was it possible to feel such elation and such misery at once! She leaned against the wall of the barn to catch her breath. Her heart drummed so loudly she could hear it. What could she do now? How could she turn back? There was nothing to do but go ahead.

⌒ Chapter Twelve ⌒

THE FOURTH OF JULY dawned cool and brilliant, as if the earth were determined to make up for the month of oppressive heat. When Theo clattered down the stairs for breakfast, Aunt Harriet made an announcement. "I have a surprise," she said, her eyes sparkling. "I spoke to Gustav Johansson yesterday and he's bringing his wagon over early . . . because we're going to take Claudia to the parade! A bit of sun and fresh air at this point could do wonders." The morning was spent in a flurry of preparation. Piled on the porch awaiting Gustav's arrival were a mattress, heaps of blankets, cushions, pillows, and parasols.

"What about the fireworks, Aunt Harriet?" asked Theo. "Could Claudia stay out for the fireworks, too?" Harriet laughed and shook her head. "We'll wait and see how the day goes," she said. "There'd be no sense in overdoing things."

When Gustav arrived, he and Stevenson lifted Claudia into the wagon as if she weighed no more than a rag doll. The wagon had been scrubbed and bleached so not a speck of dirt lay in the cracks. Claudia was settled on the mattress and bolstered by cushions and pillows. Harriet propped the parasol behind her head and Claudia leaned back with her eyes closed, taking long breaths of the warm air.

"I know I'll walk again," she said suddenly, without opening her eyes. "I know I will. I can feel it." Harriet and Maud sat on either side of her as Gustav and Stevenson led the horse away from the house. Theo ran back into the hallway for a forgotten basket, and Carl waited for her at the gate.

She wore the crisp white dress Maud had made for her graduation, the one she had worn the terrible night of Claudia's debut. It was the first time she had dressed up since, and everything seemed to bind and tug at her. She yanked the waist of the dress down and scratched at her stockings. She wished irritably that Mrs. O'Leary hadn't starched the dress so much.

She glanced at herself in the gilt-framed mirror above the message table in the hallway. Her hair was tied back with a wide, stiff ribbon. She mashed down the bow — it looked like a pair of rabbit's ears, she thought. Tonight . . . but she couldn't quite bring herself to think of that. Harriet insisted on putting up her hair, and she supposed she would have to wear this same uncomfortable dress . . . it was the only good one she had. "Only girls wear their hair loose over their shoulders," Aunt Harriet had told her last night. "Young women pile it on their heads." Theo wrinkled her nose. If she ever did become a harness-horse driver, she would cut all her hair off around her ears! She grabbed the basket and ran down the steps, slamming the door behind her.

"That's a nice dress," Carl said, leaning on the gate.

She grimaced. "It feels awful," she muttered. "You should be thankful you don't have to wear anything so stupid. You have no idea how much easier it is to do things dressed in *your* clothes . . ." Carl made no comment.

They found Gustav's wagon under a shady tree at the far end of the main street, turned so Claudia could lie watching the activity around her. Gustav led the horse away to tether it to a hitching rail. Everyone for miles around had come to Savage for the Fourth of July parade. The streets were bustling with horses and carts, wagons full of families, buggies, and people. There were women in light summer dresses and wide-brimmed hats festooned with ribbons, children weaving in and out of the crowd, and men in shirtsleeves and suspenders. From far off down the street, near the newly mowed fields where the fireworks would be displayed, the bands began to tune up. Theo could hear the thumping drums and melancholy hoots of the tubas. Gustav came back to stand briefly beside the wagon.

"My wife is coming now, with all my family," he said, shading his eyes as he looked down the street. "She tell me she will drive buggy, so I say okay." He chuckled and shook his head, looking at Claudia. "Dot little girl, she sure look fine now, Mr. Harris. Air is best, I t'ink . . . air and sun, ja?" Gustav turned to Carl, questioning him with his eyes. Carl glanced at Theo.

"I'd like to watch the parade from here, Far, if that's all right," he said, and Gustav shrugged slightly. "Well, you are almost man now . . . I said dot before, so . . . ja. You stay." He waved his hand at them and strode off down the street toward his approaching family. Carl leaned against the wagon and felt it jiggle as Harriet shifted to get a better position.

"Why don't you and Mrs. Harris sit up on the wagon seat?" Carl said, jumping up to brush it off. "You'll be able to see better, and I can tie the parasols right here . . . see?" He wrapped twine around the parasol handles and tied them firmly behind the seat. With Harriet and Maud on the seat, there was plenty of room in the wagon for Theo and Carl to sit beside Claudia. Near the front, Stevenson stood smoking his pipe and talking with some men from the town hall.

It took them awhile to get comfortable in the wagon. Carl leaned against some cushions next to Claudia, and Theo scrunched herself near his legs at the end. Claudia laughed the high, singing laugh that after all these weeks was becoming more and more frequent.

"How are you doing with that huge book Papa lent you?" Claudia asked, turning her graceful head toward Carl. He looked flustered. "It's difficult," he admitted shyly. "Mr. Bernard — from school — found some old newspaper clippings about all the controversy it caused when it was first published. Charles Darwin wrote a lot of other books, he said, about his voyages, and all the people and plants and animals he discovered." His eyes shone. "I want to read those books too . . . I want to go all around the world like that! There's so much out there . . ."

Theo glowered at the people milling past the wagon. Carl had not spoken that much to her in the last *week*. She swung her legs over the back and pretended to watch with interest the police and officials clearing the street. Claudia could make a piece of wood talk, she thought sourly. All she ever had to do was smile and laugh that laugh of hers.

But the other two didn't notice her. Claudia fussed with her pillows and Carl leaned close to her to rearrange them. Harriet bent down from her seat. "Don't let her legs flap around like that," she said, pointing. "Put that cushion there, Carl . . . no, like that. And make sure the other one is straight." He did as he was instructed, and Theo wanted to punch him.

She was shocked at herself. What was happening? At last, after so many weeks of tension and pain, Claudia was out in the open air with her family, looking almost well. There was color in her cheeks and her eyes were healthy and bright . . . so why do I feel so awful? thought Theo. Her stomach churned. Maybe she was getting sick. Maybe she was getting polio. She clenched her teeth.

Carl was gazing shyly up at Claudia. "I heard you play

157

the violin the other day," he said softly. "I never heard a violin. It sounded so . . . pure, like water, or something —" He flushed and Claudia laughed happily. "I can only play the simple tunes yet," she said. "But I can play! Oh, I never thought I'd play again! And now . . ." She stretched out her thin arms with a fluid movement as if she were dancing. "Now I just *know* I will! Theo, Aunt Harriet told me I might be on the stage again within the year!"

You act like you're on stage now, Theo growled to herself, forcing herself to smile back at Claudia. She wanted to bash the silly grin off Carl's face. She'd never seen him look like that and she hated him for making himself so foolish. She shifted herself as far away from them as she could.

"You're going to fall off the edge if you don't watch out, Theo," said Carl. She scowled and refused to look at him. Before he could say more, Claudia clapped her hands in delight. "Look — they're starting!" she cried. "Theo, look!" Theo ignored her and swung her legs viciously. The crowd fell back along the street and the parade began.

Carl got on his knees and peered down the long street. He's practically in her *lap*, thought Theo in despair. There was no question in her mind — she was sick, and after the parade she was going straight back to the house. Let Claudia have Carl all to herself, if that's what she wanted so much. Theo wrapped her arms around her stomach and hunched forward miserably.

"Are you all right, Theodora?" called Harriet, and Theo jerked upright. She couldn't bear for anyone to know something was wrong. It would just be too much. "I lost a button from my dress," she mumbled. "I was just looking for it."

The band crashed with trumpets and drums a few yards away and Theo jumped. The cymbals clanged and the drums rolled so loudly Claudia squealed and pressed a cushion to her ears. "Give me a civilized symphony any day!" she moaned through her laughter.

The drums added to the roaring and pounding inside Theo's head. She propped her elbows on her knees and leaned her chin in her hands, watching the parade through dull eyes. There was the high school band and the football team in their bright uniforms. There was Miss Frazier's Special Dance Review — the six-year-olds in their pink frocks got a loud applause. The town fire engine rolled by pulled by six white horses and followed by the fire department in their proud blue coats. Tom Henry's brand-new automobile, shipped straight from Detroit last week, drew hoots and cheers alike as it chugged past with colorful bunting fluttering from the chrome fixtures. Floats drew slowly past draped with red, white, and blue ribbons and crepe — the Women's Charity League, the Men's Shooting Club, the Teddy Roosevelt Association, its members dressed in ridiculous safari outfits. Jim Garvey's champion team of Clydesdales stepped past on hooves the size of dinner plates, followed by old Mr. Gunn leading his amazing two-tailed calf on a rope.

Carl pointed out first one thing and then another to Claudia . . . she's not *blind*, thought Theo. But Claudia exclaimed over every wonder he showed her. In her excitement she slipped down on her cushions and Harriet called out in dismay. "Claudia, you'll topple off the edge," she barked. Claudia let her arms fall back against the pillows. "Carl won't let me fall off, will you, Carl?" she laughed. "It's just so wonderful . . . it's been so long, and I never thought I'd be outside again. I can't help it."

The parade passed endlessly by in such a blur of noise and color Theo thought she would scream if it didn't end. Her head, after all, *did* ache now and she wanted to crawl home to her bed and pull the quilt over her. What was wrong with her? She'd been so full of excitement only that morning at the prospect of Claudia going out at last . . . and she'd wanted her to come to the fireworks, too! Now she was so miserable that when Carl did speak to her, all she could do was grunt in reply. No wonder he wanted to talk to Claudia instead. Who wouldn't? Claudia laughed and asked him questions and listened to everything he said.

"Theo, look!" cried Carl now. "Theo!" He shoved her shoulder to get her attention and pointed down the street. "Look who's coming!" The crowd lining the street seemed to swell with noise. This was the moment they'd all been waiting for. This was the final grand wonder of the whole parade. The wagon was jostled by people craning as far out into the street as they could. Here they came at last, the pride of Savage, the jewels crowning a tiny hamlet along the Minnesota River that might otherwise never even show up on a map. The crowd began to cheer.

From the far end of the street they appeared at last: Arion. Cresceus. Directum. And stepping like the king he was in front of them all — Dan Patch, the fastest horse in the world.

"Oh, Theo!" breathed Claudia. "They *are* beautiful! No wonder you want to work with —"

"Be *quiet!*" hissed Theo. She shot a ferocious glare at her sister. How could she be so *stupid!* People crowded around them on every side. Why, there was Mrs. Watson who had ears like a mule and could hear a whisper behind a closed door . . . and there was Otto Brunner, who made it part of his job to pass on the latest gossip. Claudia snapped her mouth shut with a stricken look at Theo. Carl stared down at his hands.

Now the horses were upon them. Despite her churning

160

stomach and the dull throbbing in her head, Theo caught her breath at the sight of them. Directum with his black coat gleaming like polished coal, Cresceus with his magnificent tail and mane sweeping the ground, Arion lifting his feet like a prince . . . was there anything more awesome in the whole world? They stepped in their powerful dignity single file down the main street of town. Ribbons were entwined in their manes and woven into their supple harnesses, flower garlands trailed from their bridles. Walking by the head of each stallion was a groom dressed in his best linen suit. The proud drivers sat in the splendor of their racing colors on the sulkies. Dan Patch led the others through a crowd that threatened to spill out into the street, and behind him on a white sulky woven with ribbons was the smiling figure of Marion Willis Savage. He lifted his cap and waved and nodded to everyone he recognized as they moved slowly along.

Dan Patch loved the crowds. Every newspaper across the country commented on his almost-human curiosity and pleasure at the bustling commotion around him wherever he went. He seemed to thrive on it. He never flinched at the countless hands reaching out to touch his glossy mahogany-brown hide. He posed calmly while camera bulb after camera bulb exploded in his face. His ears flicked forward, his neck arched, his gentle, alert eyes watching everything, Dan Patch held the attention of each man, woman, and child.

Today, Dan Patch seemed determined to outdo his reputation. He pranced on his polished hooves and bobbed his head at the crowd, first to one side and then to the other. The harder people cheered and clapped, the more the horse responded. He held his head high and surveyed the crowd, blowing curiously through his nostrils. The people laughed and exclaimed. He shook his head and sent the ribbons fluttering, and bits of his garland fell off into the street. Every tiny piece of flower was snatched up immediately.

A small girl broke free of her mother's hand and darted after a fallen rose directly under the feet of the stallion. The mother screamed and the crowd seemed to groan with one voice, but the great horse stopped still. He dipped his head to the child and snuffled her gently. Behind him the other stallions stopped as well. The child's father scooped her up and a sigh ran through the onlookers. It was true what they'd heard: Dan Patch would not hurt a fly.

The horses passed near the wagon. She could smell the hay-sweet scent of the stallion and hear the soft blowing of his breath. For that moment, nothing else existed for her. Claudia disappeared. Carl disappeared. There was only Dan Patch. She silently called out his secret name. She felt the electric power of his reply. He stopped in front of her. The groom laughed and tweaked his bridle. "C'mon, Dan-boy," he coaxed. "You still have half a parade to go."

But Dan Patch would not move. He bobbed his head at the girl sitting on the edge of the wagon. His ears strained forward and he looked at her with his friendly dark eyes. He took a step closer to nudge her with his nose and snorted a greeting. He butted her softly and Theo reached up to touch him.

The onlookers went wild with delight. What a picture the great horse made with that solemn white-dressed girl! The wagon was jostled with the crowd's pushing and suddenly Theo snatched her hands back. Dan Patch recognized her — of course! She ducked her head and tried to wriggle back in the wagon. Dan Patch shook his bridle and stretched his head toward her. Mr. Savage frowned slightly and gave the reins a twitch, and then smiled again as the horse began his stately walk down the street. As he went by, Marion Savage turned and looked searchingly at Theo. He seemed puzzled for a moment, and then the crowd demanded his attention and she was forgotten. Theo let out her breath in a whoosh, and became aware of Carl curled into a ball behind her back. She jerked around to stare at him.

"What on earth are you doing?" she muttered. He straightened up and brushed his shirt. "Theo, Dan *recognized* you!" he whispered. "Don't you see? Mr. Savage is no dummy, you know . . . if he saw me here with you, and with the horse bobbing his head around like that — well, he'd have it figured out in a minute! I was hiding, that's all."

Claudia's eyes had gone very dark. For the first time that day, she seemed pale and tired. She reached out her hands toward her paralyzed legs. "My legs are tingling," she said in a small voice. She looked up at her mother and Harriet. "Aunt Harriet, my legs feel funny . . ."

"You're tired," said Harriet firmly. "The crowd should break up as soon as the horses get down the street. I think it's time we got you back home." Harriet slipped from the seat and jumped to the ground. "Carl, go see if you can find your father and Mr. Harris. We need to get Claudia home." Maud and Harriet helped Claudia lie down on the pillows and tucked the blankets around her. Theo stood silently at the back of the wagon.

Carl returned leading the horse, and together with his father, hitched the wagon and drove back to Cargyll Street. He didn't once look down at Theo scuffing in the dirt alongside. When they got to the gate Carl slid down and spoke in Norwegian to his father. Then he muttered to no one in particular, "I'm going to find my mother and sisters . . . maybe I'll see you at the picnic and fireworks."

He started away abruptly but stopped when Gustav spoke sharply. Carl reddened and glanced at Theo. "I'll come by around ten o'clock. For the dance," he said in a rush, and ran off down the street. Theo stomped with the blankets and pillows up the porch steps and into the house.

"Don't you want to go to the picnic, Theo?" asked Stevenson. "Aunt Harriet would go with you — if you hurry, you could catch up with Carl."

"I don't want to go to the picnic!" she snapped, and Stevenson looked quizzically at Maud, who only tightened her mouth and turned to Claudia. Harriet and she settled her in the parlor bed and Maud drew the curtains against the afternoon sun. Harriet straightened and looked at Theo. "*I*'d like to go to the picnic, Theodora," she said.

Theo wished she could howl in frustration at the bewildering turmoil inside her. Her aunt's voice was so *knowing* and full of care, Theo couldn't stand it. She shook her head violently through a blindness of tears. Harriet raised her eyebrows. Theo dashed up the stairs to her room and slammed the door.

No one bothered her all that long evening. She could hear them moving around downstairs and talking. She grew very hungry but refused to sneak down and eat anything. She couldn't sleep and she was bored. The room was so hot and stuffy she yanked off the dress and sat at her desk in her shift. She sat for a long time. After a while she picked up a pencil and twirled it listlessly in her fingers. She stared at a pile of blank paper on her desk. She drew a line across the top sheet. She bit the end of her pencil.

Finally she began to write. She wrote a sentence and stopped, and then wrote another. After four sentences she didn't stop again until her shoulders were aching and it had grown too dark to see. From the other side of town came the bursting crackle of fireworks. She put down her pencil to listen. In front of her lay twelve sheets of paper covered in her small, neat handwriting. She smoothed her hand over the pile.

Then Harriet called her name and knocked on the door to her room.

∾ Chapter Thirteen ∾

"I'M NOT GOING ."

"That's ridiculous," said Harriet, and pushed open the door. She put a lamp down on the dresser and turned up the wick. She seemed imposing to Theo, with no smile in her eyes, dressed as she always was in her severe black dress. She carried Maud's silver-backed brush and comb and her apron pocket bulged with pins.

Theo sat helplessly on her chair. Her pencil rolled to the floor. Her eyes welled over and the tears burned her skin. She didn't make any noise and her face was still. She did not even turn away from her aunt.

Harriet sat on her bed and they looked at each other across the little room. There was no sympathy on Harriet's face, but no irritation either — just patience. After a few seconds Harriet reached into her pocket and brought out a handkerchief. "Wipe your face," she said. "Or else it will get all puffy."

"It doesn't matter," whispered Theo. "I'm not going." Harriet raised her eyebrows as she had done in the parlor.

"You know," she commented, "everyone gets to act ridiculous in their life once in a while. It's part of being human. In fact, it probably helps to clear the system from time to time." She stood abruptly and put a handful of hairpins on the dresser. "But it's part of growing up to recognize when to stop. And I can tell you, Theodora: it's time to stop."

"I'm not being ridiculous," Theo said. Her voice was dangerously close to a whimper. Harriet, who always understood a great number of things, didn't seem to care about her now. Theo sniffed and rubbed her bare arm over her eyes. Harriet moved behind her and with deft fingers untied the straggling ribbon.

"I know you think I don't understand," said Harriet. Theo scowled and did not answer. Harriet brushed vigorously at the long hair. "But I do, Theodora — I do. We're all human beings. I watched all of you at the parade, you know. It's very simple, what's happening to you."

"What?"

Harriet ran her fingers through Theo's hair. It felt so good that despite herself, she leaned back and closed her eyes. Harriet leaned over her shoulder. "Well," she said softly. "Well, you're in love. And you're jealous."

Theo jerked away. "That's the stupidest thing I've ever heard!" she cried. She hunched her shoulders and clasped her hands together in her lap.

"Theodora!" Maud's voice came sternly from the doorway. "What's come over you? You don't contradict people like that." She came in the room and lay something heavy-sounding and whispery on the bed. Theo refused to look at either of them. Every nerve in her jangled in mutiny. If I had any courage at all, she glowered to herself, I'd just run out of this room and . . . and what? She yanked her head away from under Harriet's hands and the hair piled precariously on her head cascaded down over her shoulders. Harriet calmly gathered it up again. Theo set her mouth.

It was a battle of wills she could fight but never win. She was no match for Harriet. She sat stiffly while Harriet arranged her hair in a loose twist on top of her head. Her aunt slid the pins in and the hair stayed firmly in place. Harriet pulled a delicate lacquered comb out of her pocket.

Maud drew in her breath. "Oh!" she exclaimed. "I haven't seen that for years, Hetty! I never see you wear it . . . I didn't know you still had it."

"Of course I still have it," grumbled Harriet, her mouth full of hairpins. "Why would I wear it around here?" She jabbed the comb into the center of the mass of hair and stepped back to survey her work. "Now the dress," she said.

Theo felt caught between the two of them. There were so many unspoken things between her mother and Harriet, she could almost see the air swirling around between them. For every word they spoke a whole history was implied, shared only by them. Theo shifted in her chair and looked reluctantly at her mother.

"What dress?" she asked sullenly. Harriet smiled . . . in triumph, Theo realized. Maud picked a dress up off the bed and held it out so the light fell over it. Theo couldn't help putting out her hand to touch the soft shimmering material. Maud held it against herself for a moment and her eyes grew very deep above the rich blue folds of the gown.

"I remember that dress," said Harriet quietly. "I remember the dance you wore it to when . . ."

"I took a few tucks this afternoon," Maud interrupted quickly, holding the dress up to Theo. "I took that bit of

lace off . . . I always thought it was too fussy. And there —
I let out the back, and tucked it here . . . It should fit."

It did fit. It felt close and supple, like nothing she had
ever worn. It did not scratch or bind her but moved when
she moved like her own skin. She turned slowly in front of
the two women and the dress whispered around her. Her
neck felt odd, cool and bare, and she held her head awkwardly because she was sure the mass of hair would fall
down. Maud took a step back.

"My little racehorse driver," she murmured, and it
seemed to Theo her smile was bewildered. Harriet looked
first at Theo, then at Maud.

"Oh, Maudie," she said in a low voice. For a moment,
confused, Theo thought her aunt was crying. But there was
a smile in Harriet's voice. "Oh, Maud — she looks just like
you, that week you came to Boston —" And again, Maud
moved to intercept her words and the room spun with unspoken things. She took Theo by the shoulders and directed
her toward the door.

"Go downstairs and show your father," she said. "Carl
should be here in ten minutes." But Stevenson had already
left to help set up refreshment tables in the large meeting
room of the town hall, where the dance was being held.
Harriet followed Theo down the stairs and into the parlor,
where she settled herself comfortably in the overstuffed
reading chair near Claudia's bed. Claudia stared at Theo in
wonder.

"You should see yourself," she breathed. Theo scowled.
What a fuss about an old dress! She struggled against her
curiosity and refused to look in the mirror. Maud hesitated
in the doorway.

"Hetty, I really do have a headache," she said finally. "I
would much rather stay here . . . honestly. Claudia and I

are right in the middle of an exciting book . . . and anyway, a girl going to her first grown-up dance should not have her mother with her." There was an incomprehensible sadness in her voice that made Theo look at her in surprise. What a strange mood had overcome Maud! She looked so tired suddenly, and yet upstairs, with that dress held against her, she'd looked so . . . *lovely.* "I wouldn't enjoy myself anyway, with this headache," Maud persisted. Harriet closed the book in her hands. Maud added softly, "Stevenson should have someone there to keep him company."

Harriet shook her head sharply. "Maud —" she said. But the yard gate slammed before she could continue and everyone looked at the door. A feeling so wonderful and terrifying shot through Theo she almost sat down, dizzy. Maud looked back at Harriet as she went to answer the doorbell. "It's *all right*, Hetty," she said. Claudia squeezed Theo's hand and Theo screwed up her face and went to meet Carl.

He was exactly the same Carl. She wasn't sure why she had expected anything different. He was waiting for her the way he always did. His shirt was clean and pressed and tucked into his best Sunday pants. His boots were polished and he wore a stiff black bow under his chin. His eyes were just as blue and clear and had the same somber, polite expression they ever did. "Hello, Mrs. Harris," he greeted Maud. In the hallway he poked his head into the parlor and said, "Hello, Dr. Kerr. Hey, Claudia — do you feel better now?"

"I'm feeling fine now, Carl . . . I just needed to rest."

But he did not speak to Theo. Her face burned. He glanced at her once and looked away quickly. He studied his boots as they walked out the door and down the steps. Theo shivered. She knew this would happen. She looked so stupid in this dress with her hair piled like a bale of hay on her head . . . But by the gate, as if it took every ounce of courage in him, Carl turned to her and took a deep breath. "You're beautiful," he whispered. And the whole awful, bewildering day was swept away from her as if it had never been.

The entire town of Savage had turned out for the dance. Everyone from school was there, even Gyp Grimer with his hair slicked down and his hand on the arm of a skinny girl. He leered at Carl and yanked the girl away toward the refreshment tables. Carl grinned at Theo. "Someday he'll yank the wrong girl or the wrong mule, and they'll haul off and kick his face in," he whispered to her. She stifled a giggle. They stood awkwardly near the door and looked around the hall.

"There's Papa," said Theo, and Stevenson put his pipe in his pocket and came toward them. He looked for a long time at Theo, and then without a word he turned to Harriet. "I know," nodded Harriet in such a soft voice it hardly seemed like hers.

"You are a lucky man," Stevenson said to Carl, clearing his throat. Harriet took his arm and they walked away. Carl glanced at Theo quickly. Suddenly he reached over and took her hand. She jumped.

"Theo, you have to hold my hand if you're going to dance with me," he said. "You *are* going to dance, aren't you?"

"That's what we came here for, isn't it?" she muttered, and Carl sighed. He held her hand tighter and looked at her seriously.

"Theo," he said, "sometimes I think you are really an awful girl. I do, Theo. I thought we were friends. Sometimes you talk to me and tell me everything you think about, and sometimes . . . like today . . . you act like I'm some nasty stranger."

"I don't!"

"Oh, yes, you do," he insisted. "Look, could we just be friends tonight? I know you probably hate wearing that dress and everything . . . I mean, I feel like an idiot in this collar and tie. But you have to believe me, Theo. You really look so —"

"All right," she interrupted hastily. "It's only that I . . . I don't know how to dance." He smiled at her, a slow smile like the sun lifting above the morning pastures. "I don't either," he said. "So we can just pretend we know exactly what we're doing."

They wore themselves out tripping over each other's feet, and laughed so hard they had to stop to catch their breath. During a pause in the music they drank fruit punch with orange peels floating in it. Theo got trapped into a long conversation with Miss Schroeder, and Mr. Bernard clapped Carl on the back when he learned that Carl would be going on to high school after all. The music started again and Theo was whisked onto the dance floor by her father. She was startled to discover he knew how to dance very well.

"Now that you're a young lady, I see I have neglected some important elements of your education, Theodora," said Stevenson gravely. "You have read fine books, know something about art and music, and are familiar with rudimentary scientific knowledge, but you do not know how to dance."

"I think she dances very nicely, Mr. Harris," said Carl. Stevenson bowed his head.

"That is because you are a true friend, and because your own education in that area is lacking as well," he pronounced, and Harriet, coming toward them from the refreshment tables, threw back her head and laughed loudly.

"I will give Mr. Johansson a short lesson," she said firmly.

During the next whirling dance, Theo and Carl watched each other being pulled around the floor by Stevenson and Harriet. "If your friendship survives this night, it will be forged on a base of granite," announced Stevenson mournfully, handing Theo back to Carl. Theo grimaced.

"I would rather drive horses," she said.

"I would rather read," Carl agreed.

But something in the air of the soft summer night made it impossible for them to keep apart. Even though their shins were sore from being kicked and Theo's hair was working loose from the pins, even though Carl was sure he might choke in his tight collar and tie, they danced. They danced and could not keep their eyes from each other. Carl never let go of her hand. He communicated through his touch and his eyes, and they spoke words less and less, but Theo did not feel a moment of silence between them. She was intoxicated with the whirling movement and the music and the feeling of Carl's arms around her.

"I thought you liked Claudia," she murmured once, and he knew exactly what she meant. He brushed his face against her hair. "That was stupid," he smiled.

Everything in the world slipped away except the magical space around her and Carl. Within that space were all the wonderful unspoken things and the music shimmering like light. Carl held her closer. His feet no longer knocked against hers. She no longer tripped on the hem of her blue gown. She gazed deep into his eyes and she could see where she was going. Through his hand she knew him, as if there was only one heart between them. She knew his secret name and called to him without a word. It was his true name, the name of wisdom and of the longing to *know*, and when she called to him he answered. And the night slipped around their magic space like joy.

Someone bumped lightly against her as she danced. The world rushed back into their magical place. Carl tripped on his bootlace. Theo almost lost her grip on his hand. She looked up. Harriet and Stevenson were dancing. The music slowed into a waltz and she turned from Carl to watch them. Carl glanced at them too, troubled. "You want something to drink?" he asked. She shook her head without taking her eyes from the dancing couple.

Harriet and Stevenson danced together as if they were a single human being. The black dress stood out in startling contrast with the light-colored summer gowns of the other women. Harriet seemed taller and more powerful than any woman there. Her movements were perfectly matched to Stevenson's. Their faces were close together and they held each other with their eyes as if there was no one else in the room.

A terrible apprehension rippled through Theo. She did not want to meet Carl's eyes now. But when she looked around the floor it seemed all the other dancers were dancing in exactly the same way, and no one noticed her father and her aunt. But Theo knew they were not dancing the same way as everyone else. She knew they were alone together in a different place, because she had just been in that place with Carl.

"Why don't you get something to drink, Theo?" said Carl uneasily. "Your face is real hot." She put her hands to her cheeks and let him lead her to the tables where the ladies from the Hospital Auxiliary were serving punch. Amelia McCarthy, with her dark blond hair piled in curls all over her head, simpered when she saw Theo.

"Where did you get such a lovely gown, Theodora?" she asked in the little-girl voice Theo hated.

"From a box," growled Theo. Amelia tossed her head

and smiled at Carl. "You haven't asked me to dance, Carl," she invited. Carl looked at her helplessly.

"I'm an awful dancer," he said. "I'm awful, aren't I, Theo? She won't dance with me anymore because I've ripped the hem of her gown." Amelia twisted her mouth in scorn and slapped at her little brother's hand when he came to beg her to get him a drink. Carl let out his breath in relief when Amelia was tugged away by the sash of her dress to the refreshment tables.

"Her mother should've drowned her when she was born," muttered Theo.

"You're being really awful again," said Carl. He took her arm and pulled her with him outside. The summer night was cool, and the smell of new-mown hay hung like perfume in the air. Around the steps of the town hall stood a few groups of people talking or laughing quietly at the end of the long festive day. A mother rocked a baby while her husband talked to a friend. Three men argued hotly about how fast Tom Henry's new automobile could go on the straightaway outside of town. A couple swayed in the shadows under a huge spruce tree to the music drifting out the windows. Theo sat on the wide steps and Carl settled down next to her.

"I feel terrible," said Theo in a small voice. She wanted to lean her head against Carl's shoulder, to get back something of the magical space around them. She looked at Carl nervously. They were not meant to be out here like this, alone . . . Miss Schroeder said girls at dances should have chaperones until they were eighteen.

She narrowed her eyes. Harriet was the one who should have a chaperone! But she refused to think about what she had seen on the dance floor. She scraped her feet along the rough stone steps and sighed. Carl draped his arms over his knees the way he did when they sat talking in the cottonwood grove by the stream, and seeing it made her feel calmer. Carl yanked the bow tie from his collar and stuffed it in his pocket.

"You're going to start with Mr. Turner tomorrow," he said suddenly. "You haven't said anything about it all day! Aren't you excited?"

"Yes . . ." She stared into the darkness. How far away everything seemed! The parade, the horses . . . "I wrote a new story today," she said in a low voice. "I finished it just before you came by. It's different from my other ones . . . I don't really know why I wrote it." She hesitated and Carl smiled at her. "It's about old Amon Szabo — the rat killer," she said carefully. "I keep thinking about him, and wondering . . . who he is. Where he's from. Something sad happened to him . . . can't you hear it in his voice? He had to start his whole life all over again. I think he is so lonely . . ."

Carl leaned his shoulder against her own. The warmth from him crept through her. "So it's a real story," he smiled at her.

"Well, it's sort of . . . made up," she said. "I just wrote what I imagined happened to him."

"That's still real," he said. "Will you let me read it?"

She nodded slowly. "I do want you to read it, Carl," she said. "But I don't know if it's any good or anything. I mean, it might just be . . . well, it's not the same as all the horse ones."

"I want to read it," he said.

Harriet came out the door behind them and Stevenson followed her down the steps. The music had stopped and

175

other people came through the door. The clock tower chimed one o'clock as they walked through the quiet streets toward home.

"You're not walking all the way back to the farm tonight, are you?" Stevenson asked Carl. He had his pipe in his mouth but had not lit it.

"No, sir," said Carl, shaking his head. "My father asked Mr. Brunner if I could sleep in that room back of his store. I'm all set." Harriet opened the gate, but Carl did not follow them into the yard. Theo watched her father and Harriet go up on the porch, where they leaned against the railing and spoke in low voices.

"Well, I'll see you tomorrow," Theo said lamely. "Thank you. It was nice . . ." When Carl did not reply she tugged at the sash on her gown, self-conscious. "Tomorrow I'll look like myself again."

"You looked like yourself tonight!" cried Carl in a low voice. "Theo, I . . ." He looked at the ground and then, suddenly, he leaned over and kissed her. His nose bumped her cheek but his mouth was very soft on her skin. Without a word he turned and strode back down Cargyll Street. She was stunned. Her cheek burned. She looked toward the porch and saw the faint glow of her father's pipe. She could not see if Harriet was with him, so deep were the shadows. She closed the gate after her and wandered into the yard.

She wondered if a person could blow up inside, from such a chaotic mixture of emotions and thoughts. She put her hand to her face where Carl had kissed her. From the porch came Stevenson's low laugh. So Harriet was still there with him . . . She did not understand her father at all. He was always so distracted, a preoccupied, kind man with whom she had little conflict . . . but who else was he? There was some other part of him that Harriet seemed not

176

only to know but to claim as her own. Theo whacked a stick against a shrub. She wanted to rush up the steps to the porch and grab her father. This is *my* father! Leave him alone! Harriet was still in that place she shared with Stevenson — a place Theo did not understand.

The door opened and Maud stood backlit by the lamp in the hallway. Her hair hung loose down her back and the light spun through it. Stevenson turned to her and Harriet moved from the shadows, and suddenly Theo found herself crying.

She had never felt so completely alone. Carl was a dream disappeared into the night, and up on the porch three people were moving through an inexplicable dance that she could never be part of. She thought of Maud patiently picking out stitches and taking tucks on this lovely mysterious gown all afternoon while Theo sulked in her room. Where had the gown come from? She lifted the skirt and rubbed the silky material over her burning face. She thought of Harriet's hands as she arranged her hair, and how much she loved the touch of those strong, sure fingers, and how Harriet would always listen to her . . . She thought of her father's face when he had first seen her in the beautiful gown. What did it mean to them? What memory did they all share when they looked at Theo in that dress?

She stared toward the porch and wiped the tears from her eyes. "There was someone I loved, and who loved me," Harriet had told her. "There was someone I loved . . ." Theo gasped softly. Stevenson? Her father! But Harriet had chosen to be a doctor. . . . And then Maud. . . . She gazed at them, stunned. They were standing close together talking. Once in a while she heard a quiet laugh, and once Harriet leaned her head briefly on Stevenson's shoulder, and once Stevenson drew Maud close to his side . . . Theo's legs trembled as she stood hidden by the roses.

"Theodora, are you going to stay out there all night?" called Maud. Theo still hung back, unwilling to come closer. But could anything really be wrong? Had anything been done that was wrong? They did not seem unhappy, the three of them, smiling out into the dark yard where she was standing. The crickets sang under the steps and somewhere high in the dark leaves, a mockingbird burst into his night song. Her father laughed.

"Hear that, Theo?" he called. "It'll be dawn soon."

"Mockingbirds sing all night, Papa," she answered, and walked across the yard to join them. They watched her as she came up the steps, lifting the gown carefully so she would not trip. All at once she knew she did understand the unspoken things. After tonight, after Carl . . . she understood. She held her head high. Tomorrow, when she saw Carl . . .

Tomorrow! It was *already* tomorrow! In only a few hours she would have to go to the farm and find the old trainer Bill Turner. She would drive the horses on the International Stock Feed Farm! Excitement tingled down her arms and legs. For the first time, the beautiful blue gown seemed confining. The petticoats tangled around her legs and the tight-fitting waist made it difficult to breathe. Tomorrow . . . no, today! . . . she would put on her comfortable boy's clothing and pin her hair under a cap, take up the long leather reins and feel truly, for the first time, the rush of speed against her face.

"You are beautiful, Theodora," Maud whispered, and gave Theo the briefest hug around her shoulders. Theo looked at her mother and then at Harriet. They looked so alike, those sisters . . . but how much easier it was to love

Harriet! Why was it so hard to feel close to her mother? As she went into the house, Theo heard Stevenson say, "She looks just like you, Maudie . . ." and then the door closed behind her. She went slowly up the stairs, hung the blue gown carefully on a hanger, and crawled into bed.

⌒ Chapter Fourteen ⌒

THEO SLEPT only a few hours before she woke heavy-headed and unable to sleep again. It was still dark, but the air smelled of the dawn mist. Outside her window Theo saw the low fog hanging in the leaves, and knew the pastures would seem like a fairy-tale realm, the trees floating like islands in the pale lavender mist. She dressed quickly in her old muslin dress, her fingers stumbling in excitement. Even in her bare feet she made a slight noise at the bottom of the stairs and Claudia stirred in her bed.

"Are you going already, Thee?" she called in a whisper. Theo paused. "It's still dark out."

"I couldn't sleep," Theo whispered back. "I was going to sit out on the swing awhile."

"I can't sleep either. Will you sit here with me instead? Close the door so you don't wake anyone."

Carl would not arrive at the stream for almost two hours, and she wanted to sit under her tree by herself to think. But Claudia's face watched her hopefully from the darkness, and Theo came to sit near the bed on the floor. She didn't light a candle. Claudia turned her head to look at her. "Tell me about the dance," she begged. "I miss dancing so much . . ."

"Well . . ." Theo picked at the fringe of the bed cover. If Claudia had been able to dance, she would have danced with Carl last night. No one would have expected anything different than that he should dance with both sisters. But Theo remembered the parade and shuddered. If Claudia had been able to dance, the evening would have ended very differently. "It was all right," she answered cautiously.

"Did Carl dance with you the whole time?" Claudia persisted.

"Yes," said Theo. "He asked me to go, didn't he?"

Claudia dropped her head back on the pillow and sighed. She didn't say anything for several minutes. It was so quiet they could hear the hollow ticking of the grandfather clock at the end of the hallway.

"Why are you angry at me, Thee?" asked Claudia at last. Her voice sounded thin in the darkness, as if it could disappear. "Mama said you were upset and wouldn't go to the fireworks. She didn't tell me why, but I could tell you were angry with me."

Theo wished she could shrug her shoulders and explain everything away with headaches and worries about the dance. It would have been much easier. But something in the still, dark parlor on the edge between night and dawn made it impossible to hide. She remembered Claudia's words to her the day she'd moved her arms: "Since I've been sick we don't talk." She took a deep breath.

"It was because of Carl," she said. "I was angry because of Carl."

"What did I do to Carl?" Claudia asked, puzzled. Theo braided the bed-cover fringe and watched it unravel.

"You didn't do anything *to* Carl . . ." she said in a low

voice. "Well, yes — you did. You made him like you. You kept laughing and asking him questions . . ."

"But, Thee! I was so happy to be outside — I haven't been out of this room in more than a month, until yesterday! I didn't mean to . . ." Claudia blinked her eyes rapidly. Don't you cry, thought Theo. Don't you dare cry and make me feel horrid.

"Oh, Claudia!" she cried. "Don't you understand? Don't you know that all you have to do is laugh and . . . and . . . all you have to do is just *be* there, and everyone loves . . . and I may as well be a little bug on the floor!"

Claudia was silent again. Her eyes blinked. At last she spoke, and her voice trembled. "You really didn't want me to go yesterday, did you? You don't *want* me to get better, do you!" Claudia was crying now and Theo pounded the rug with her fist. Claudia wasn't even trying to understand! She was so used to being the center of everything around her, she *couldn't* understand.

"That's not true, and it's horrid of you to say it," said Theo. "I just feel like I get lost when you're around. I can't help it, Claudia. I don't know how to laugh the way you do, or talk about things or play music . . . and I'm not pretty . . ."

"You're not *pretty*?" gasped Claudia. "Are you an idiot? Didn't you even look in a mirror last night?" Theo glared at the floor. "You think Carl liked *me*?" continued Claudia, as if everything had suddenly become clear to her. "That's what you were angry about?" She twisted the heavy bed-covers into a knot with her thin hands. "If you hadn't been so busy pouting off the end of the wagon yesterday, you would've noticed that Carl hardly took his eyes off you," she said indignantly. "The only reason I talked to him was because I was so happy to be outside — and because he looked so miserable. You didn't once look at him, Thee. You didn't do anything but grunt. He looked like a kicked dog."

"That's not true!"

"Yes, it is. And what's more — no one thinks you're a bug on the floor but you!" cried Claudia. "It's not fair if you always compare yourself with me. I'm *me* — I can't be any different."

It was true. Everyone seemed to agree she'd acted like a fool yesterday — Harriet had told her she was ridiculous, and Claudia, and probably Carl, too . . . But no — Carl had danced with her the whole evening, and she couldn't have mistaken that magical place. And after, when he'd . . . Theo put her hand to her cheek and was glad it was too dark for Claudia to see her blush. No, Carl wouldn't kiss someone he thought was ridiculous.

"Thee, I think you're an amazing person," whispered Claudia. She reached out her hand and stroked Theo's hair, letting the long strands slip through her fingers. "Yesterday, when those horses went by . . . I thought they were the most lovely, strongest creatures I'd ever seen. I know why you want to be around them, Theo. But you're so much braver than I am — yes, you are. I could *never* do what you're doing — all by yourself. I've had help all my life — I've had everyone encouraging me and giving me everything I needed . . . You're doing this *all on your own!*"

"You did everything on your own, too!" cried Theo. "No one else played the violin for you! No one else practiced all those hours!"

Claudia nodded. "I know," she said. "I know what I've done, and I know what I can do. It's just a lot easier to do it when people help you along and believe in what you're doing."

That was true, also. But Theo had people who believed in her. Carl believed she could do whatever she set her heart on. And Aunt Harriet — she believed in her. And Mr. Savage, even though he thought she was a boy. And old Amon Szabo, the rat killer, who knew her secrets and somehow knew how very important they were to her. And even . . . Dan Patch. Could a horse believe in someone? she wondered. Of course! A horse could sense and trust and *know* things without needing words. If you were racing down the track with a quarter-mile left to go and every muscle of the horse was stretched to its limit, and you asked him to go faster still — why, he would do it, if he *believed* in you! That was how races were won. That was how legends were made.

"I'm not angry at you, Claudia," Theo whispered, leaning her head on her sister's shoulder. Claudia's thin arms stole around her neck. The hallway clock chimed and Theo saw the darkness outside the window had given way to a shimmering dawn.

"I have to go," she said. "I'm going to drive a horse today, Claudia! Today I'm going to begin learning how to drive!"

She was soaked with dew by the time she reached the hollow tree on the bank of the stream. Carl was not there yet. The wild grapevines that draped over the branches were hung with small green fruit that would begin to ripen soon to purple. The sun was still below the curve of the hills. She reached into the tree and pulled out Carl's clothing.

She dressed quickly, shivering in the cool air, and wondered why everything felt different. For more than a month she had changed into these same clothes while Carl waited for her by the fence — but this morning, she was glad he was not there, and watched nervously for him as she struggled to pull on the stiff pants. When she folded up her own clothes, she took from the pinafore pocket the story she had written about Amon Szabo, "A Different Kind of Wolf." She flipped through the pages and frowned. She had written it so fast she hadn't had time to reread it. She looked up and saw Carl climbing the fence and coming toward her. Quickly she folded the pages and stuffed them deep into her pants pocket.

"I hardly slept at all," Carl announced. His eyes had dark circles under them. "That bed at Mr. Brunner's felt like rocks."

She was inexplicably flustered. She'd forgotten to pull back her hair and pin it up under the cap, and she wished she had. But now Carl was with her, she was reluctant to do it. Her hair was soft, still in waves from last night that rippled down over her shoulders. He glanced at her and she looked away.

They sat at a distance from each other. Theo threw pebbles into the stream. Wasn't this just the way they'd always been, all summer long? Wasn't she back in her comfortable boy's clothing, looking like Carl on their ordinary working day? No — it *was* different now, and suddenly she missed the familiar time *before*. Even Carl's eyes seemed different . . . a darker blue? Just tired? No, it was how he looked at her from those eyes . . .

"What did you put in your pocket just now?" he asked suddenly. "Was it your story — the one you said I could read?"

She nodded reluctantly but did not take it from her pocket. There was something new between them, and she did not feel the same as she had sitting on the steps after the dance. Her stories were a private world, a haven . . . if that changed too, then nothing would feel safe.

Carl stretched out on his back and looked at the sky

184

through the pattern of leaves and grapevines. The sun glowed on the tips of the grasses. A kingfisher shrieked and raced down the stream past them. In the distance a horse whinnied and was answered by another. Theo was not sure if she heard the pounding of hooves or the thumping of her own heart. Carl plucked a piece of grass and chewed it.

"You won't be able to pass for a boy much longer," he commented without looking at her. Her face burned and she didn't answer. Carl sighed and rolled over on his stomach, poking the grass-stem into a small anthill. "Why do you want to hide everything about yourself that's beautiful?" he asked softly. "You were so beautiful last night, Theo. I couldn't believe it was you. No, that's not true . . . I *could* believe it. It's just that you never showed it to me before . . . that *you*. And I know you have that story for me in your pocket." He studied the ants running over the anthill. "I know you have it, and you've hidden it from me, and you aren't going to let me read it. You aren't, are you? Because you want to hide it. I wish I knew why."

She was sure she could never answer him. The wad of folded-up paper pressed against her leg suddenly seemed the only safe, *known* thing left to her in the world. The space between Carl and her was unexplored territory . . . it frightened her just to look at him, and yet — and yet, if she could have, she would curl up next to him on the ground and feel his heart beating next to her own . . .

"We're going to be in high school at the end of the summer," Carl said in a troubled voice. "And I want . . . I mean, you're my *best friend*, Theo. You're the best friend I ever had and there's no one like you in the whole world. But I'm so afraid that once we don't do this anymore . . ." He swept his arm around him at the farm. "Once we stop working here, you'll just hide away from me."

She licked her dry lips. "Carl — " she said. "Oh, I get so mixed up about everything! I don't even know why I do things anymore. But I don't want to hide from you . . ." She lowered her head and went on in a rush, "You're my best friend, too. I don't really have any other friends, and . . . and I like you a whole lot."

Carl smiled and heaved himself up to sit facing her. "Do you?" he said. "Because I like you a whole lot, too."

She slowly took out the story. Giving it to him placed a seal on something between them. He leaned toward her and took the folded papers, and put them carefully in his pocket. He stood up and held out his hand.

"We better get going," he said gravely. He kept his hand out, and she took it in her own. She still held it as they walked down the last slope toward the yard gate. She stared with wonder up at the gleaming onion-dome roofs and the bright fluttering flags. Had they always been this brilliant?

ᕙ Chapter Fifteen ᕗ

BY THE END of that day, Theo was convinced she would never sit on a sulky after all. Bill Turner, the trainer, was a man of sparse frame and even sparser words. His face was as brown and creased as an old leather buggy seat exposed to decades of sun and snow. His movements were deliberate and conservative. His voice, when he spoke at all, was gruff. But there was an underlying gentleness to his manner with horses, and Theo could see that nothing else mattered to the old trainer except harness horses.

When she reported to him, he glanced at her with his lined face impassive. For a moment, she thought he would deny ever having been spoken to by Marion Savage. He reached out one knobby hand and pinched the muscles in her arm. "How old are you, boy?" he barked.

"Almost sixteen, sir," she gulped. That, at least, was not a lie. Bill Turner tightened his mouth and stared at the ground. "So Mr. Savage thinks you have the makings of a driver?" he asked, as if he thought nothing of the opinion of his boss. Theo nodded. Bill Turner shook his head. "Nope," he said. "You have no muscle, boy. These ain't ponies . . . these're stallions. An' don't think they're all as gentle as Dan, 'cause they ain't. Most of 'em are hellions. You need muscles."

He turned abruptly away from her. She stared at him. Was this a test? She couldn't believe the old trainer would go against Mr. Savage's instructions, but he was walking away as if he meant to do just that. She took a step after him.

"Mr. Savage said muscles would come with time and work," she called. "The horses *listen* to me, Mr. Turner." The trainer stopped in his tracks without turning around. She held her breath. At last he growled, still with his back turned, "Go in number three harness room an' get that old harness hangin' by the door." She ran to get it and brought it back to him, determined not to trip on the straps and reins trailing behind her on the ground. He gestured with a curt nod of his head and she dropped the harness in a heap.

"Now," he said. "You sit there an' you straighten that thing out, the way you think it oughta go. You jest lay it on the ground as straight as you kin get it. Come get me in Arion's wing when you think you got it right." And he stumped briskly off.

Theo squatted down by the huge tangled pile of straps and poked at it. She didn't know where to begin. She closed her eyes, trying to visualize the way the harnesses looked on the horses she'd seen countless times in the yard. But when she opened her eyes, nothing she could imagine matched this mess of straps and buckles in front of her. She pulled tentatively at bits of the harness. As soon as one piece seemed to fall straight, another would be twisted beneath it.

She worked for twenty minutes and at last stood with aching legs to survey what she'd done. She had figured out the front from the back and was fairly certain the straps and buckles were matched up in the right places. It still looked a confused mess on the ground, but she went to find Bill Turner.

He stared down at her work with his hands on his hips. He checked his tarnished old wristwatch. "Twenty minutes," he stated. "Race'd be over 'fore you even got your horse harnessed, boy." She twisted her hands together behind her back. The old trainer sighed and toed the harness with his foot. "Well, I seen worse," he conceded. "You ain't got it twisted in a figure eight, at least. Now — you know what every one of them pieces is called?" She shook her head wearily.

So the day was spent with the harness. Each piece was named, examined, unfastened, fastened again. When a horse was led into the yard, Bill Turner made her explain and name the harness pieces on each. Her arms ached from lifting harnesses from tall horses and carrying them back to the rooms where they were kept and hanging them in

188

order on the hooks. Her right foot was bruised where a nervous colt had stepped on her.

"You walk behind 'em like that, sonny, you gonna lose all yer toes," was Mr. Turner's only comment. "Lucky you didn't get yer head kicked in."

She dragged herself through the fields at the end of the day. She was streaked with dirt and stunk from the oil and sweat on the harnesses, and she was too exhausted to think about Carl walking beside her. He grinned at her sympathetically. "You should do what I do," he suggested. "Why don't you have a swim? I jump in that stream back of the forge before I go home. Look — that little pool's big enough."

She longed to float in the cool water and let it wash over her bruised, grimy skin. But what could she wear to swim in? Carl was watching her and she blushed. "I can't swim when you're here," she muttered. He shrugged.

"It wouldn't matter to me," he said. "You could swim in your shift. I have five sisters . . . we always go swimming together." But there was an unfamiliar tremor in his voice and he avoided her eyes. She shook her head stubbornly.

"I'll just go on ahead," he said. "You can swim if you want. It'll help your muscles, to cool off." He was gone across the stream before she could answer, loping up the slope and disappearing over the rise without looking back. She watched him go and missed him at once.

For three days, Theo struggled with the harnesses. By midday of the third day, she was able to throw a harness with reasonable accuracy over the back of a horse. All the straps hung as they should, ready for her to buckle. She could bridle a horse if it was a calm one and did not throw its head around, and she could run the reins back without twisting them. She could recite the name of all the pieces

189

and describe their functions. Bill Turner nodded briefly.

"Now the sulky," he said, and she groaned silently. Would she have to take *that* apart, too? But learning the sulky proved less complicated, and by the end of five days, Theo could completely harness, bridle, and hitch a horse to the sulky. She had learned to watch carefully and ask almost nothing. Bill Turner hated questions. She didn't dare ask him when she might actually sit on a sulky behind a horse. But early on a Monday morning, he led a plodding swaybacked old horse from one of the stalls.

"This here's Brown City Lad," he told her, jerking his head at the old horse. "Laddie. He was a good pacer in his day — good as any. He's trained more drivers than I can count. What I don't tell you, he will. You listen to him, mebbe you'll turn out half-decent."

She harnessed up the quiet horse. He turned his patient head to watch everything she did, blowing kindly through his nostrils. He stood without moving, lowered his head for the bridle, opened his mouth for the bit, and backed without hesitation between the shafts of the sulky. Theo fell in love with him at once. It was the first time she had seen Bill Turner smile. He ran his old hand down the swayed back and scratched the long ears. Laddie butted him gently on the chest.

"We've been a lot of miles together, haven't we, old boy?" he said. "If there's a horse heaven, this'un will be with the angels. He's a wise ol' man, he is." And Brown City Lad, his racing days no more than a distant memory in his great horse heart, took Theo out on the track as if he knew exactly what his job was. Bill Turner walked at his head, and a trackhand followed, leading a riding horse.

"Now, boy, after I give you a coupla pointers, I'm gonna ride alongside of you, and you're gonna *walk* right 'round this here track," he said. "You try anything more'n a walk, it's all over — understand? There's some wouldn't have you out this soon, but I figure there's only one way to learn to drive . . . an' that's to drive. Now, Laddie'll do whatever you tell him. He ain't got no surprises up his sleeve. You listen to him, and you listen to me."

For several weeks, Theo learned to drive Brown City Lad. She learned the reins and the curve of the track and the way the sulky moved. She learned to feel the horse through the reins. She went from a walk to a slow jog, and finally to a lively pace that left Laddie blowing violently at the end of it. Bill Turner slapped him on the neck. " 'Bout time you earned yer keep, lazy-guts," he smiled. "I ain't fooled by you one bit . . . all that blowin' and huffin'. You ain't no more worn out than . . . Boy! Boy!" He stomped up to Theo. "What're you gettin' off fer? You just gonna let the horse loose here on the track?"

Theo scrambled back on the sulky, abashed. Laddie was such a sensible horse that she had forgotten the driver had to stay in the seat unless a person held the head. In the time it took a driver to slip from the seat and walk to the head of an unattended horse, the horse could bolt and injure itself and others severely.

On the day Brown City Lad jogged at a training pace along the track with a small group of two-year-olds, Theo felt like a real driver. Laddie seemed not only to be training her, but also to nudge and correct the colts being trained alongside of him. One of the drivers grinned over at Theo as he passed by. "Don't know why we bother to drive 'em at all," he called. "That Laddie, he'd do the whole job for us if we let him — prob'ly do it a whole lot better, too!" She turned her head to grin back and Bill Turner, cantering along at the center of the track on his riding horse, barked out at her: "Keep your eyes to yourself, boy! Concentrate on what yer' doin'. Where yer head goes, yer horse is bound to follow." She stared straight ahead at the steady back of Brown City Lad. But the smile was still on her face. She took a deep breath. She was a driver!

August broke into warm golden days and cool evenings that promised the first breath of autumn. The goldenrod along the roads glowed in the sun and the hayricks in the fields rose from the stubble like miniature mountains. Stevenson began to clear the shed near the kitchen for the wagonloads of wood that would be stacked inside. Harriet dug a light woolen shawl from her traveling trunk and draped it around her shoulders in the evenings.

"Do you always wear black, Aunt Harriet?" asked Claudia after dinner one night when she and Theo had finished sewing buttons on the shirtwaists old Mrs. Schmitt had made. Claudia held one of the shirts up to the light. "You'd look awfully good in this blue-striped one," she mused, looking at her aunt. "It's only going to be wasted on Theo, you know. She rips everything a week after she gets it."

"I do not!"

"Yes, you do!" laughed Claudia. "Mama said she's embarrassed to keep asking Mrs. Schmitt to mend things. It's all that running around in the fields after the horses . . ." Theo threw a spool of thread at her. Harriet folded all the new shirtwaists into a neat pile. From the other room came the sound of a steady clickety-clack, clickety-clack. Claudia made a face.

"Ever since you found that typing machine thing, Aunt Harriet, Mama doesn't come out of her study. She says she can get three times as much done as she can with her pen, but I don't see how she can even *think* with all that noise!" she said.

"Before too long, writers won't be able to do without one," Harriet smiled. "I couldn't believe it when I found that one at Brunner's store. Otto said he got it for himself and then gave up on it, so he let me have it for what he paid for it."

"I tried it," said Theo. "I love it." She imagined writing her stories on the wonderful new machine, seeing each letter stamped on the clean white page in even, neat rows. She even loved the strange clickety-clack of the keys as they went up and down. They did not sound too different to her ears from the distant staccato drumming of the horses training on the track.

She smiled to herself. Tomorrow was Saturday, and Carl was bringing over the first load of firewood. He'd promised to bring her story with him and she could hardly wait to hear what he thought of it. She was wonderfully tired from her first full week of driving. Bill Turner had grunted with what could be taken for approval late that afternoon, after she'd unharnessed Laddie and brushed him down. "Well," he'd said, "You're a scrawny thing, boy, but Laddie seems willin' to work fer you." She had taken this as a compliment. Laddie, in all his wisdom, seemed perfectly capable of deciding for himself whether a young driver was worth training.

Stevenson came out of his library into the parlor. "Too much noise," he said, indicating Maud's study with a nod of his head. "I can't think straight!" He settled himself at the little writing desk near the fireplace and spread his casework out. He was so tall and lean he dwarfed the desk like an overgrown schoolboy. Theo giggled and was about to tease him out of his serious work-face and into a smile when Harriet stood abruptly and pulled her shawl around her. She bent to kiss Claudia. "Dream of dancing," she said, and smiled the way she always did when saying good-night to her. Then she said goodnight quietly to Stevenson, who only grunted a distracted reply without looking up from his papers.

"Is it a difficult case, Papa?" asked Claudia. Did Claudia ever feel any of the unspoken things? Theo wondered. She watched her father as Harriet left the room, but he was only shaking his head at Claudia's question.

"No, it's just a boring one," he muttered. "And I won't have time to work on it tomorrow because we've got to get the wood stacked, and on Sunday your mother is having those women in for a meeting . . ."

"Oh, not the ones who want Mama to go to Washington with them to lobby for the vote!" cried Claudia. She rolled her eyes at Theo. "Don't you get sick of hearing about the voting question?" she complained. "It's all Mama ever talks about anymore." Stevenson closed the file he was working on and leaned back in the chair until it creaked.

"It's not just the vote," he chided her. "It's the vote, and it's wanting equal pay for equal work, and wanting the right to own property. You remember Paul Karpinsky, sweet-heart?" Claudia wrinkled her nose in disgust. Paul Karpin-sky was a violinist like herself, also an alternate with the City Symphony. He was a smug young man who made no secret of his opinion of women musicians.

"Well," Stevenson continued. "Paul Karpinsky was paid more than double the fee you would get for a single per-formance with the symphony. And he couldn't play half as well!" Stevenson took out his pipe and lit it. Claudia stared at him.

"How do you know that, Papa?" she asked. He shrugged.

"I'm a lawyer." He smiled. "I thought you knew that,

sweetheart — about Paul. About all the men, for that matter." Claudia shook her head and frowned.

"I didn't . . . I just played," she said slowly. "I hardly thought about the money, really. I mean, you and Mama were paying my room and board, and I was just so happy to play with the symphony, I didn't think . . ."

Theo lay awake for a long time in her narrow bed, watching the shadows thrown by the moon across her ceiling. Through the wooden floorboards she could faintly hear the clickety-clack of the typing machine. The *typewriter*, Harriet called it. Maud was working late into the night in preparation for her suffrage meeting on Sunday. Theo knew that some of the important women coming to visit her mother were traveling a distance by train because Maud did not want to leave Claudia. She wondered drowsily if they would be able to persuade Maud to go to Washington, D.C. Which would be stronger, her devotion to Claudia or her devotion to the cause of women's rights? Theo turned on her side and watched the leaves dancing with the moon.

The summer was racing by like one of the flashing horses on the track. School would start in a few weeks. She shifted in the bed again. Downstairs the sound of the typewriter stopped abruptly and she missed the steady, comforting rhythm of it. In the sudden silence, the realization hit with the force of a tornado.

What had she been doing, all these long weeks of summer? What had she been thinking of? All her restless longings would come to nothing. All those weeks of hauling water buckets, running errands, struggling with harnesses . . . all for nothing. She remembered the long morning talks with Carl, the tired, happy walks with him back to town together in the late afternoon, and felt only the nothingness of what lay ahead. Everything she'd dreamed of, everything that had begun to come true for her . . . all would come to nothing.

She remembered the gruff instructions of old Bill Turner as she sat behind Brown City Lad pacing down the curving track, and knew she had been living a foolish dream . . . and for what? What had she thought would ever come of any of it? School would start — high school, with all the studying, and the strange new role she'd have to play . . . young *woman*. Long skirts, hair up. And it was true, what Carl had said: she wouldn't be able to pass for a boy much longer. She lay trembling under the quilt and squeezed her eyes shut.

She'd avoided mirrors for weeks. Her once-loose muslin dresses were too small for her. She felt comfortable only in Carl's large clothes, but soon even those would fail to hide her. There was nothing she could do about it. The tall, thin boy she had been was disappearing.

And what had she done it all for? She clenched the quilt in her hands. It wasn't as if she hadn't known this would happen! Everyone had told her — Harriet, her mother, even Carl . . . everyone. They all knew it would have to come to an end. Why had *she*, alone, ignored this? What had she imagined would happen? This week — perhaps already — Bill Turner would have a talk with Marion Savage.

"Well?" Mr. Savage would ask. "How's it going, Bill? How's that young man I sent you working out? Think he has it in him? Will he make a driver?"

And Bill Turner might stare into the ground the way he always did before answering a question. He might clear his throat and Mr. Savage would smile at his crusty manner.

196

Then Bill Turner might finally, without further fuss, say simply: "Yup."

And that would be it. She'd be taken on as an apprentice driver. Years of work would lie ahead . . . years before she could drive in a real race. Oh, maybe she'd get to drive a few heats here and there on the local tracks, but it would be years and years before she could drive one of the great horses that broke the bonds of earth and raced into the realm of dreams!

But it could never be. How could it be — was she to spend her life dressed as a man? Her body ached with tension as she lay in the bed, and such a grief filled her she wanted to howl into the moon-bright sky. What happened to people who had to give up their dreams? How was it possible to come so close . . . no, to actually *have* the dream in her grasp, and then for the stupidest reason imaginable, have to let it slip away as if it had never been? Because she was a *girl*.

She stared fiercely out the window. If she could not drive horses, she did not want to do anything else. That was all there was to it. She would quit school — she was fifteen. She could do it. She would just *make* Mr. Savage understand! *He* would know she could do it. All he would have to do would be to forget she was a girl. Did it really matter? Did the horses care? No! All that mattered on the track was speed. All that mattered was that a human being could call deep into the mysterious heart of a horse and command him to fly along the track until the relentless hands of the stopwatch were left far behind. And how could she give that up? She *knew* she had it in her to be a great driver. She knew it. She curled up in a tight ball beneath the quilt and felt she was losing everything in the world.

The typewriter started up again downstairs. Maud was setting her words in neat rows along the clean sheets of paper. Word after word . . . sentences of words, paragraphs of words, words she was bringing out from somewhere deep inside herself, because she had to say them. Words she believed in, words about women and justice and freedom. Perhaps they were the words she would take with her to Washington, D.C., words she would speak aloud before government committees full of men, words that would have to shake down empires of resistance and change the world. Theo listened as she lay under the quilt. The steady clickety-clack of the typewriter keys lulled her to sleep, beating through her like the hooves of a racing horse. She smiled drowsily. Maybe Maud would let her use the wonderful new machine again. She could type all her stories into neat, even rows of words . . .

ᗧᑌ Chapter Sixteen ᑌᗧ

SHE SLEPT until it grew too hot for her under the covers. She woke groggily to a steady thunk-thunk coming from outside the house. She scrambled from the bed. Carl must already be here, she thought. He'd come to bring the wood and help Stevenson split it and load it in the shed. He'd promised to bring her story today. He'd had it for a long time and he hadn't said anything yet. Maybe he didn't like it . . .

She leaned out the window and saw the team of mules

hitched to the gatepost with the heavy hauling-wagon behind them. Stevenson had bought their winter's supply of wood from Gustav Johansson, who had spared his son for this morning during the busy harvest season to bring it to town.

She flew down the stairs barefoot and almost ran into her mother. "Theodora, for goodness' sakes, you can't go outside with all those axes lying around with no *shoes* on," she said wearily, pushing a strand of hair from her face with a flour-covered hand. The stove in the kitchen was burning full-blast, and Maud was helping Mrs. O'Leary bake the pies and cakes for the next day. Her face was smudged with flour and Theo laughed. "It'll be a long day before I can teach your mother to bake," agreed Mrs. O'Leary.

"Mama, you look like a clown!" cried Theo, jamming her feet into her boots. She rolled her stockings down around her ankles and Mrs. O'Leary rolled her eyes at her. Maud said dryly, "And you look like a ragamuffin!" She sighed. "I never thought I would say such a thing," she confessed to Mrs. O'Leary, "but I can't wait until school starts and she's *forced* to look like a decent young woman!"

Theo clattered down the back steps and found Carl, shirtsleeves rolled up and his suspender slipping off his shoulder, splitting logs and throwing them into a pile. He straightened when he saw her and leaned the ax against the chopping stump. "Thought you'd sleep all morning," he grinned. "I gave up on your help."

"Theodora, I don't want to see you using that ax," called Stevenson from the shed, where he was piling the split logs. "It's too heavy for you. No sense in losing a foot."

"Mr. Harris, Theo's real strong now," said Carl. "You should see how strong her arms are. She almost beat me at arm wrestling the other day." Stevenson emerged into the sunlight and gave Theo a measured look. "You should see what she does at the farm," Carl insisted. Stevenson waved his hand in defeat.

"Go ahead, then," he grunted, lifting an armful of wood. "Far be it from me, of all people, to dictate what a woman can do!"

But Theo had never used an ax before and found the heavy steel head unwieldy. She banged it down on the log Carl set up for her and it bounced. She set her teeth and raised the ax again. Thunk. A tiny chip of wood shot up and hit her arm.

"You have to set your legs apart," said Carl. "You have to bring it up from your shoulders, Theo . . . no, not like that. That's your elbow. It'll just bounce that way. You have to follow the ax down with your shoulders . . . see?" Carl split eight logs before she severed one into two raggedy pieces.

"There's more chips than log," she muttered, surveying her work in dismay. She worked alongside Carl until she thought her own back would split like the wood, and gradually the pile of logs disappeared into the shed. They were covered in sweat and wood chips, and Mrs. O'Leary made them eat their lunch sitting outside on the back step.

"I have to get home soon," said Carl, wiping his hands on his pants. "My father's cutting the bottom hayfield today." He pulled a folded wad of papers from his pocket and smiled at her shyly. "I brought your story, Theo."

She pretended to pick crumbs off her dress. Carl opened the folded pages and spread them on his knees. "I didn't get a chance to read it until the middle of the week," he said slowly. "And then I wanted to think about it for a while, and I wanted to read it again." His face was flushed when he looked at her. "I didn't want you to think I'd forgotten about it."

"I knew you didn't forget," Theo said quickly.

Carl smoothed the pages carefully. "It's a real good story, Theo," he said at last. "I . . . I was surprised." He shook his head. "No, I mean . . . I wasn't surprised it was *good*. Just that it was so — " He stopped and looked down at the pages. "It made me cry, Theo," he said softly. "Not because it was a sad story . . . I mean, I know it's about someone who loses everything that's important to him and has to start all over again. But I could hear *you* in the words. Your voice. Like you *knew* what you were writing, and I believed you . . . and so I cried."

"But I don't really know. It was all made up . . ."

"Oh, Theo!" cried Carl. "There's lots of ways of knowing something. I know things . . . I don't know where they come from, but I *know*. You wouldn't be able to make this all up" — He jabbed his finger at the pages — "You wouldn't have been able to write this at all, if you didn't know!"

He handed her the story and she stared down at her small, neat handwriting. She remembered when she wrote it, how alone she had felt in her room, how frightened of herself. The story had come from somewhere she did not understand, come straight through all her turmoil of emotions and turned into words on a page . . . she stared at the words now, and thought *she* might cry.

Carl clasped his hands around his knees. "Mr. Brunner lets me read the magazines in his store," he said slowly. "Some of them have stories in them, and your story is better than most of them, Theo! It is! Why don't you send your story to one of those magazines? I copied down the addresses for you —"

"No!" she said. She shook her head. "No. I just want to write them for myself, Carl. I mean, I want you to read them . . . but I know you, and anyway . . . anyway, they're just little stories, Carl. They aren't very important."

"I think they're important," muttered Carl. "And I don't think I'm the only person who'd think so, either."

There was a heavy thud inside the house and Theo heard Claudia cry out. She pushed past Carl and dashed through the kitchen to the hallway. Maud and Harriet were already in the parlor. Claudia lay tangled in her blankets on the floor by the bed. One arm was twisted under her and her face was white with shock and fear. Maud whimpered and threw herself on her knees beside her, reaching out her arms.

"Don't!" cried Harriet. She knelt next to Maud. "Don't move her — wait a moment. If she's hurt her back . . ." Claudia watched her aunt with frightened eyes. Harriet gently pulled the blankets from around her. "Lift your right arm," she commanded. Claudia lifted her free arm from the floor. "Wiggle your fingers," said Harriet. The thin fingers moved. Harriet visibly relaxed. She peered into Claudia's eyes. "Turn your head slowly . . . no, that way. Good. Nod it." Harriet sank back on her heels. "She's all right," she said to Maud.

"What were you *doing*!" cried Maud. "Claudia, how did you fall out of bed?" Stevenson, his shirt littered with wood-chips, had joined her on the floor. He knelt close to Maud and one of his hands clasped hers tightly, and the other smoothed Claudia's forehead.

Harriet, forgotten, rose from the floor and stepped back. Only Theo saw the look of grief pass over her aunt's face, as if Harriet were suddenly understanding something terribly important just as it was being taken away. As if she was seeing it at the very moment she lost it — something she hadn't known was important until it was too late. Theo wanted to wrap herself within Harriet's arms, to comfort and be comforted . . . but already the moment had passed. Harriet turned briskly to Carl.

"I'm glad you're here," she said. "We need another pair of strong arms to lift Claudia back on the bed." Claudia was crying now, held between her mother and father. Stevenson rocked both her and Maud in his arms.

"Sweetheart — can't you tell us what you were doing?" he pleaded.

"Oh, Papa!" she sobbed. "I thought I could *walk*! Mama . . . I felt it. I did! That tingling in my legs — just like in my arms, before I moved them. I was so sure . . ." She struggled to catch her breath. "I wanted to walk so much, and everyone was so busy and I was alone and . . . I thought I could just get up and walk. I'm sorry . . ." Now Maud was crying, too. Stevenson bowed his head and his knuckles were white as he held Maud's hand.

The whole day was ruined. The sweet warm sunshine day, her mother humming in her study and Carl talking to her about her story . . . ruined. Theo stifled her angry tears. Carl would lift Claudia in his arms and lay her carefully on the bed, and then he would leave for the farm to help his father with the haying. And Maud and Stevenson and Aunt Harriet would spend the afternoon around Claudia . . .

How could Claudia have been so stupid! How could she have thought she'd be able to stand and walk — after all this time? Hadn't she known how dangerous it would be? No, she'd wanted attention — that was it. Everyone had been busy and she'd been alone listening to the busy sounds.

Theo watched, stony-faced, as Carl and Stevenson lifted Claudia gently from the floor. Harriet supported her legs and Maud picked up the trailing blankets. Theo swallowed the fear-taste in her mouth. What if Claudia had *really* hurt herself? What if she had undone all the good of the last months — all Harriet's endless massage with the expensive liniment that Theo's wages at the horse farm bought, all Maud's tireless washing and turning and moving the paralyzed limbs hours after hour? She turned away abruptly, but Claudia reached for her hand.

"I didn't mean to scare everyone," she pleaded. "I didn't think. I really thought I could do it, Thee! I did! I could *feel* my legs! I wanted to so much I was afraid to call for help. I thought it might go away, and I . . . I wanted to do it *all by myself*. You understand, don't you, Thee?"

How could she not understand? How could she stay angry? Theo blinked back her tears. Claudia *would* walk! She would. That was more important than anything. She said goodbye to Carl in the parlor and stayed with Claudia all the long afternoon.

On Monday morning Carl caught up with Theo as she was crossing the railroad line and climbing down the bank to the field. He was unusually somber, and when they reached the cottonwoods, he said, "I'm giving my notice today. School starts in about three weeks. I'm not going to work at the blacksmith's after that." His eyes blazed in his brown face and he gazed past Theo into some far-off realm. "I'm *never* going back, Theo! I'm going to school, and then I'm going to university . . . I am. I don't know how. I don't have any money. But I *am*."

She was preoccupied with Carl's words as she harnessed up Brown City Lad; Bill Turner snapped at her twice for her clumsiness. She settled herself on the sulky seat and took up the reins, and the old trainer stumped off at Laddie's head toward the track. From across the yard Theo saw

Marion Savage talking to Dennis O'Connor. When he spotted her he came to meet her at the track entrance.

"Well, son — seems you passed Mr. Turner's test," he said, his eyes dancing. "He thinks you've got promise. It was like pulling teeth to get him to admit it, wasn't that right, Bill?" The trainer ignored Mr. Savage's teasing. "It'll take years, though . . . you know that, don't you, son? Great drivers aren't made in a day. Even Harry Hersey was a boy once — and now look at him! He drives the king of horses — Dan Patch!" He clapped her on the shoulder. "Just you remember that when you want to up and quit because Mr. Turner works you to the bone, son. Just remember Dan Patch." He looked at her intensely for a moment, and Theo was sure she saw the faintest shadow of a question in his eyes. But he turned to run his hand over Laddie in a caress. "You're worth your weight in gold, aren't you, Laddie-boy?" he crooned softly. He glanced thoughtfully again at Theo before walking back down the boulevard toward the yard.

She drove Laddie until she thought the old horse would drop from exhaustion. She drove a quiet mare named Jenny Bird. She drove a skittery gelding who had a strong aversion for the inside rail, so she had to fight him away from the center of the track. She drove another mare named Ophelia, mad as the character in Shakespeare's play after whom she was named. Ophelia hated other horses. She hated being harnessed and fretted about being brushed. She hated the pigeons that swooped over the track in bright flocks. For days, Theo drove horse after horse. The days slid into one another almost without definition. She hid her troubling thoughts behind the clouds of dust on the track and let the constant staccato beat of hooves drown out her anxiety.

Every day, an excited tension and anticipation ran

through the International Stock Feed Farm as horses were readied for the state-fair circuit. Every day, the boxcars stopped on the railroad siding that ran in front of the barns. Horses were blanketed, their legs wrapped, the boxcars filled with fresh-cut meadow hay. Then the train would whistle and move off, carrying the pride of the farm to all the corners of the nation.

Everyone kept an eye on Dan Patch. No matter what other horses were being groomed and readied, Dan Patch was everyone's favorite. Somehow he belonged at once to everyone and to no one but Marion Savage. Between the great stallion and the neat, quiet man something immense seemed to pulse with promise. Last year in Lexington, Dan Patch had broken his own world record. Could he do it again? Could Dan Patch cut a second, five seconds, ten seconds off his amazing speed around a one-mile track? And could he do it — oh, was it too much to hope for! — could he do it at the state fair this September in his own state of Minnesota?

Everyone believed in Dan Patch. Theo heard his name spoken everywhere as August wore on. She heard it in Brunner's Mercantile and on the steps of the bank. The men who gathered outside the barbershop and on the benches by the town hall spoke the name and asked the same questions over and over. Could he do it? She heard children shrilling out the name as they raced and played horse down the dusty summer roads.

She even heard the name spoken by the women who had come to meet her mother and persuade her to go with them to far-off Washington, D.C. "Too bad for us Dan Patch isn't a mare!" they joked. "What a boon for our side that would be!" Even Maud smiled when Theo spoke his name. "He's not an ordinary horse," she conceded. "He makes people

206

believe in themselves, doesn't he? He makes people *hope*. I can't understand it."

But Theo understood. No one who had ever watched the stallion would have difficulty understanding. No one who had ever seen him burst into his heart-stopping strides and fly down an empty track toward immortality would ever question why this animal held the promise of a new century in his great dark eyes.

ᴄᴏ Chapter Seventeen ᴄᴏ

SUMMER WAS FAST DISAPPEARING along the streams and vine-tangled copses of trees where the leaves had already begun to tip with color. The cornfields were higher than a man. Pumpkins swelled on the vines and the apples began to deepen with red. In town, woodsheds were filled and cellars piled with coal. Women began the laborious task of canning and preserving the mounds of fruits and vegetables that would carry them through the long Minnesota winter.

Theo woke in the middle of the night. She listened for the mockingbird to begin his predawn song, but there was no sound outside the old wooden house. It was hours before sunrise. She was shivering, and she pulled up the heavy quilt folded at the end of her bed.

In less than two weeks she would have to put on the new shirts and tuck them into the long straight skirts girls wore to high school. She would have to learn to put up her hair like Maud and Claudia and Harriet. But she did not think of it as a new beginning — for her, in a week and a half, everything would be over. Her mind had given her no peace for a minute. Even behind the jogging horses it tumbled over and over inside her. She felt she was slipping down to the end of a rope hanging over a bottomless ravine. She could not hold on. And she could not let go.

It seemed to her that everyone was watching her. Maud wore a pensive frown. If Theo caught her eye, her mother would bite her lip and look away. If Maud seemed about to speak, Theo would see her father give her a quick shake of the head, and Maud would say nothing. Harriet spoke too cheerfully. Only Claudia seemed herself, if more distracted. She was trying a "mental exercise," as she termed it, designed by herself, which she practiced several times a day. It involved visualizing herself walking . . . walking around the room, up the stairs, down the street, in the garden. She furrowed her brow and imagined walking every step.

But Theo knew everyone else was waiting to see how she would bring about the end of her job at the International Stock Feed Farm. Would she just not show up one day, and would young Theo Stevens simply disappear off the face of the earth? But how could she leave without saying goodbye to the grooms and stablehands she had befriended, to old Amon Szabo the rat killer, or even to Bill Turner? And most of all, how could she walk away from Marion Savage himself, who had recognized her dream and given her a chance to follow it?

Yet how could she face him and tell him she had been deceiving him all these months? Marion Savage was a businessman, an entrepreneur, a millionaire with a genius for promoting his product . . . he could be stubborn, perhaps a bit blind to things outside his own enthusiasms, but everyone agreed he was as honest a man as you could find anywhere. Theo could not bear to imagine the look on his face when she told him the truth. So she dangled at the end of her rope in silent panic, and her last week at the horse farm began.

It was difficult not to get swept up in the excitement of the place, despite her dilemma. Dan Patch, just returned in his private railway car from another state, could not help showing off for the grooms and stablehands. He threw up his head and rolled his eyes in mock wildness. He arched his neck in triumph and eyed the paddock full of brood mares. Then he stood still and surveyed his kingdom, and it seemed to everyone that Dan Patch was *laughing*.

"Look at him!" cried Sam, a sandy-haired groom. "He's pullin' yer leg, Buddy! Look how he's laughin' at you! He's got you all worried he's a wild'un all of a sudden, don't he?" Theo paused as she unharnessed a mare. Bill Turner had turned aside to talk to a groom. She peered around him for a better view of Dan Patch. The stallion shook his head and snorted, stepping closer to her. The mare quivered violently.

"That mare don't like stallions, boy! I told you that before," barked Bill Turner. She hastily led the mare to the far side of the yard and ran the brush over her back methodically. After a moment she stopped and leaned her head against the mare's shoulder.

She was not surprised when Amon Szabo sidled around the corner of the barn and came up to her. She had come to expect his sudden appearances. He had his favorite terrier with him, carried in the pocket of his baggy coat so only the sharp ears stuck out. Tip was old and fierce, his face scarred from years of battles with rats.

"You, girl-boy Theo," called Amon softly. He tilted his

grizzled head to the side and squinted at her from his animal eyes. "You fall down, you so much sad? Horse hold you up?"

She tried to smile and ran her hand down the mare's neck. "I'm not going to fall down," she said. "I was just thinking."

Amon Szabo hissed quietly as he hunkered down in the shade along the barn wall. The terrier popped out and sniffed the base of the wall. Amon chuckled. "He never stop hunting," he said. "He hunt 'til he dead." He didn't speak for several more minutes while Theo slowly brushed out the mare's coarse mane. She was desperately glad for the rat killer's company. He knew her secrets and he knew — she was sure — that she did not know what to do.

"Real monsters never too big," he said finally. "Monsters in here —" He tapped his chest. "They feel so big, such big we think we die. But they no real, that's all. They not real monsters."

She tried to puzzle out his meaning. Maybe she thought her problem was bigger than it really was? Perhaps she was making more of it than she needed to? Perhaps, if she just went up to Mr. Savage and simply explained . . . but she shook her head violently, and Amon Szabo fixed her with his black eyes.

"You very brave girl," he said. "I think my own girl, she be brave like you, if she live. She hunt wolf, maybe. Girls not wolf hunters. But my girl, she such brave wolf hunter maybe." He paused and Theo watched the fleeting grief on his face, gone so quickly she hardly knew she'd seen it. "Is brave to follow dream in heart. But dream-path change, like wolf-path. I follow wolf — sometimes here, sometimes there. Like dream. But dream not change, that's all. Wolf not change. Just path."

What was old Amon telling her? She gazed at Tip, digging a hole furiously near the barn wall. "I don't know how to tell him," she mumbled at last. She looked at him helplessly. "I feel like I am losing the only thing that's important to me."

"Sometimes lose everything," agreed Amon. "Then die, inside. Yes, I know this *losing*." He shook his head emphatically. "But dream not die." Amon peered up at the sun and yawned. He stood. "You want tell boss-Savage? That you girl?" he asked. She nodded miserably. "Then, time will come. You see. Don't worry — you know. It come." He stumped off around the edge of the building.

Theo dragged home through the fields. Carl had not come to work that day but had stayed home with his father to help bring in the hay. The hayfields all around the town were being cut, and that took precedence over anything else. Livestock could not make it through the long, frozen winter without hay.

She arrived home to find Claudia sitting on the edge of the bed with Harriet supporting her by the shoulders. Stevenson, home early from his office, was standing near them. Theo stopped in amazement at the door.

"Where's Mama?" she asked.

"She went to town," said Claudia, her eyes shining. "But I can't wait! I can feel my legs, Theo! I knew that tingling meant something. And I've been doing my mental exercises every day. I can walk! I know I can!"

Harriet patted her arm and looked worried. "Don't rush it, Claudia," she said. "Your muscles haven't been used for a long time — they're very weak. You need to build them up —"

"It will build them if I walk!" cried Claudia. "Why do you want to keep me from walking? Just set me up, Papa! Please, Papa . . . just let me try."

Claudia's face was tense with hope and fear, and Theo had never heard such a desperate pleading in her voice. Once Claudia had wanted to play the violin, because the music broke her free into the joy that was at the heart of who she was. Now she wanted to walk, to free herself of the paralysis that kept her from being herself . . . same dream, different paths. The dream was *freedom*. "Dream-path change . . . but dream not change . . ." Was that what Amon Szabo meant? Were dreams what made a person free?

"Let her try, Papa," Theo said. "Aunt Harriet, let her try! She has to . . . really."

Stevenson looked at Harriet and Harriet looked back at him. Each found something in the other, and Theo saw them find it. Harriet nodded and Stevenson put his arm around his daughter.

"All right, Claudia," said Harriet. "All right. We can try."

They stood on either side of Claudia and tucked their arms under hers. Harriet nudged Claudia's feet straight with her foot. Claudia took a breath and closed her eyes. Theo held her breath.

"We're going to lift you up now, sweetheart," said Stevenson, and Harriet added, "Keep your legs as straight as you can. We won't let you fall."

Claudia stood straight and tall between her father and her aunt. For a moment no one said a word. Claudia's entire concentration was on her legs. Theo had seen the same concentration on her face countless times before a performance. Claudia would sit with her violin on her lap and she would look down into herself. She would find the music deep inside her.

"Let me go," said Claudia. "Let go of my arms."

Harriet and Stevenson exchanged another glance. Theo

concentrated along with Claudia and willed her legs to root firmly on the ground.

"I'm standing," Claudia said quietly. "I'm standing. Let me go."

Stevenson slowly drew his arm away from her and after a moment, Harriet did the same. They held their hands poised inches from Claudia's body. But they did not touch her. Claudia stood alone.

She took a long, ragged breath and lifted her head. Her eyes widened and she looked straight at Theo. "I'm doing it," she breathed. "I'm standing. All by myself."

"Yes!" Theo said. Then Claudia swayed. She clutched at her father and he lowered her gently again to the bed. Claudia buried her face in her hands. Harriet seemed to sway herself, and the blood drained from her face. Suddenly she leaned against Stevenson and his arms went around her, holding her close to him with his head bent on hers.

No one moved. The earth had stopped spinning. There was her father and Harriet in an endless embrace, Claudia in exhaustion on the bed, and herself like a planet spun loose from its orbit into silent, uncharted space. And into that silence came her mother, Maud.

The world began to spin again. Harriet broke away from Stevenson, her eyes flying to her sister with a look of misery. She ran from the room. Before Maud could follow, Stevenson took her hand and they seemed to stare at each other for an eternity. Theo wanted to scream at all of them. *Say something!* she raged to herself. Someone *say* something! Claudia! Claudia! She stared wildly at her sister until Claudia raised her head.

"Mama," she called hoarsely. "Mama! I stood by myself. I did. I can feel my legs." Her voice strengthened with each word, and at last Maud turned to her and sat on the edge of the bed with a dazed expression. She looked across the room to Theo.

"You smell like a horse," she said in a flat voice. Theo stumbled from the room and ran upstairs, slamming her door. She lay facedown on the bed and refused to think. It grew darker and still she did not move. When a small tap came on her door she stiffened and did not answer. The tap came again, louder.

"Theodora," said Maud through the door. "I know you're awake. I'm going to come in." The door was pushed open and her mother shut it quietly behind her. The bed sagged when Maud sat, and Theo turned sharply to the wall. After a long pause she felt her mother's hand stroking her head. Over and over Maud's hand moved through her hair. Tears ran down Theo's face and into her nose.

"It's all right, you know, sweetheart," said Maud finally. Theo sniffed viciously.

"I *hate* her!" she cried, muffling her words in the pillow.

"No, you don't," said Maud gently. "You don't hate her. You love her. Harriet is wonderful, and no one can help loving her."

"Papa . . ."

"Your father always loved Harriet," whispered Maud. "He knew her long before he met me. He wanted to marry her . . . but she wanted to be a doctor, so she said no." There was a long pause. "Then he met me one weekend, when I went to visit Harriet in Boston. I met him at a dance . . ." Theo felt Maud's smile right through her hand. "I loved him at once . . . and he loved me, too. He does, sweetheart. I just wasn't his first choice."

"But now —" She was so choked she couldn't finish. Maud pulled her over to look directly in her eyes. The smile she'd felt through her mother's hands was still in her eyes.

"It really is all right," Maud repeated. "You mustn't be so upset! We've talked about it many times over the years — all of us. Harriet and I don't have any secrets. I love her . . . she's my sister. And I couldn't have done without her, these last months."

"Aunt Harriet's a lot like Claudia, isn't she, Mama?" Theo twisted herself until she was half-leaning against Maud. "And you're like me."

Maud smiled thoughtfully. "We're all our own persons," she said. "We each have our own particular selves . . . but yes, I can see that Claudia is a bit like Harriet."

"Everyone loves Claudia, too," Theo stated flatly. Her mother looked at her in surprise.

"Claudia is a performer," she said. "She has to get a response from people . . . it's part of who she is. In that way, you *are* like me, Theodora. We work more privately . . . we're more solitary. We need time to think — and that's who *we* are. Claudia admires you, Theodora. She looks up to you quite a bit."

"To *me!* She looks up to *me!*" gasped Theo. Maud pulled the quilt around her.

"You're both so busy admiring each other, you don't stop to see yourselves," she said, and her eyes twinkled very like Harriet's did. "If you saw yourself as Claudia sees you, going to that farm every day dressed like a boy . . ."

Theo turned her face away and Maud sighed. After a moment she leaned over to hug her. "You better go down to your aunt," she said. "She's feeling awfully hurt. She's going back to New York soon and —"

"She's leaving?"

"She has a life of her own, sweetheart," said Maud. "She came to help us with Claudia. She thinks Claudia could be walking on her own in a few weeks . . . that there will be

215

a complete recovery from the polio. It's time for her to get back to her own work."

"But will Papa . . ."

Maud smiled sadly and shook her head. "It's been very hard, you know," she said in a low voice. "On all of us."

On all of us. Theo looked up at her mother's reflective face. So she hadn't been the only one to struggle with the layers and layers of unspoken things. " '. . . whole different worlds, each one of them all by themselves and all alone . . .' " said Theo in a whisper. Maud looked puzzled. "It's just something Carl said once, about families," Theo explained.

When Maud stood up in the darkness, she seemed to Theo taller somehow, more powerful. "We're all alone until we love," she said quietly. She took Theo's hand and pulled her from the bed. "Come on downstairs before your aunt goes to sleep."

Harriet was reading in her little room next to the parlor. The light from the lamp washed down one side of her face, leaving the other side in shadow, and Theo thought that in her sadness, she was even more timeless and beautiful than ever. She could not imagine, suddenly, how it would be not to have Harriet living in the house.

Harriet placed her book carefully on the little side table when Theo came to the doorway. They looked at each other a long time.

"I love you, Aunt Harriet," whispered Theo, and Harriet came to her and pulled her close. She smelled of leather-bound books and soft wool clothing, and of the same indefinable sadness that belonged to Amon Szabo. They held each other without saying a word.

216

⌒ Chapter Eighteen ⌒

A FIERCE PERSISTENCE running through her blood woke
Theo the next morning. She hopped from the bed and
pulled her clothes on with quick, jerky movements. She
wanted to run. She sniffed the cold, sharp air, raced down
the stairs, and out along Cargyll Street in the early morning
mist. Carl met her by the tracks.

"Race with me!" cried Theo.

"What's got into you?" he laughed. She tugged at his
hand and he raced her over the fields. Where the hay had
not been cut they had to leap and plow their way through
until they were gasping for breath. Still Theo ran, in bounds
that could never match the bounding of her heart until at
last, gasping with laughter, she jumped the stream and
landed with a thud on the other side. Carl splashed through
and fell to the ground beside her. He rolled on his side and
grinned.

"You are a crazy girl!" he said. "What'd you do that
for?"

"I don't know . . . I don't know!" she cried, her chest
burning. "I felt like running the minute I got up." But even
the running did not still the restless energy within her.

"Theo," said Carl. "I was going to tell you before, but —
well, I'm not coming back to the farm after today. There's
the haying, and then school starts, and . . . I'm not coming
back." He watched her somberly, and she bowed her head.
They walked slowly toward the farm, and after a short time,
Carl said, "I'll see you in school every day, Theo. We can always sit together on the train. It'll hardly be any different . . ."

"It won't be the same at all," she said. "It's already dif-

217

ferent." He didn't say any more, but let her think to herself until they reached the gate into the yards.

Today was the day, then. She had to do it. Somehow she had to bring to an end the deception . . . say goodbye. That was the strange urgency racing in her blood this morning! Yes. Somehow she must have known, today was the day. She could not imagine how it would happen. But Amon Szabo had told her the time would come and that she would know. She had to believe him. She smiled into Carl's troubled eyes.

"It'll be all right," she said softly.

As usual, the yard was a hubbub of early-morning activity. Trunks of supplies, blankets, buckets, harnesses, and sulkies were all being loaded into the long boxcars waiting on the railroad tracks. Horses clattered nervously in the yards while grooms struggled to wrap their legs and fasten the blanket buckles. Steam rose in clouds from the horses' backs in the cool air. Ramps into the cars were lowered with a rattling of chains. A dozen horses were being sent east this morning, to the big state fairs in Pennsylvania, New Jersey, and Delaware. Bill Turner hardly looked at Theo when she came up to him.

"This here's a real busy mornin', boy," he grunted. He waved his arm impatiently toward the barn. "Take Laddie out an' give him a good workout. I'll meet you on the track later." She went slowly into the barn to Laddie's stall and led him out. This was the last time she would ever harness him up. He snuffled at her sweetly with his velvet nose and her eyes blurred with tears.

Even the track was a busy place. Horses worked out on it all day, but during the racing season there were mock heats which Marion Savage and the trainers studied with critical eyes, their thumbs on the buttons of their stopwatches. During the racing season Mr. Savage did not spend much of his time on the porch of his mansion on the bluffs across the river watching his horses through binoculars. He stood at the track himself, or drove, or held lengthy discussions with his trainers. Theo led Brown City Lad up the short rise to the track and waited until a trackhand had time to hold him while she settled into the sulky. Even Laddie seemed infected by the excitement. He threw up his head and sidestepped, and the trackhand chuckled as he held the bridle.

"Ol' Laddie knows what's goin' on," he said. "He'd be out there racin' if we let him." He squinted at the far side of the track. "Looks like Bert's got his lot workin' out already," he commented. At the half-mile post a group of dark forms flew along the rail. "An' there's Moonlight! What's he got him out there for? He's supposed to be goin' to New Jersey today. Guess they're gettin' the kinks outa his legs . . ." The trackhand gave Laddie a final pat and waved to Theo as she turned him onto the track. "You gonna have to drive good today," he grinned. "This place is more crowded than a city street . . . why, even Dan'll be out here later on. An' when he's out here, watch out! The wind when he goes by'll blow you halfway 'cross the county!"

She took Laddie at a slow jogging pace around the track. Within seconds the group of horses passed them, breathing hard and drumming the track with their flashing hooves. Laddie paid them no attention and jogged steadily on. The sulky wheels made a soft whooshing noise under her. A flock of pigeons dipped over the track and lifted, so the rising sun caught the undersides of their wings. Theo opened her mouth and drank in the cool brightness around her. She eased Laddie across the track to the outside rail near the entrance gate and Bill Turner stumped up to her.

"You're lettin' him be lazy, boy," he grumbled. "I want him slow, but don't let him fall asleep. You ain't on a pleasure drive."

She took Laddie on another circuit around the track. A few horses passed her and she looked over at the group of drivers, trainers, and grooms that leaned against the fence near the entrance. She caught a glimpse of a light-colored suit. Marion Savage had come early to watch his horses warm up. She brought her eyes back to the horse pacing rhythmically in front of her.

Her head was empty of thoughts. After days of torment she felt utterly relaxed. There was nothing else but this single moment, this horse, this morning. She eased Laddie into the far turn and began the jog up the back stretch. From there she looked across the field in the center of the track, and saw another horse being led through the entrance gate.

She knew him immediately. Dan Patch. Her hands tightened on the reins and Laddie shook his head in mild protest. She began to pull him up as she approached but Bill Turner waved her on. Behind her three other horses were waved on. Dan Patch watched them all eagerly.

"Once more around, boys!" called Marion Savage. "Then let's bring them all in." From time to time the track was cleared so one of the champions could have a clear race against the watch. Theo saw the two thoroughbred running horses, Cobweb and Mag, being held near the gate. Dan Patch was going to race the clock! Cobweb and Mag were used to run ahead of the stallion to inspire him to his greatest speeds. Already a sizable crowd of onlookers had gathered along the track fence. Anyone who could take a break had come to watch the great horse.

Laddie was blowing a little by now and the harness along

his back rubbed a ridge of white foam lather up from his dark hide. She let him find his own pace down the back stretch. He jogged patiently to the finish and then wheeled calmly under her direction back toward the entrance gate. Close behind her, three more drivers slowed and brought their horses in. By the time she pulled up in the center track to wait for a trackhand, there were seven horses coming in at the same time.

Dan Patch calmly watched the activity as he stood by his groom. Mr. Savage was talking with two trainers, and more people joined the onlookers at the fence. Even Amon Szabo, Theo saw, had slipped through the crowd and was standing slightly to one side watching the track. He caught sight of Theo the same moment a trackhand came up and took Laddie's bridle. As the trackhand waited for the horses in front to move through the gate, the rat killer sidled over and stood near her. He ran his hand along Laddie's flank but did not say a word to Theo.

Suddenly, a flurry of commotion broke out among the horses on the boulevard leading up to the track entrance. Theo craned her neck around the driver in front of her. Above the shouting came the shrill, high scream of a stallion. Marion Savage and the trainers dashed down the bank toward the boulevard.

A stallion being groomed in the yard had spooked and bolted away from his handler. Now he wheeled in the crowd among the horses and sulkies, rearing and squealing in panic. The other horses fussed between the shafts of the sulkies. Within seconds there was a swirling melee of dust and frightened horses. Men shouted and ran in to grab at bolting horses, and others scattered to head off the loose stallion.

221

"Who had Tar-Boy?" yelled Mr. Savage. "Careful, Pat — get Moonlight away from there! Get him back!"

The nervous Moonlight struggled violently between the sulky shafts when the wild-eyed Tar-Boy dashed by. He backed and tried to buck, and the sulky tipped dangerously. When the trackhand trying to hold him scrambled clear, a man making a wild grab at Tar-Boy's halter crashed into him. Moonlight, completely panicked now and held only by his driver, skittered backwards and jammed his sulky into the wheels of the sulky next to him.

The groom holding Dan Patch exclaimed under his breath. He looked around him quickly. Only Dan Patch and Brown City Lad remained on the track. He called over to Amon Szabo. "Hey, Amon! Give us a hand, will ya? Somebody's got to catch Moonlight before he goes berserk. I don't think anybody has hold of him."

He gave the lead on Dan Patch's bridle to the old rat killer. "Just hold him for half a minute, will ya, and let me see if I can get hold of Moonlight." Amon Szabo took the lead-rope and the trackhand leaped the fence and ran toward the confusion.

Almost imperceptibly, Amon Szabo moved with Dan Patch closer to Brown City Lad. The two horses greeted each other softly, blowing and nuzzling inquisitively. The trackhand holding Laddie chuckled. "These two are wonderin' what all the commotion's about," he grinned.

Amon Szabo narrowed his glittery eyes. He jerked his head at Laddie. "I take," he hissed in his rasping voice. "These horses gentle like kittens. I hold both — you go help." He pointed with his free hand toward the boulevard.

The trackhand looked questioningly at Theo. "It's all right, Nate," she said calmly. "Laddie's not going anywhere. You better go help." Nate hesitated a moment and then pressed the lead-rope into Amon's hands. He climbed the fence and was lost in the milling throng. Theo was alone on the track with Amon Szabo, Laddie, and the great Dan Patch.

The old rat killer held both lead-ropes. Laddie nibbled gently on Dan Patch's cheekstrap. The old man looked back at Theo as she sat on the sulky behind Brown City Lad. His face had no expression. He made no gesture. He simply watched her. An uncanny silence settled around her.

Through the strange silence she saw the confusion on the boulevard begin to settle, and the horses and men move slowly toward the barns. Tar-Boy had been caught and meekly followed his handler behind the others. Moonlight, lathered in sweat, his eyes still rolling, was held by two men next to the boulevard as the others went by. Marion Savage spoke briefly to one of the men. The onlookers who had scattered when the confusion began gathered again and moved back toward the fence. Mr. Savage laughed at something a trainer said and they, too, walked back toward the entrance gate.

Amon Szabo spoke. "Time here," he hissed. His black eyes bore into her own. "Time. *Now*."

It would never come again, this moment. This chance. This one single instant in time. It had to be now. It was the only thing she could do with this one breath in her body. If she blinked, if she hesitated, if she even *thought*, the moment would pass. It would never come again. She slipped from the seat of the sulky behind Brown City Lad. She took two short steps.

And settled herself in the sulky behind Dan Patch. She took up the reins. She placed her feet firmly in the stirrups. The sulky rolled under her. She felt the enormous power waiting between the shafts. She took a deep breath and nodded her head. Amon Szabo unsnapped the lead rope. Theo was driving Dan Patch.

She turned him out onto the track. He stepped before her majestically. His great heart lifted and her own heart filled to answer. The sulky whispered on the track. Dan Patch began to pace.

Behind her she heard the shouts of the onlookers and felt a rush of air, as if the whole crowd were running after her. But it was too late. Dan Patch was the fastest horse on earth. She lifted her head and held the reins tightly in her hands. She knew she was not driving Dan Patch. She could never hold in such immense power as she felt through those reins. No, he was taking her with him. He was in control.

The drumming hooves pounded straight into her blood. She gave herself to the surge of sound carrying her along. She trusted him utterly. He called to her, called her secret name from deep in his heart, from the speed he was weaving out of the air. And she called back to him, so there were no longer two hearts but one vital beating heart between them. His name sung on her lips. She tasted it in the dust and wind and in the joy racing through her.

Time did not exist. They raced forever along an endless track that stretched like a gleaming ribbon before them. The wind swooped down to join them. The sun fell across their path like a carpet spread before a king. And then, with no more effort than the faintest quiver of air, Dan Patch lifted free of the earth and flew like pure light into the place where dreams are born.

This was his kingdom. He took her there because they shared the same heart. Everything in her but that heart fell away, but with that heart she could see and hear and taste and touch more clearly than she could believe. Dan Patch took her to the very center of his kingdom and there she saw all the tracks and paths and roads merging into that one single realm. And with nothing but her heart, she saw everyone she loved in the world.

She saw her sister Claudia — not self-centered and vain, but so in love with beautiful music she made the very air around her dance with joy. And there was her Aunt Harriet, walking the heartbreaking path she'd chosen to reach her dream, who for one brief summer saw in her sister's home everything she herself had given up. There was Maud, her mother, who worked with passionate determination so other women could fulfill their dreams, and made that work *her* dream. Through the pounding hooves and the pounding of her heart, Theo saw them all.

Everyone was there: Stevenson, who dreamed of justice, and Gustav Johansson, who pulled his dream with bare hands out of the raw prairie earth, and Marion Savage, who saw everything he believed in through the heart of one mahogany-bay horse. And there was Amon Szabo the rat killer, who had lost his home and his family and his work — and who had come across the sea to begin again. He found his wolf-dogs in a pack of feisty terriers, found his hungry wolves again in the grain-thieving rats, and found the daughter he had lost in a tall girl hiding in the clothing of a boy . . .

On and on the great horse took her. On and on the mighty hooves pounded deep into the realm of dreams. Carl was there, holding out his hand to her, with eyes that looked far into the distance to see the greatness of things, and who saw Theo there in that greatness. She threw back her head and the horse went even faster. Into her lungs surged the wondrous wind until her blood and bone and muscles were fed on speed.

But at last the earth reclaimed them. The track looped around on itself and even Dan Patch had to follow. The sulky whirred under Theo once more as she raced along the hard dirt toward the finish line. Dan Patch never broke his breathtaking strides. Earth or air, it was all the same to him. But Theo felt a terrible sadness rushing through her. The wondrous kingdom was gone forever. Never again would she taste such perfection in her heart. And Dan Patch felt her falter. Once more he called to her down the long leather reins. He called the name of courage and she lifted her head to listen. She gripped the reins and answered him as they flashed by the three-quarter mile post.

It seemed to Theo that every person on the farm was massed by the fence watching them. In front of them all waited Marion Savage. Theo transferred the reins to one hand and held them firmly. With her free hand she reached up and pulled off her cap. She plucked the pins from her long dark hair and let it fall free. It streamed out behind her. She shook her head. Nothing felt more wonderful than the wind through her hair.

Dan Patch slowed to a walk and a groom ran up to take his head. He darted an incredulous, frightened glance at Theo. Slowly she slipped from the sulky seat, and Dan Patch was led away. She stood without moving as Marion Savage walked up to her. Bill Turner stomped angrily behind him and beside him scurried Amon Szabo. But Mr. Savage put out his hand to stop them from speaking, and his eyes looked steadily into Theo's. She looked as steadily back. Mr. Savage stepped close to her.

"And did he take you there, to that place you were looking for?" asked Mr. Savage so quietly only she could hear.

"Yes," she whispered. "I called his name and he took me." Her legs began to shake. She set her teeth but did not drop her eyes. Marion Savage put his hand on her arm to hold her steady.

"Theodora," he said. "I wondered how you were going to tell me who you were."

Her eyes widened and he smiled into them, leaning closer to her. "The day of the parade," he whispered. "Remember? Dan came up to you . . . I knew then."

"You knew all this time?" she gasped, finding her voice. "And you still let me drive?"

"Why not?" said Mr. Savage softly, gazing past her to look at Dan Patch standing calmly with his groom. "Why not? I could not have stopped you. One way or another, you would have driven that horse. Our dreams are the most powerful forces on earth."

Dan Patch turned his head and watched them both. He bobbed his head and snorted happily. Mr. Savage smiled. "Dreams are strange things, aren't they?" he asked her. "All my life I dreamed of this . . ." His eyes swept around the track and over the fields to the barns. "But it wasn't really *this*, was it? Because I have this now, and I still dream. It is something even bigger — something you can't touch with your hands or see with your eyes. It's something always a promise ahead of you —" The stallion whickered. He pranced and his ears pointed eagerly at them.

"It's something Dan himself taught me," continued Mr. Savage, still holding Theo steadily by the arm. "About dreams. You aren't meant to catch them. You don't *want* to. They always have to be ahead of you, just beyond your sight . . . something you have to imagine. Something you have to *race* with. And you don't ever want to win over a dream." He chuckled and shook his head. "But don't ever tell Dan Patch that. He's determined to try."

Her legs were shaking uncontrollably now. There was anger on the faces of some of the men in the crowd, and Bill Turner turned away from her and stomped off without a word. Others watched her in bewilderment. But the only person who mattered was Marion Savage. She saw in his eyes kindness and complete understanding. He took her hand a moment in his own, until Carl ran up to her through the crowd. Then Mr. Savage turned and walked over to his horse.

Carl put his arms around her and she did not mind that the entire farm was watching. Dan Patch raised his head and whinnied. She called out a silent goodbye.

Carl's eyes were shining. "I saw you!" he whispered to her as they walked off the track. "I saw you, Theo. You were the most beautiful person in the world!" He held her hand tightly and she found the strength in her legs. Amon Szabo slipped through the crowd and walked on the other side of her. She lifted her head and smiled, tasting the clear morning air.

ᵔᵕ Chapter Nineteen ᵔᵕ

THE TRAIN STREAMED through early September wheat fields and orchards bursting with apples, over wooden bridges and dusty roads. Theo lay her cheek against the cool glass window. A farmer sitting in his mule cart flashed by, his hand raised in greeting. A horse and buggy kept pace briefly, and from it a small boy peered up at the train windows. Once she saw an automobile laboring up a hill in a cloud of steam.

Carl dozed next to her in the compartment, and across from her sat her father nodding to the steady tickity-tickitytack of the wheels over the rails. Against his shoulder, with her head turned to the other window, sat Claudia. Claudia, feeling Theo's eyes on her, turned and smiled. "The last time I was to a fair I was a child . . . but it was only last year," she said quietly. She stretched her legs out in the cramped space. Theo shifted on the seat, longing to pull up her long skirts so the air could get to her legs, and Claudia watched her and smiled again. "I remember I could hardly wait to wear long skirts," she mused. "I thought I'd really be grown-up then . . . funny, isn't it? A lot more than that has to happen before a person grows up."

"Women shouldn't have to wear such stupid clothes," grumbled Theo. "Mama is right. I hope they change that along with voting and all those other things. As soon as I'm done with school and on my own, I'm going right back to men's clothes, and I don't care what anyone says!"

She pressed her face against the glass again. They had been on the train since early morning and she was stiff with the sitting. Her thoughts flashed by like the scenes outside the train window. So much had changed in the last two weeks.

Claudia was walking. Two days after she stood in the parlor, the day after Theo drove Dan Patch, Claudia got up and walked across the room. She had to be carried back to bed, but by the evening she was up again, walking unsteadily into the hallway. Harriet pleaded with her not to strain anything, to take it slowly, but Claudia would not stop. Day after day she walked. She walked around the parlor and out into the kitchen. Up and down the hallway she walked, her hand on the wall, her right leg sliding on the floor. She walked outside, and one day, to everyone's amazement, she walked down the porch steps.

She made her faltering, determined way up and down

the street. Even at night she would not stop, and Theo heard her as she lay in bed, walking back and forth along the hallway. Her steps grew more even and her pace steadier. Every day she would run her hands down the calves of her slender legs, feeling for muscles. One day Claudia walked to meet Theo and Carl as they got back from school on the train. Her face flushed with pride, she held Carl's arm as they walked down Cargyll Street, and Theo felt only gladness.

"Theo!" said Claudia now, her eyes dancing. "What do you think — will Papa let me ride the Giant Swing? It was always my favorite, back in Indiana. I wonder if there'll be a Giant Swing . . ."

Theo squirmed on the seat, trying to kick her legs free of the confining skirt. She heard the crackle of paper in her pocket and reached in to pull out a thick creamy envelope. How many times had she read this letter since it arrived a week before? She turned the envelope over in her hands.

"Miss Theodora Harris, Driver," she read. "Number Eight, Cargyll Street, Savage, Minnesota." She slid out the single sheet of matching paper and read it, although she knew it by heart. The handwriting swept in bold upward strokes across the paper, and when she held the page to the light, she saw the translucent watermark. The letterhead was an embossed engraving of a horse's head. The ears pricked forward eagerly, the eyes alert and knowing — there was no mistaking the look of a king. Under the engraving were the words DAN PATCH 1:55¼.

Dear Miss Harris (otherwise known as Theo),

Dan Patch and I would be honored by your company

at the great Minnesota State Fair on September 8,
1906, at three o'clock in the afternoon in the grand-
stand, where Dan Patch will do his best to race his
dream once and for all. Dan cares a great deal for his
friends and knows when they are cheering him on, so
please come with your family and sit in the special seats
I have reserved for friends.

Yours most sincerely,
Mr. M. W. Savage

Enclosed with the letter had been four train tickets and
four passes to the grandstand. She held the letter against
her cheek with the same joy she had felt a week ago when
it came in the mail. The state fair was in a town north of
Minneapolis, a long morning's train ride away. Maud had
gone to Washington, D.C., two days earlier, traveling with
Harriet, who was returning to her hospital in New York.
Before she left, Harriet pronounced Claudia fit and able to
continue her interrupted life. So the four tickets went to
Theo and her father, Claudia — and Carl.

Carl's rough blond head was lying close to her shoulder.
If she moved slightly it would rest against her . . . but the
train jolted over a bridge and Carl woke. "You must have
been tired," Theo said. "Did you try to read that entire
science assignment last night?"

Carl rubbed his face ruefully. "I got behind . . . there's
still all the haying," he admitted. "I had to read six chapters.
It'll be better in winter when all the crops are in." A momentary look of discouragement passed over his eyes.

"You'll do it, Carl," said Theo swiftly.

He gazed out the window. "I *have* to do it," he said.

Theo folded the letter and put it back in her pocket, and

231

Carl suddenly reached in his own pocket and said abruptly, "I have another letter for you, Theo. It came Thursday, but I wanted to wait until today to give it to you, because . . ."

"A letter for *me*? How do you have a letter for me?"

"Well . . . you'll probably be angry with me," he said in a rush. "That's why I waited 'til today — it's hard to be angry when you're going to a fair."

She burst out laughing. Who on earth had sent her a letter through Carl? But he looked serious, and turned the plain brown envelope over in his hands. There was a single sheet of paper inside which he took out and unfolded. Theo caught a glimpse of neat rows of words . . . this letter had been written on a typewriter. There was a letterhead on this one, too, but she couldn't make it out. She reached for it, but Carl held the letter against his chest, as if to protect it.

"Please try to understand, Theo," he pleaded. "I think it's really important. More than you think . . . and you're my best friend, and —"

"Oh, for goodness' sakes, Carl!" she snapped. "Let me *see* it!"

He handed it to her without another word. She had to read through it twice before she could comprehend what it was about.

"Dear Mr. Johansson," she read. "Thank you for sending the story titled 'A Different Kind of Wolf' to our magazine. It is quite an unusual story and well-written, and the editors were impressed. Your friend does indeed have extraordinary writing ability, especially as you say she is only sixteen years old. We would most certainly like to publish her story in our magazine, but we would have to do it under her name — and for that, we need her permission. We sincerely hope you will be able to persuade your friend to give us that, and to reveal who she is. You say she has written many stories. We think she may be a true writer. Perhaps she will be brave enough to send us more someday."

Dazed, Theo read the letter a third time before thinking to look at the letterhead. "Harper's Weekly," she read. "Malcolm Dunn, Editor-in-Chief." And at the bottom, in a scrawling blue signature, "Malcolm Dunn."

She folded the letter and slipped it back in the envelope. She handed it to Carl and stared out the window without seeing anything of the countryside sweeping by. After a moment, Carl cried in a low voice, "Theo! It was too good to hide it. Please don't be angry!"

"I'm not angry," she said. The window glass cooled her face. From the corner of her eyes she saw Carl watching her anxiously. She reached again for the letter and without a word, held it with both hands in her lap.

"I copied your story, Theo," Carl told her doggedly. "That's why I kept it so long. Miss Schroeder gave me some paper and I copied your story. I got the address from those magazines at Mr. Brunner's store. I picked the magazine with the best stories in it, Theo . . . that's the one I sent your story to. It was miles better than the stories in any of the other magazines. And I *did* ask you . . ."

"And I said I didn't want to," she remarked. He was silent. She unfolded the letter again and read it slowly. "A Different Kind of Wolf" . . . her strange little story about old Amon Szabo the rat killer, who had to begin again from the rubble of his ruined life. Her story had traveled all the way to New York City. It had been read by the editor of a big magazine. They wanted to print her story out in neat, even rows of words on the pages of a magazine that people would read all over the country. Under the title would be her name: Theodora Harris. Theodora Harris, Writer. She wiped the palms of her hands on her skirt over the pocket which held the other letter, addressed to Theodora Harris, Driver. She narrowed her eyes. Theodora Harris, Writer. Old Amon Szabo's words had found their way into her story: "Same dream . . . different paths. Dreams have such many shapes. Dream the same. Shape always changes . . ."

She turned to Carl. "I'm not angry," she told him softly, and wondered why she was not. Her stories were a secret haven no longer. She looked at him in wonder. Carl. He had risked her anger because he believed in her. "Thank you," she said.

"So will you do it, Theo?" he asked. "Will you tell them who you are and let them publish your story?"

The train screeched to a stop at the station near the state fair grounds. The platform teemed with people. It was a crowd of summer dresses and parasols, wide-ribboned hats, racing children, buggies and horses, porters dressed in braided uniforms, men in summer coats and bowler hats, and frantic policemen trying to direct it all. Stevenson said something through the noise to Claudia as he reached to the rack above them for their bag.

Carl sat still, waiting for Theo's reply. She held the plain brown envelope to her nose and sniffed the faraway scent of it. "I will say they can publish my story," she said.

Carl threw both arms up with fists clenched, like a victorious prizefighter. They looked at each other in delight. Suddenly she leaned forward. He moved his head and she felt his lips on her own. The shrill whistle of a porter blasted directly beneath their window and they broke apart, flushed. They clung to each other with their eyes.

Stevenson struggled with the heavy bag and Claudia was bent over lacing her boots tightly around her ankles. No

234

one had seen them. Carl flashed Theo an embarrassed, joyful grin, and she answered with one of her own. They were swept out into the heat and glare on the most important day of the Minnesota State Fair.

Theo was so full of wonder she thought she might burst. She trailed through the fairgrounds behind Carl, her father, and Claudia. She tumbled through a fantasy of sights and smells and sounds, until she had to close her eyes from the intensity of it all. The food she ate tasted richer than anything she had ever eaten, the colors of the bright tents danced before her eyes, and the air was filled with music.

All through her private joy she felt the anticipations and tension of the crowd: Today Dan Patch would race in his own state and try to shatter his own world record. Would he do it? Was it possible for any horse to go so fast? The clown-faced ice-cream vendors, the hot-air balloon men, the acrobats and the sword-swallowing man, the Tattooed Lady and the World's Strongest Man, the Mummy of Ancient Egypt, the gypsy with the dancing dogs, the organ grinder with his monkey — they all wondered the same thing. Could Dan Patch break his own extraordinary record? Somewhere in the barns behind the grandstand, hidden in a quiet stall knee-deep in summer straw, Dan Patch waited. From deep in his magnificent heart, could he hear his dream calling him?

Stevenson found a patch of shade near the band gazebo and spread a blanket on the grass. Claudia sat with Theo and nibbled on a candy apple.

"You can't go on the Giant Swing, and that's final," said Stevenson sternly. "I know you're a grown woman of nearly twenty, Claudia, but you are also recently risen from your sickbed, and I could not look your mother in the eye if I —" Claudia twirled the sticky apple under her father's nose.

"I'm as strong as an ox, Papa," she scolded him. "If it were up to you, I'd still be home in bed. Thank goodness Aunt Harriet is a doctor with eyes in her head. *She* could see I was fine! And she expressly said I could go to the fair —"

"She did not, however, give her permission for the Giant Swing," said Stevenson.

Theo laughed. "You know we never win an argument with Papa," she said. "That's why he's a lawyer. Where ever has Carl got to?" She shaded her eyes and searched through the crowds that strolled by on all sides of them. Carl had gone to scout out the best way to the grandstand. In another moment she saw him returning, weaving his way through the sea of skirts and hats and parasols.

"It's shortest to go around by the tents," he said. They had to walk slowly with Claudia who, despite her protests, still tired easily. But her eyes shone and she stood steadily in the mass of people waiting to get in the grandstand gates.

Forty thousand people converged on the fairgrounds that day and funneled through the gates into the grandstand. In the sultry afternoon heat, the colorful bunting draped from the grandstand roof wilted, as the mercury in the thermometer hanging on the wall of the huge structure crept up to ninety degrees. The heat quivered over the track like a dark mirage.

Stevenson found the seats reserved for them in the section roped off for friends and family of Marion Savage. They settled on the benches and waited. Forty thousand people waited with them. Thousands of people checked their watches. The officials in the booth above the finish line talked among themselves. The anticipation of the crowd swelled like a living wind confined within the tiers of the grandstand. Then, like a wind, a sigh ran through forty thousand throats. Two horses walked out onto the track trailing their sulkies.

"Where's Dan Patch?" asked Claudia, straining to see. "What horses are those?"

"Those are the front-runners," explained Theo. "Mag and Cobweb — they have to gallop way out ahead of Dan Patch, so he thinks he's racing them. Otherwise he gets bored. They have to gallop — no other pacers could keep ahead of him, no matter how much of a lead they had."

The front-runners moved into position ahead of the starting post, one on the rail and the other near center track. Suddenly a hush fell over the crowd. They sensed the great horse before they saw him. Forty thousand necks craned. The heat seemed to crackle in the air.

Dan Patch stepped out on the track. The crowd roared. But Theo sat wrapped in silence, staring at the horse who had taken her with him to his kingdom of dreams. She did not hear the cheering crowds. She did not see them. She saw only Dan Patch. Tentatively, she called out his secret name. Would he hear her? Would he remember her? She closed her eyes and concentrated, putting all her heart into the call. She called the name of speed and perfection and freedom, and her silent call sang out over the thousands of people, out over the burning track to the big brown horse. And he heard her call. He turned his head. His ears strained forward. He paused for a fraction of a second. But he answered her. Then he moved out onto the track.

He paced his two warm-up heats without breaking into more than a fine sheen of sweat. He turned his head toward the crowd as he went by. The staccato pounding of his hooves was like music, and the people waved their hats and chanted his name: Dan Patch! Dan Patch! After the second heat he walked in a slow circle near the gate. He did not even appear to be breathing hard. His attention was always on the crowd, his eyes alert and keen. He walked a final slow circle as once again the two front-runners were positioned ahead of him. Dan Patch bobbed his head and pawed the track. He was ready.

This time there was no sound from the crowd. This was it. This was when Dan Patch would strive to break his unbelievable record. The sun shimmered on his dark coat and glinted along the shafts of the sulky. The front-runners broke into a gallop. The starter's gun was raised into the air.

Dan Patch leaped forward into the sun-drenched dust. His great hooves beat the earth. His heart swelled. He pulled closer to the galloping runners. In a storm of dust they flashed like thunder past the official's stand. The starting gun popped with a puff of smoke and the pins on the stopwatches clicked. Dan Patch began his race against time.

His legs ate up the track. Stride after stride, faster than flesh and blood, he seemed to pulse with a mighty heat, as if he and the sun were brothers racing across the timeless space of sky. He rose through the light until all four of his flashing hooves were off the ground.

Dan Patch passed the quarter-mile post and began the wide turn onto the back stretch. He was no more than a dark spot surging through the golden dust. As he passed each marker-post a flag dropped so the driver would know they were within the time they strived for. The front-runners, galloping to their limit, began to fall back. Stride by stride Dan Patch pulled up upon them. His great head stretched almost into the back of the driver ahead of him. Not a breath came from the crowd as they watched him sweep along the far side of the track and pass by the three-quarter-mile post. The dust whirled up like a prairie storm. The crowd in the stands began a low chanting.

"Patch! Patch! Patch!" they called. They leaned into the turn with him as he raced down that last terrible stretch to the finish.

Dan Patch broke through the mirage of heat into the clear air flying on hooves of perfect speed. The crowd rose to meet him. On and on he came, growing larger with every stride, until he bounded down the last hundred feet past the grandstand like something hurtled from the infinite forces of the universe. He flashed across the finish line so fast there was no time to catch a breath. Far past the line he finally slowed, turned, and jogged back toward the official's booth.

There was not a single stir from the grandstand. Every person waited. Every person held their breath. The officials leaned their heads together. They checked and rechecked their watches. Then the announcer stepped forward and lifted the megaphone to his mouth.

"Well, folks — here you have it. Dan Patch has raced the mile in *one minute fifty-five seconds flat*, breaking the world's . . ."

But his voice was drowned out by the wave of sound that rose from forty thousand throats. The cheers swelled up and spilled down over the track, until the grandstand seemed to sway and move of its own accord out toward the most incredible horse on earth.

But Theo sat utterly still. She did not know that thousands of people streamed joyfully out toward the great stallion. She did not know that fifty policemen struggled to hold them back. She did not see the driver lifted on the shoulders of the crowd in triumph, nor did she see the wreath of roses draped around the pacer's neck. She did not see Dan Patch lower his head as he sucked air deep into his heaving lungs, and she did not see Marion Savage lean his head against the horse's face with tears in his eyes.

Carl reached for her hand. She let him lead her after Stevenson and Claudia as they struggled through the press of people. Stevenson shouldered ahead of them, trying to clear a path for Claudia. The commotion was so great there was no possibility of speaking until they had made their way to a far corner of the fairgrounds. Close to a fence at the very back of the grandstand Stevenson spread the blanket out in the shade of the building, then left to buy lemonade from a concession stand nearby. Claudia groaned in relief and lay back, cushioning her head with her arm and closing her eyes.

Carl sat close to Theo. She leaned against him and stared up at the high blue sky. The sun had sunk toward the prairie and the afternoon shadows lay long and dark against the grass. They sat quietly for several minutes.

Something sidled through the shadows on the other side of the fence. Theo frowned. It was a strangely familiar movement, but it did not emerge at once. The corner of the building was half in shadow and half in glaring sun, and she could not see. For several seconds nothing moved. She squinted as the shadows seemed to draw together and shuffle toward her along the fence. She stumbled to her feet, put her hand briefly on Carl's shoulder so he would not follow, and went to the fence.

"Girl-boy Theo," hissed Amon Szabo. "Is it you? Is it you in such a pretty way?"

"It's me, Mr. Szabo," she answered. The terriers stood on their hind legs eagerly against the fence, and she knelt to pat them. The old rat killer hunkered down on the grass. He peered at her from his black eyes.

"Dream still there?" he asked, tapping his chest above his heart. He cocked his head at her.

She smiled. "Yes," she answered. "Yes. The dream is still there."

~ Author's Afterword ~

THE RECORD DAN PATCH SET that afternoon in September 1906, at the Minnesota State Fair, was not broken by another horse for over twenty years. Dan Patch himself never paced a faster mile. He retired a few years later to the lovely pastures of the International Stock Feed Farm.

Dan Patch and his owner/partner, Marion Willis Savage, died one day apart in 1916. After a short illness, the great horse fell to his side in his box stall and began to pace. The magnificent legs flew back and forth, sending the straw high into the air. Perhaps he paced his fastest mile in those few minutes, but we will never know. But it is certain that the greatest racehorse who ever lived died racing.

Thirty-six hours later, M. W. Savage, lying ill himself in a hospital bed, heard of his beloved horse's death. Perhaps he lost the will to live . . . perhaps he knew that he had come, with Dan Patch, as close as any living being can to winning a race with his dreams. Marion Savage died that very day.

The story of Dan Patch began almost one hundred years ago on a small farm in Oxford, Indiana, in 1896. There a small brown colt with crooked legs was born who would become the fastest pacing horse in the world. Marion Savage once wrote: "I was born with a great desire to raise high-class harness horses, and when à boy I commenced to raise some [colts]. . . . From that time on I dreamed of and planned for the day when I would own a 'Stock Farm' on which I could carry out my fond desires."

And Dan Patch carried out those "fond desires" far beyond his wildest imaginings. During the twenty years the horse lived and raced, his name became literally a household word. M. W. Savage, with his genius for advertising, used the name of his famous pacer to endorse dozens of products from tobacco to wood stoves, from automobiles to children's toys. Songs were written for Dan Patch, and dance steps were named after him. Dan Patch was the very first "sports hero."

The key to the worldwide fame of the horse lay in his exceptionally charismatic personality. An editorial in the *Chicago Tribune*, in August 1903, read: "It is no wonder Dan Patch has friends. He is an amiable and sociable horse. He likes people. He likes to turn his head and look at people when he is on the track. He likes to listen to the band. He likes things in general. He has a good time. He is a good mixer. That is why he has friends as well as admirers. That's why, when the news goes out that Dan Patch has paced another wonderful mile, one will find that all of Dan Patch's human acquaintances are visibly, and sometimes bibulously, gratified. Dan Patch is a good fellow."

Dan Patch was a real horse and Marion Savage was a real person. You can find the town of Savage on a map today, a little to the south and east of Minneapolis, Minnesota. But you would not find the great barns or the oval track. They are gone, and no one knows the secret place where Dan Patch was buried. The legend of Dan Patch must live entirely in your imagination and dreams, as it does in mine.

Marion Willis Savage had two sons. The younger son,

Harold, inherited his father's passion for harness horses. Harold in turn passed that love on to his own son, Richard, who in turn passed it on to his daughter Deborah . . . who wrote this book.